# AMULETS AND ALIBIS

## THE CLARISSA BELL MYSTERIES
### BOOK THREE

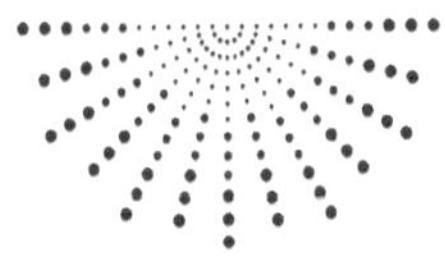

## TRACY HIGLEY

# CHAPTER ONE

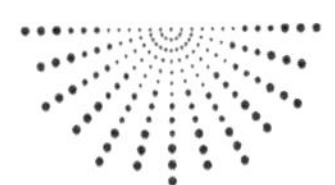

$\mathscr{I}$'d made a fundamental error in my career planning.

Standing at the podium of Cairo's Continental-Savoy Hotel, facing an overheated roomful of wealthy Europeans who'd come expecting tales of murder rather than ceramic chemistry, I realized I should have specialized in something less prone to explaining bloodstains to authorities.

Ever since Carter's discovery of Tutankhamun's tomb two years ago, every European with War profits fancied themselves the next great explorer.

But Dr. Bradford had been quite clear this morning—secure three major pledges from these potential donors, or face relegation to what he ridiculously called "the dirty jobs."

"—which demonstrates the sophisticated copper-calcium chemistry of New Kingdom faience." I gestured toward my carefully prepared slides while hoping desperately that someone, anyone, might ask about firing temperatures rather than firing weapons.

No such luck.

A gentleman in the third row shot up his hand like a schoolboy with the answer to everything.

"Dr. Bell! Surely you must tell us about the murder investigations! Far more thrilling than pottery techniques, wouldn't you say?"

Ladies fanned themselves with ivory-handled fans while gentlemen adjusted wilted white linen collars. The mahogany podium felt slippery under my increasingly damp palms.

"I appreciate your interest." My voice hardened. "But I'm here to discuss archaeological methodology, not criminology—"

"Oh, but Dr. Bell!" A lady in an elaborate feathered hat preened forward. "Surely criminal investigations are far more fascinating than dusty old pottery! Tell us about those stolen blue artifacts!"

I yanked at the lantern slide projector. The mechanism jammed with the determination of a tomb door sealed for three millennia, then lurched forward to display an unimpressive pottery fragment.

"Perhaps we might discuss pottery breakage rates instead?" I suggested brightly. "Remarkably similar mortality statistics to criminal investigations, but with significantly less paperwork."

The gentleman persisted. "But the stolen artifacts! The conspiracy! Surely that's more exciting than broken pots?"

"Only if one enjoys kidnappings and poisonings. Personally, I find intact ceramics infinitely more appealing than intact corpses."

I'd lost control of my own lecture. Supposedly, these people —Bradford's potential donors— invited me to speak about ancient Egyptian artifacts, not perform like a trained seal recounting criminal adventures. Yet here they sat, treasure hunters masquerading as patrons, with their attention focused entirely on the wrong aspect of my experience.

*Specimen: Audience (Wealthy Collector Variety), Notable Characteristics: Selective hearing regarding scholarly content, irritating ability to reduce complex research to entertainment value.*

A voice from the back cut through the murmurs. "Dr. Bell, your methods for authenticating lapis lazuli pigments must be quite sophisticated. I'm curious—what would you recommend for pieces that have been recently... relocated from private collections?"

The room fell silent except for the gentle whisper of expensive fans. I craned my neck but couldn't see the speaker.

"Authentication procedures," I managed, my throat dry. The question carried uncomfortable specificity—few understood the connection to systematic forgeries or the shadowy "Operation Indigo" network we'd uncovered. "Such work requires laboratory analysis and documented provenance. Hardly suitable for drawing room discussion."

"How delightfully modest," he called out. "Though I suspect your expertise extends beyond laboratory work. After all, fieldwork requires such... practical knowledge."

I straightened my shoulders, channeling every ounce of Oxford-trained dignity.

My thoughts unavoidably turned to my former investigative partner. Benedict Quinn would have found this audience's bloodthirsty curiosity grimly amusing, probably would have made some sardonic observation about today's wealthy collectors and yesterday's gladiatorial spectators.


But four weeks of silence had made it clear our professional collaboration—and whatever else it might have been—was permanently concluded.

Four weeks since he'd vanished without explanation after we'd recovered some of the stolen pieces—though the mastermind behind Operation Indigo remained frustratingly elusive.

"Very well. Since you're curious about my previous investigations, I can provide context that relates directly to the preservation challenges facing Egyptian cultural heritage."

The room settled into expectant silence, perfumes and tobacco smoke creating cloying layers in the still air.

"The artifacts in question were part of a systematic theft ring targeting items with specific blue pigmentation—ancient Egyptian pieces that contained advanced mathematical and astronomical knowledge. The conspiracy involved government officials, museum consultants, and private collectors who systematically removed genuine artifacts containing advanced mathematical and astronomical knowledge—pieces that challenged accepted narratives about ancient Egyptian capabilities. We discovered that authentic pieces were being replaced with sophisticated forgeries, their scientific content deliberately altered or suppressed."

I skipped the more lurid details, of Rosamund Fairchild's murder of my mentor, Gregory Sutherland. The way Elias Hawke's body sounded as it hit the floor after the bullet from an unknown gun found him. Even the murders at Lady Blackwood's estate, still fueled by Operation Indigo's puppet master.

I paused, noting how several faces had sharpened with interest that seemed more calculating than scholarly.

"While we identified some of the network participants, the mastermind remains hidden, and several key pieces, including what Dr. Jasper Thorne called the 'Astral Sphere,' were never recovered. The investigation revealed how easily legitimate scholarship can be corrupted when cultural heritage becomes profitable commodity rather than protected legacy."

A murmur of fascinated whispers rippled through the audience, carrying fragments of "conspiracy" and "stolen treasures" that made my jaw clench.

From the corner of my eye, I caught movement—a figure near the back wall discreetly photographing my slides without permission. The realization that someone might be gathering intelligence about my research sent a chill down my spine despite the afternoon's oppressive heat.

During our previous investigations, we'd discovered how thoroughly the artifact theft network monitored potential threats. Quinn had warned me that Operation Indigo had eyes everywhere—even in academic circles.

"Perhaps," I said, my voice steadier than I felt, "we might return to the original topic of New Kingdom ceramic techniques? I have several fascinating examples of—"

A sharp rap on the wall interrupted my desperate attempt

at redirection. A hotel messenger appeared in the doorway, bearing a silver tray.

"Dr. Clarissa Bell?" His crisp uniform and formal bearing suggested this wasn't ordinary hotel correspondence. "Urgent delivery, madam."

So urgent, it needed to interrupt my lecture?

The envelope resting on the polished tray was expensive—heavy cream paper with elegant script and a distinctly formal weight. A small embossed symbol at the bottom caught my eye: a tiny blue flame, rendered in a deep blue.

The small embossed symbol made my chest tighten with recognition. Blue pigmentation had been the connecting thread in the systematic thefts—not common Egyptian blue, but precious lapis lazuli reserved for the most significant pieces.

My hand trembled slightly as I broke the wax seal, awareness of every watching eye in the suddenly silent room. The invitation's contents were equally elegant and ominous:

*The honor of your presence is requested aboard the luxury steamship* Nefertiti *for a ten-day cruise from Cairo to Aswan.*

*Your expertise in ancient Egyptian astronomy and pigment authentication would grace our scholarly gathering.*

*Please join Professor Nigel Montague and distinguished guests for an exclusive examination of recently acquired artifacts.*

*Departure tomorrow at dawn from Bulaq dock. Private cabin arrangements prepared.*

The invitation was unsigned. But it had to have issued from Professor Montague.

My heart warmed a bit at being sought out by the kindly professor-turned-curator from the Graeco-Roman Museum, whose assistance during previous investigations had earned my trust and gratitude.

The invitation was professional recognition, an opportunity to work with respected colleagues while enjoying the comfort of Nile luxury travel.

But I couldn't accept. I needed to focus on my career, not adventures in artifact acquisition.

I exhaled in a huff. After five weeks of peaceful digging in the sand, carefully sorting pottery sherds and documenting glazing techniques far from murder investigations and international conspiracies, a distracting opportunity had found me again.

"Dr. Bell?" The messenger waited patiently while the audience watched. "Is there a reply?"

I looked up at the expectant faces surrounding me—Bradford's potential donors, the suspicious questioner still watching with calculating interest, the photographer who'd slipped closer during the distraction. Tomorrow morning, I could be sailing south toward Aswan in comfort, or I could remain in Cairo, examining pottery while wondering what "recently acquired artifacts" were aboard that luxury steamship.

The choice should have been simple. I was an archaeologist, not a detective. I'd proven definitively that criminal investigation led to chloroform, kidnapping, and narrow escapes from burning buildings. The sensible course was to decline politely and return to work where the most dangerous thing was the occasional structural collapse of ancient walls.

But... Professor Montague had requested my expertise specifically. And that blue flame symbol suggested connections to the unresolved mysteries that haunted my dreams—the missing artifacts, the shadowy mastermind who'd orchestrated thefts across three countries, the stolen mathematical knowledge that could rewrite our understanding of ancient Egyptian achievements.

I folded the invitation with deliberate care, tucking it into my portfolio while the assembled audience watched.

"Please inform the sender," I said, surprised by the steadiness of my own voice, "that I require time to consider this generous invitation."

As the messenger departed and I returned to the podium to conclude my lecture with determinedly dry commentary about firing temperatures, I couldn't shake the feeling that my peaceful scholarly interlude was about to end.

The lecture concluded to polite applause. As the audience

dispersed in clusters of whispered speculation about invitations and detective stories, I remained at the podium, staring at the blue flame insignia on the envelope.

Five weeks ago, I'd believed my adventures in criminal investigation would remain a part-time effort. I'd returned to legitimate archaeology with relief, grateful to exchange life-threatening conspiracies for the peaceful challenge of reconstructing pottery, where the most dangerous thing was paper cuts from catalog cards.

But all it took was Professor Montague's elegant invitation to drag me back toward the sort of adventure that invariably ended with me explaining my presence at crime scenes to skeptical authorities.

The blue flame insignia seemed to pulse with malevolent life in the afternoon light, like a tiny beacon calling me back to the world of international conspiracies and people who viewed murder as acceptable business practice.

*Specimen: Peaceful Academic Life (Recently Deceased), Cause of Death: Mysterious invitation bearing familiar color of impending doom.*

I closed my portfolio, already calculating what arrangements would be necessary if I were foolish enough to accept this invitation.

After all, what was the worst that could happen on a scholarly cruise filled with distinguished academics and valuable artifacts?

*Rather a lot,* my rational mind whispered.

*And you know it.*

# CHAPTER TWO

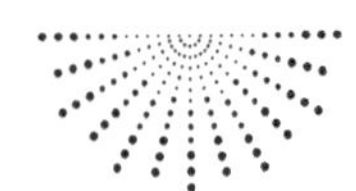

The excavation tent at Giza had become a furnace, the canvas walls radiating heat like a kiln, and I was holding a pottery sherd upside down.

"You've been staring at that fragment for ten minutes," Annie observed, looking up from her field notebook where I had her sketching small amulets from yesterday's finds. A letter with Fredde's familiar handwriting peeked from beneath her documentation sheets—their regular correspondence a bright spot in the desert isolation.

"Either it's the most fascinating piece of Old Kingdom domestic pottery in existence, or you're avoiding making a decision about that invitation."

I set down the sherd—definitely not fascinating—and reached for my water canteen. The metallic tang of overheated water made me grimace. "Professor Montague specifically requested my expertise."

Annie set down her stylus beside the neat rows of cataloged amulets. "You're still wondering about your father's connections to that smuggling network, aren't you? Another cruise ship full of his sort of people—wealthy collectors treating Egyptian heritage like parlor entertainment. No wonder you're hesitant."

"I'm an archaeologist, not a detective." The words felt rehearsed. "My responsibility is to legitimate scholarship, not chasing conspiracies."

"And yet you brought the invitation back here instead of declining immediately." Annie fixed me with the look she'd perfected during our year of partnership—gentle but relentless. "You're burying yourself in pottery because you're afraid to admit you're struggling with Quinn's disappearance. The blue flame symbol is just an excuse—you're curious about Operation Indigo because it connects to him."

Before I could respond, the tent flap burst open. Dr. Bradford stood silhouetted against the blazing afternoon light, looking like he'd been chased across the desert by creditors.

"Dr. Bell! Wonderful news! The Ashford Foundation has agreed to increase funding."

I became suddenly fascinated by my pottery fragment. I hated this part of the job. "What's the catch?"

"Catch? There's no catch. Merely... expectations."

I sensed that the conditions attached to this generous funding development involved me.

"However," Bradford positioned himself between me and the tent opening like a general blocking retreat, "They were quite specific about expecting our most prominent team member to represent our work among influential circles. He was particularly impressed by your reputation as someone who can... navigate complex situations."

My hands stilled on the cataloging materials. "You can speak plainly, Dr. Bradford."

"Thank you, I shall. The invitation you received earlier today. It represents an extraordinary opportunity. Ten days among some of Egypt's most distinguished collectors and scholars, examining artifacts aboard a luxury ship. The potential to expand our network justifies—"

"You heard about the invitation."

"Professor Montague wrote to me directly." Bradford drew himself up. "I assured him you'd be delighted."

"You accepted on my behalf?" The catalog card crumpled in my grip. "How wonderfully autocratic of you."

"The funding implications were too significant to risk delay. Continued support depends on our team's visibility among influential collectors." Bradford mopped his forehead with a handkerchief that had seen better decades. "Surely you understand the practical necessities of archaeological finance."

Annie's chair scraped softly through the packed the sand as she rose. "Perhaps Dr. Bell should be allowed to make her own professional decisions?"

Bradford directed his answer at me. "Archaeological expeditions require funding. Funding requires patron satisfaction. You're here to satisfy patrons."

I tried to smooth the card, fingers tense. "And if I refuse this 'opportunity'?"

His smile held all the warmth of limestone after sunset. "I would naturally respect your decision. Though future expedition positions might prove... limited. Other directors are less understanding about team members who decline opportunities that could benefit multiple projects."

Professional blackmail, delivered with administrative efficiency and wrapped in concern for the greater good of archaeology. Word travels fast among archaeologists—Bradford would ensure every dig director from Alexandria to Aswan heard about my 'unreliability' if I refused.

"The steamship departs at dawn." He consulted his pocket watch as though setting a countdown. "I've taken the liberty of arranging your absence from site duties. Professor Montague was quite insistent about the urgency."

The excavation brushes scattered across my worktable seemed to mock my pretense of scholarly control. I'd been using cataloging work like a shield against uncomfortable truths—about Father's possible involvement, about Quinn's silence, about my own inability to confront either situation directly. External forces had once again organized my life without consultation, reducing me from respected archaeologist to convenient pawn in other people's strategic games.

"I'll need time to prepare," I said, my voice steadier than my hands. "And Annie must be allowed to accompany me."

"Naturally. Though I should mention—You were also requested to share any expertise you might have regarding recent... investigative developments. Apparently, your reputation extends beyond purely academic circles."

Bradford departed, leaving Annie and me alone in the tent's oppressive atmosphere.


"Well," Annie said after several moments of contemplative silence, "at least you'll have excellent accommodations while dodging whatever dangers this invitation actually represents."

By evening, my apartment had erupted into packing chaos. After the expansive dig site where problems could be walked off among ancient monuments, my cramped quarters felt like a specimen jar with the lid screwed tight. The windows hadn't opened since the hotel painted them shut three seasons ago.

Annie had taken to her own hotel accommodations—still paid for by my father, and still more upscale than mine—to pack her own belongings. Meanwhile, I struggled to put together a wardrobe suitable for hobnobbing among the elite, while stopping every few minutes to seek relief from my tiny electric fan—one of my apartment's modern conveniences, when it worked.

A knock at the door elicited a sigh of relief. Annie must have finished with her packing and come to rescue me.

I swung it wide. "You're just in time—"

But it was not Annie.

Benedict Quinn stood in my doorway, his linen suit looking like he'd stepped off the cover of *Adventure Quarterly*, despite Cairo's punishing heat.

"Good evening, Dr. Bell."

That quirky half-smile did nothing to dislodge the four-week-old stone in my chest.

"What are you doing here?" I crossed the room to wrestle

with the painted-shut windows, needing air and escape in equal measure.

The electric fan chose Quinn's arrival to explode in a shower of sparks, mechanical failure punctuating his appearance with acrid smoke.

Even my appliances were abandoning me.

"Stupid fan," I muttered, unplugging the smoking contraption. Then reconsidered and plugged it back into the wall.

"I need to speak with you about something important."

"Oh? Important? After four weeks of silence?" I returned to wrestle with the sticky window. The tang of smoke was killing my overdeveloped sense of smell, which had always been a blessing and a curse.

"Clarissa, I'm sorry—"

"Save it." I yanked at the window frame with unnecessary force.

After our second collaboration at Lady Blackwood's estate and Quinn's honesty about his true occupation as British Intelligence, not to mention the lovely Christmas we spent together, I'd believed something had changed between us, that we were moving toward something... significant.

Instead, a few days after returning to the Giza dig, my messages to Quinn had gone unanswered, and I'd not seen him since.

"Listen, Clarissa, please. It was my handler who forced the communication blackout—"

Heat flooded my chest and rose up my throat like molten metal. "Oh, how convenient. 'My handler made me do it.' What are you, a poorly trained dog?"

"Operation Indigo is still active. Someone's still collecting the stolen pieces. There's an upcoming clandestine auction. Aboard a Nile cruise."

The leather portfolio containing Montague's invitation seemed to radiate significance from my writing desk. "Is that right?"

"My superiors want me aboard, undercover as a wealthy collector."

Seriously?

I glanced at the clothes strewn about the room and my steamer trunk. It couldn't be more obvious that I was packing. Had his trained eye picked up on it?

"That sounds like a lovely vacation for you. I hope you enjoy it."

"My superiors want me aboard, maintaining a low profile." He paused, studying my expression with the attention of someone defusing explosive devices. "The cover requires a wife. To appear legitimate among married passengers."

The temperature in my already stifling apartment seemed to spike beyond endurance.

My hands curled into fists. "You can't be serious."

"I've already told them you agreed."

Already ag—before ASKING me?"

"The mission parameters required immediate confirmation. I know how this appears—"

"How this appears?" My voice pitched an octave higher as I turned away deliberately, presenting my back. "You vanish for four weeks without explanation, then reappear presuming I'll participate in your convenient charade?"

Quinn moved cautiously around my writing desk. "Your reputation made you specifically valuable to my handlers. The 'detective archaeologist' designation carries weight in intelligence circles."

"The designation that's turned me into a performing seal for wealthy collectors." I crossed my arms tightly across my chest. "I returned to legitimate archaeology to avoid being anyone's trained monkey."

"I'm confused. Are you a seal, or a monkey?"

That quirky half-smile appeared—the one that used to make my stomach flutter and now just made my hands tremble with barely leashed energy that wanted to throw something fragile and satisfying.

I wasn't playing this game. "It's quite likely these aren't just wealthy tourists. Some of them are probably connected to the network that stole the Sphere and killed people to protect their operation."

Quinn's expression hardened with genuine concern. "The auction was organized secretly, which explains the last-minute timing. Someone is consolidating stolen artifacts, possibly including pieces that were never recovered from Hawke's organization."

"And you assumed I'd abandon my archaeological work to provide cover for your intelligence mission? What's the job description—smile winningly while you rifle through people's personal effects? Provide alibis while looking decorative? I'm an archaeologist, not a stage prop with advanced degrees."

Quinn's voice was equally sharp. "I assumed you'd want to stop whoever killed your mentor and stole artifacts containing mathematical knowledge that could transform our understanding of ancient Egyptian achievements." He frowned. "I assumed you'd care about preventing cultural heritage from disappearing into private collections where scholars will never access it."

"You broke communication not because you were ordered to, but because you chose obedience over...whatever we were developing." My throat tightened.

Quinn's careful composure cracked slightly. "The communication blackout was necessary for operational security. Personal feelings couldn't compromise—"

"Personal feelings." The words tasted bitter in the stifling air. "How wonderfully clinical. And now you need a wife to complete your cover story."

"A fake wife. For professional purposes only, maintaining appearances during a dangerous investigation that could prevent—"

"Get out." I gripped the back of my desk chair until my knuckles went white, the words cutting through his explanations.

Quinn remained motionless for several seconds. When he finally spoke, his voice carried quiet resignation.

"The steamship departs at dawn. If you're aboard, we can discuss terms. If not..." He moved toward the door. "I'll find another way to complete the mission."

His footsteps echoed on the stairs, fading into Cairo's evening sounds—distant conversation, children playing in courtyards, the eternal whisper of wind through ancient stones that had witnessed far more drama than this.

I turned again to face the stubborn window, hands pressed against glass that refused to budge, much like my circumstances.

Quinn was right about one thing: whoever had organized this auction likely possessed stolen artifacts that needed to be retrieved.

And tomorrow morning, I could either remain in Cairo cataloging pottery fragments while wondering what dangerous game was being played aboard that steamship, or I could sail south toward Aswan as someone's fake wife, armed with archaeological expertise and a month's worth of accumulated fury at presumptuous men who organized my life without consultation.

Once again, the choice should have been simple. I was an archaeologist, not a spy.

But that blue flame symbol...

I leaned my forehead against the window.

Quinn appeared in the street below.

I rapped my knuckles against the glass.

He paused but didn't turn immediately.

When he did, the look he tossed over his shoulder carried something that made my traitorous heart skip despite everything—not just self-congratulation, but something vulnerable that reminded me why I'd fallen for him in the first place.

I mouthed a single word, the decision made before my rational mind could intervene:

"Wait."

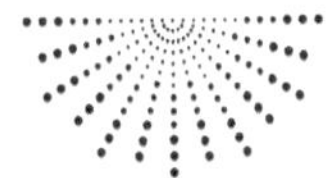

*T*he word escaped before I could properly categorize it as a catastrophic tactical error.

Quinn stepped back into my apartment moments later, closing the door with a quiet click. "Clarissa, believe me. I wanted to reach out. But my handler received intelligence that Operation Indigo operatives were monitoring our communications. The surveillance created unacceptable risk."

"To whom, exactly? Your precious mission or my inconveniently female feelings?"

"To you." His voice dropped. "The people we're investigating have already killed to protect their network. My handler believed—and I agreed—that complete separation was the only way to ensure your safety."

The broken fan made a desperate, grinding attempt at revival, then surrendered with a sound like dying clockwork.

"How considerate of you both." I straightened a stack of research notes that required no straightening. "And now that you've determined I'm expendable again, you've returned to request my services as decorative spouse."

"My superiors believe Operation Indigo is still active." Quinn remained near the door, respecting the invisible boundary I'd established. "The Sphere wasn't stolen from

Karnak Temple randomly—someone specific wanted it, and they're collecting similar pieces. That's why they need me on this cruise. But they believe our previous—interactions—will make our cover story believable."

I pulled out the invitation and traced the blue flame emblem. "And you require a wife because...?"

"Because wealthy collectors travel with their wives. Because private auctions expect established couples. Because unmarried men draw attention and questions that compromise investigation."

Quinn's expression remained neutral, but his fingers adjusted his perfectly aligned cuffs.

"Clarissa, you're the leading expert on the exact artifacts being targeted. Your knowledge of pigment authentication could identify which pieces are genuine versus forgeries—and more importantly, which pieces are worth killing for. Without your expertise, I could spend the entire cruise cataloging expensive forgeries while the real artifacts disappear." He hesitated. "And you've proven remarkably effective at extracting information from suspects who underestimate you."

I sorted his statement into its component parts: practical mission requirements, professional acknowledgment, and backhanded compliment.

*Intelligence Agent (Species: Quinn), Notable Characteristics: Strategic deployment of partial truths, selective explanation of motives, ability to appear reasonable while manipulating.*

"Well, as it happens, I've already been invited to this cruise." I held up Montague's invitation, enjoying the momentary surprise that fractured Quinn's composure. "Professor Montague specifically requested my expertise. Bradford has already insisted I attend."

The balance of power shifted perceptibly, like excavation soil after unexpected rain.

"You didn't mention this."

"You didn't ask. You assumed I would accompany you as wife, not that I might have my own invitation as scholar."

Quinn absorbed this information with rapid recalculation.

He stepped closer, eyeing the blue flame insignia with focused attention.

"This changes the operational parameters. Montague invited you personally? With this specific marking?"

I handed him the invitation. "The same blue shade we've encountered before. I suspect whoever's behind this auction is using established connections to gather specific people and artifacts."

Quinn studied the invitation with narrowed eyes. "The timing is concerning."

I reclaimed the paper with archaeologist's possessiveness. "And yet you're perfectly willing to drag me into this situation as your convenient wife."

The amber glow of the oil lamp caught something unexpected in Quinn's expression—a brief flash of what appeared to be genuine remorse before professional neutrality reasserted itself. A bead of perspiration tracked down his temple despite his immaculate appearance, the only sign that even Benedict Quinn wasn't immune to Cairo's evening heat or our charged proximity.

"I wouldn't have let anything happen to you."

"How reassuring. But it doesn't matter anyway. You can't be undercover, and I can't be your fake wife. Professor Montague certainly knows us both."

"But this is even better! Montague knows me as a rich antiquities dealer. And now I have a perfectly legitimate reason to accompany you, as myself. After our whirlwind romance and nuptials, of course. Montague would expect your husband to join you for a trip like this."

"I'm not pretending to be your wife."

"What about fiancée?"

The suggestion hung in the air like smoke from ceremonial incense—enticing and potentially hazardous.

"An engagement would explain both my recent absence and our current proximity," Quinn continued. "We could claim I was abroad arranging family matters before our marriage. It would allow you to maintain your professional identity as Dr. Bell while explaining our connection."

The logic was infuriatingly sound. An engagement would preserve my name while providing plausible explanation for our relationship. It would allow separate accommodations while justifying our frequent interactions during investigation.

I folded my arms. "Even if I agreed to this charade—which I haven't—there are conditions."

Quinn's expression remained neutral, but I detected the subtle shift in his posture.

I shuffled my research notes, avoiding direct eye contact as I formulated my terms. "First." The sharp tap of my boot heel against the floor tiles punctuated my demands. "I am the invited expert. You are my *guest*, as my fiancé—not the other way around."

His eyebrows rose, but then he shrugged one shoulder. "Agreed."

"Second, we maintain separate accommodations. Annie must also be allowed to come as my companion."

"Annie's presence is sensible, but she must be in a separate accommodation as well. As a ladies' companion, not your friend."

"Fine. Third," I continued, "you will not make decisions regarding my involvement without consultation. I am a partner in this investigation, not a subordinate agent to be deployed at convenience."

"That could complicate operational security—"

"Non-negotiable."

We stared at each other across my cluttered desk—a battle of wills conducted in silence until Quinn nodded once.

"Fourth," I said, noting his eyeroll, "any information discovered about Operation Indigo will be shared immediately. No convenient omissions out of misplaced chivalry or 'operational security.'"

A muscle tightened in Quinn's jaw. "Some information remains classified—"

"Then I'll discover it myself, likely at inconvenient moments that compromise your precious mission."

The silence stretched between us like a taut excavation rope.

"Have you reached the end of your demands?" Quinn finally asked.

"I reserve the right to add conditions as circumstances warrant."

Something dangerously close to amusement flickered across his face. "That's not how negotiations typically function."

"I don't typically function as someone's fictional fiancée. Extraordinary situations require extraordinary terms."

Quinn reached into his waistcoat pocket and withdrew a small velvet box with the ceremonial gravity of someone handling ancient artifacts. "In the interest of authenticity, my handler provided this."

He extended it to me, and the box opened to reveal a ring that betrayed uncomfortable knowledge of my preferences—a central lapis lazuli stone framed by small diamonds, set in aged silver with hieroglyphic symbols etched into the band. Not ostentatious, not modern, but precisely what I might have chosen for myself.

"Your handler has surprisingly specific knowledge of my taste in jewelry."

"Not my handler. Me." Quinn's gaze held mine. "I selected it."

The admission disturbed carefully maintained categories. I'd filed our relationship under *Professionally Terminated* after the weeks of silence. This ring suggested revision might be required.

"'Well then, *your* knowledge of my jewelry preferences is simultaneously thoughtful and terrifying," I tried to focus on academic details rather than emotional implications. I squinted at the engraving but would need my spectacles to read it. "What does it say?"

"'Truth emerges from darkness.'" Quinn kept his distance,

allowing me to examine the ring without pressure of proximity. "It seemed appropriate."

Appropriate or alarming, depending on one's interpretation. The ring represented both deception and investigation—a false engagement concealing the search for genuine truth about Operation Indigo. The symbolism was elegant, manipulative, and disturbingly appealing.

"We'll need a convincing engagement narrative," Quinn continued. "How I proposed, when we decided—"

"You're the expert at inventing lies, so I'll leave that to you."

I stared at the ring box on my desk, the perfect circle of lapis lazuli catching the lamplight like a trap closing around my independence. The delicate piece looked incongruously fragile against the scattered pottery fragments and measuring tools that defined my real life.

Quinn remained silent, but I could feel his attention on my hands as I finally, reluctantly, slipped the ring onto my finger. It fit perfectly—which was somehow more infuriating than if it had been wrong. My hand trembled slightly as I adjusted to the unfamiliar weight, a physical reminder of the deception we were constructing.

The apartment's confines seemed to contract around us, forcing acknowledgment of the physical performance our arrangement would require—linked arms, meaningful glances, the casual intimacies expected of an engaged couple. Playing the role would require dismantling carefully constructed barriers between us.

I reached for my cup of tea, long grown cold.

"We should establish clear boundaries for public behavior," I said, retreating behind academic specificity. "Acceptable forms of address, appropriate physical contact—"

"Perhaps we should practice."

My teacup stilled halfway to my lips. "Practice what, exactly?"

"Looking like an engaged couple rather than adversarial colleagues." Quinn gestured to the conspicuous distance between us. "Currently, we resemble negotiators at a peace treaty, not people planning marriage."

"An accurate assessment of our actual relationship."

"Which will immediately signal deception to anyone watching. Engaged couples typically demonstrate greater comfort with proximity."

I set down the cup with deliberate care, my shoulders tensing. "What do you suggest?"

"May I?" Quinn indicated the space beside me.

I nodded stiffly, and he crossed the invisible boundary. He settled beside me, close enough that the familiar scent of his cologne registered—sandalwood and leather notes that triggered unwelcome memories of previous investigations. The sticky dampness of my collar against my neck seemed to intensify as the apartment's heat rose with our proximity.

"Engaged couples touch casually." He demonstrated by adjusting a strand of hair that had escaped my practical knot, his fingers barely grazing my temple.

The gesture was achingly familiar, and my treacherous pulse responded despite my intellectual resistance. I forced myself to remain still, cataloging this as unwelcome physical evidence of unresolved attraction.

"They communicate without words. They anticipate each other's movements." He reached across me for Montague's invitation, and I found myself automatically shifting to give him space—the kind of unconscious accommodation that comes from intimate familiarity. "Yes, like that."

"I anticipate you'll be insufferable about this arrangement."

Quinn's unexpected laugh vibrated through the space between us. "Accurate anticipation. We might convince them after all."

I checked my small ladies' pocket watch attached to my belt —dawn was approximately seven hours away.

"I should contact Annie." I manufactured distance from the unsettling proximity, moving toward my small writing desk. "And pack appropriate attire for this charade. She'll need to know about the... arrangement."

"I'll send a telegram to my handler confirming our partnership." Quinn straightened his burgundy waistcoat. "The ship departs at dawn from Bulaq dock. I'll arrange transportation."

"I'll meet you there. Separate arrivals maintain the story that I received my own invitation."

Quinn paused at the threshold, his expression momentarily unguarded. "For what it's worth, I truly regretted the communication blackout. And I've missed you."

The admission hovered between us like delicate pottery fragments—broken pieces that might reassemble into their original form or might remain permanently damaged, depending on restoration techniques.

"Dawn," I said, neither accepting nor rejecting his explanation. "Don't be late."

After he departed, I remained motionless, staring at the open velvet box on my desk. The hieroglyphs caught lamplight —*truth emerges from darkness*—a promise and warning simultaneously.

*Subject demonstrates concerning willingness to sacrifice academic stability for dangerous liaisons.*

I headed downstairs to place a call to Annie, informing her of the charade, then paused on the threshold, struck by the absurdity of my situation.

"Well," I muttered to the empty room behind me, addressing my academic credentials hanging crookedly on the wall, "at least this adventure won't require explaining myself to the Egyptian Antiquities Service."

The fan gave one final, defiant sputter—rather like my common sense.

Perhaps I should have specialized in something sensible. Like explosives.

# CHAPTER FOUR

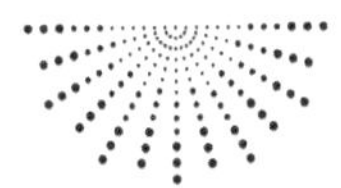

The gangplank to the Nefertiti trembled under foot, as if the vessel itself were anxious to be away.

Even the ship's name exemplified the Tutankhamun-inspired frenzy sweeping through Western society since Lord Carnarvon and Howard Carter's discovery. From the Egyptian motifs on the stewards' uniform buttons to the papyrus-shaped brass railings, everything on the British-owned luxury tourist steam ship catered to passengers' desire to consume ancient Egypt as fashionable entertainment while understanding little of its actual significance.

Annie walked beside me, carrying my hatbox with all the solemnity of a temple offering.

"Remember," I murmured, "I am here as an archaeological expert, not as Benedict Quinn's appendage."

"Of course, Dr. Bell." Annie's voice was suspiciously sweet. "Though that rather spectacular ring suggests otherwise."

I glanced down at my left hand where Quinn's hieroglyphic engagement ring glinted in the morning sun. The ancient Egyptian symbols caught the light. *Truth emerges from darkness.* A taunting reminder of our fabrication.

"I could always claim it's an archaeological specimen," I muttered.

Annie's laugh sparkled in the dry air. "I doubt even the most gullible passenger would believe you wear priceless antiquities on your finger."

We approached the ship's entrance where a uniformed officer with the ramrod posture of a career military man stood greeting passengers. His weathered face creased into a professional smile as we reached him.

"Welcome aboard the *Nefertiti*. I am Captain Mason." His eyes flicked briefly to my luggage, which contained more books than clothing. "You must be Dr. Bell, our archaeological expert."

"Yes, I—"

"She is indeed," came Quinn's voice from behind me. He materialized at my side with infuriating stealth, placing a hand at the small of my back. "And I'm Benedict Quinn, her fiancé."

My spine stiffened involuntarily at his touch.

Captain Mason's eyebrows rose slightly, but his smile remained fixed.

"How delightful. Congratulations on your engagement."

His careful phrasing made it clear he found our situation unusual. I forced my face into what I hoped was a besotted expression.

"Thank you, Captain. The engagement is quite new."

"Very new," Quinn added, his thumb tracing a small circle against my back.

"Well, we're honored to have you aboard." The Captain's eyes darted between us. "I do hope your trip won't involve any... unexpected complications."

"Complications?" I asked.

"I've been made aware of your previous adventures in Egypt, Dr. Bell." The Captain adjusted his gleaming brass buttons, each one embossed with the ship's logo. "The *Nefertiti* prides itself on discretion and comfort. Our wealthy patrons expect a certain level of... tranquility."

Quinn's hand pressed more firmly against me. "I assure you, Captain," he said smoothly, "we're simply here to examine artifacts. The only mystery we plan to solve is where to find the best viewing spot on deck."

The Captain looked unconvinced but nodded. "Sinclair will show you to your cabins. Professor Montague sends his apologies, by the way. He's been delayed in Alexandria but will join us at our first port of call."

I glanced at Quinn. Odd that the man organizing this cruise, and its auction, was not even present for the embarkation.

A sharply dressed ship's steward appeared to escort us.

Quinn and I followed him into the polished interior of the ship, with Annie trailing behind.

Quinn leaned close enough that his breath warmed my ear.

"Smile, darling. We're madly in love, remember?"

I whispered through clenched teeth. "Touch my back again without warning and you'll need a medical examination."

The steward led us, with Annie trailing, down a corridor of gleaming mahogany, each footstep muffled by plush carpeting. The walls were adorned with framed hieroglyphic reproductions, transforming the narrow passage into a floating museum.

"Your cabins, Dr. Bell, Mr. Quinn." Sinclair opened adjacent doors with a flourish. "You'll find they share a connecting door for... convenience." His expression remained professionally neutral, but the implication hung in the air.

"How thoughtful," I said faintly.

"Will there be anything else?" Sinclair asked.

"No, thank—"

"Actually," Quinn interrupted, "could you tell us more about the auction? My fiancée is particularly interested in items with lapis lazuli. Have you seen the pieces?"

Sinclair's face remained passive. "I'm sorry, I don't have any information about that. But I can tell you the welcome reception begins in thirty minutes on the upper deck. Most passengers will be attending."

Annie and I entered the spacious cabin, complete with four-poster bed, writing desk, and a small private balcony overlooking the Nile. Egyptian-inspired fabrics in jewel tones decorated the walls and bedding.

Annie immediately began unpacking my trunks. "Quite luxurious for a research expedition."

"This isn't research," I sighed. "It's theater."

Halfway through unpacking, a tentative knock sounded on the connecting door. I approached it warily, acutely aware of the symbolism of this threshold.

"Yes?" I called through the wood.

"May I come in?" Quinn's voice held a note of amusement. "We should discuss our strategy before meeting the other passengers."

The gentle lapping of Nile water against the hull provided a rhythmic counterpoint to my racing heartbeat. I unlocked my side and swung it open to find Quinn leaning casually against the frame. He'd changed into a linen suit.

"Interesting architectural challenge," he said, gesturing to the door between our rooms.

"Not at all. It will remain firmly locked from my side."

"Of course," His eyes crinkled. "Though it might raise questions if the steward notices during turndown service."

"I doubt it'll create a scandal," I replied dryly.

"I should warn you... I sleep-walk," Quinn added with mock seriousness. "You might wake to find I've cataloged your hairpins and dated them to the early Bronze Age."

"How terrifying. I'll be sure to barricade the door with my complete collection of pottery classification manuals. Even your lockpicking skills can't overcome five volumes on Predynastic ceramics."

Annie cleared her throat meaningfully. "I'll just finish unpacking your evening clothes, Dr. Bell. For the dinner tonight where you'll need to appear madly in love with Mr. Quinn."

I shot her a betrayed look that should have reduced her to archaeological dust. "That's quite enough, Annie."

"I'm simply ensuring accuracy, Dr. Bell," Annie replied, innocently arranging my evening gloves. "Future archaeologists might uncover evidence of your passionate romance. Wouldn't want to confuse the scholarly record."

Quinn's poorly disguised chuckle did nothing to improve my mood. He stepped fully into my cabin, surveying the space. "Have you given any thought to how we'll approach the other passengers? We need to identify potential Operation Indigo players without arousing suspicion."

"I thought I might try the radical approach of introducing myself as an archaeologist and discussing artifacts."

"While I play the besotted fiancé?" Quinn smiled. "Not entirely a stretch."

Before I could formulate a suitably cutting response, a commotion in the corridor drew our attention. The door to my cabin remained ajar, giving us a clear view as a familiar figure strode purposefully past, followed by a younger man carrying an official-looking case.

I froze. "Was that—"

"Inspector Hassan," Quinn confirmed, his posture instantly alert. "What's he doing here?"

I moved to the doorway in time to see Hassan disappear around the corner. "Nothing good for our investigation, I imagine. His presence is hardly coincidental."

"The plot thickens," Quinn murmured. "And before we've even left the dock."

"Shall we attend that welcome reception?" I suggested. "I suddenly find myself very interested in meeting our fellow passengers."

"After you, my dear fiancée."

I smoothed my travel dress, a practical cotton creation in a shade of green that Annie insisted brought out my eyes. "Annie, please continue organizing my tools and clothes. I want everything cataloged and secured."

She nodded, eyes sparkling with suppressed amusement. "Enjoy your first public appearance as a couple."

The upper deck of the cruise ship had been transformed into an elegant reception area. White-jacketed stewards circulated with trays of champagne flutes, while passengers gathered in small conversational clusters. The ship's gramophone played a muted jazz record, the latest sensation from America that seemed jarringly anachronistic against the ancient landscape. The Nile stretched before us like a tawny ribbon, and through the windows, I caught glimpses of feluccas with their distinctive triangular sails drifting along the shoreline, a design unchanged since pharaonic times.

Quinn's arm lightly circled my waist, and this time I managed not to flinch.

"Remember," he whispered, "we're in love."

"I'm trying to forget," I muttered. Then regretted the possible interpretation.

We'd barely accepted champagne when a commanding voice cut through the ambient chatter.

"Dr. Bell. What a surprise."

I turned to face Inspector Hassan, whose impeccable suit and severe expression seemed unchanged since our last encounter. Beside him stood a young Egyptian man with intelligent eyes and a deferential posture.

"Inspector Hassan," I forced warmth into my voice. "I could say the same. What brings you aboard the *Nefertiti*?"

"Official business. Received some last-minute information about an auction taking place on board." He raised an eyebrow at Quinn. "I assume that is why you are here, Mr. Quinn? Perhaps you can tell me if all is, as they say, 'above board' with this auction?"

Quinn smiled. "I'm just an invited guest, I'm afraid. My dear Clarissa has me tagging along."

Hassan's gaze shifted pointedly to my left hand where the engagement ring caught the light. "Ah. I see congratulations are in order." But the scowl that accompanied the remark was hardly congratulatory.

Quinn's arm tightened around my waist with possessive ease. "Thank you, Inspector. We're delightfully, deliriously happy."

I managed not to choke on my champagne, but it was a near thing.

"How curious that you never mentioned your engagement during our previous... investigations, Dr. Bell."

My fingers curled reflexively around the stem of my champagne glass as Hassan's gaze lingered on my ring, the pressure threatening to snap the delicate crystal. My mind raced. "It happened rather suddenly."

"It would seem so. Almost as sudden as your appearance on this cruise."

Beside me, Quinn maintained his pleasant expression, but I felt the almost imperceptible tension in his arm against my back. We needed to tread carefully.

The young man beside Hassan shifted.

Hassan noticed and made a perfunctory introduction. "This is my assistant, Faraj. He will be helping me catalog the artifacts for the auction."

Faraj wore a modern European suit, but his tarboosh—the traditional red felt hat—marked him as part of Egypt's emerging professional class navigating between worlds.

Faraj extended his hand eagerly. "It's an honor to meet you, Dr. Bell. Your paper on New Kingdom pigmentation techniques was extraordinary."

I warmed to him immediately, and not just because of the compliment. "Thank you, Faraj. Are you interested in archaeological chemistry?"

"Very much so. I've been studying—"

"Faraj will be examining all items before the auction," Hassan interrupted. "To ensure nothing of national importance leaves Egypt illegally."

The undercurrent was clear: he suspected the auction might include stolen artifacts.

"A wise precaution," Quinn commented smoothly. "Perhaps Clarissa could assist? Her expertise with pigments is unmatched."

"That won't be necessary. I prefer official channels." Hassan straightened the sleeve of his impeccably tailored jacket, revealing a glimpse of his government-issued identification bracelet.

A booming aristocratic voice turned us to the door.

"I say, you must be the famous Dr. Bell!" A tall, handsome man in his late thirties approached our group. His auburn hair was slightly too long for fashion, and he wore his expensive linen suit with the careless confidence of inherited wealth.

"Lord Percival Ashford," he introduced himself, taking my hand and holding it a moment longer than necessary. "Your reputation precedes you. The archaeologist who solves mysteries! Absolutely fascinating."

I extracted my hand. "You're too kind, Lord Ashford. I'm simply an archaeologist."

"And my fiancée," Quinn added, his arm reasserting itself around my waist.

Lord Ashford's eyes widened with exaggerated dismay. "Engaged! What a tragedy for the rest of mankind." He turned to Quinn, hand on his chest. "You're a fortunate man, sir. Very fortunate indeed. I shall have to content myself with mere friendship and scholarly admiration."

The conversation shifted as more passengers joined our circle. A young woman with dark brown hair and sapphire blue eyes drifted over, dressed in a sky-blue day dress that screamed Parisian fashion.

"Lady Penelope Fairfax," she introduced herself in a cultivated mid-Atlantic America accent. "How lovely to meet fellow enthusiasts of Egyptian culture."

Her gaze lingered curiously on Hassan before moving to me. "Dr. Bell, your lecture series at the Cairo Museum was divine. I attended your talk on pigmentation analysis."

Another woman hovered at the edge of our group, plump and nervous in an outdated navy dress. She clutched an oversized beaded reticule like a shield.

"Mrs. Beatrice Pemberton," she introduced herself when I caught her eye. "From Manchester. My late husband collected Egyptian pieces. Nothing scholarly, mind you, just beautiful things."

Her eyes darted anxiously between faces as she spoke, particularly lingering on Lord Ashford.

As the conversation flowed around topics of archaeology and Egyptian history, I cataloged our fellow passengers.

*Lord Ashford: aristocratic specimen, possibly predatory, excessive cologne suggesting compensation for intellectual inadequacy.*

*Lady Penelope: decorative exterior with unexpectedly observant gaze, categorization incomplete.*

*Mrs. Pemberton: nervous demeanor suggesting either natural timidity or specific anxiety, further observation required.*

Meanwhile, I noticed Hassan watching Quinn and me with undisguised suspicion. His skepticism was warranted—our sudden engagement would seem implausible to anyone who had seen us work together before, particularly someone who had witnessed our frequent professional disagreements during previous investigations.

"So how did you two meet?" Lady Penelope asked, her innocent question landing like a trap.

Quinn and I answered simultaneously:

"At a museum lecture—" I began.

"Through mutual colleagues—" Quinn said.

We stopped, exchanging alarmed glances. Hassan's eyebrows rose fractionally.

"What my fiancée means," Quinn recovered smoothly, "is that while we were introduced through colleagues, we truly connected at one of her museum lectures on pottery glazing techniques."

"How... romantic," Lady Penelope said with the dubious tone of someone who'd expected champagne and moonlight rather than pottery and kiln temperatures.

"It was the way she differentiated between Middle and New Kingdom firing temperatures," Quinn continued, his eyes meeting mine with unexpected warmth. "Such passion for the smallest details. When she explained how a mere two-degree variance could completely alter the chemical structure of copper-based pigments, I was utterly captivated."

The genuine admiration in his voice—and the specificity of the details of my work—caught me off guard. I found myself staring at him, momentarily forgetting our audience.

"Clarissa had no idea I was courting her for months," Quinn added with a wry smile. "Too absorbed in her work to notice. I finally had to be rather direct."

"Direct?" Lord Ashford asked.

"Hmm. Yes. I—uh—proposed in the middle of her excavation site," Quinn grinned. "Got down on one knee in a pit of pottery shards. Most uncomfortable proposal in archaeological history."

I briefly imagined Quinn proposing in an excavation trench—the precise depth of sacrilege that would have my colleagues using my dissertation as kindling for their cook fires. Oxford would revoke my degree by telegram before he finished the question.

"Most uncomfortable acceptance, too," I added, surprising myself. "I was so shocked I dropped a Dynasty XVIII alabaster jar fragment. Nearly fell on his head."

Something in Hassan's expression shifted, a barely perceptible softening. Whether he believed our ridiculous story or simply enjoyed watching me construct historical fiction on the spot, I couldn't tell.

The ship's whistle sounded, announcing our imminent departure. As passengers moved toward the railings to watch Cairo recede, Lord Ashford lingered by my side.

"You must tell me about your work with blue pigments," he said, taking my hand and holding it a moment longer than propriety dictated. "I have several pieces with remarkable blue coloration in my collection."

Quinn's casual smile never wavered, but something dangerous flickered in his eyes. Was it the mention of blue pigment? Or Ashford's flirtatious manner?

"Perhaps you could show Dr. Bell your collection another time, Lord Ashford," Quinn suggested, his voice pleasant yet somehow unyielding. "When we're not on our engagement cruise."

"What sort of blue, Lord Ashford?" I tried to sound merely academically interested. "Ancient Egyptian blue or lapis lazuli?"

"Both, actually. I find the symbolism fascinating." He absentmindedly touched a small pin on his lapel—a stylized blue flame in what appeared to be enamel work.

My heart rate picked up. "What an interesting pin," I commented. "Family crest?"

"This? Oh, just my old school society." He smiled with the casual ease of someone discussing the weather rather than a potential conspiracy. "The Brotherhood of the Blue Flame. A philosophical club—ancient wisdom, that sort of thing. We have like-minded members in archaeological circles. Nothing terribly exciting, just gentlemen with an interest in the... deeper aspects of history."

The Brotherhood of the Blue Flame.

The blue flame symbol matched exactly the insignia on my invitation. Montague must also be a member.

But perhaps it had nothing to do with Operation Indigo, after all.

"How interesting," I managed, my voice steady despite the revelation. "I'd love to hear more about it."

Quinn's hand appeared on my elbow, his grip gentle but insistent. "Darling, I believe they're serving dinner soon. We should prepare. You know how particular you are about your evening toilette."

As he guided me away, I resisted the urge to step on his foot.

I glanced back to see Hassan deep in conversation with his assistant Faraj, both men watching our retreat with unreadable expressions.

# CHAPTER FIVE

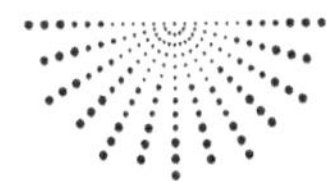

*M*orning light spilled across the *Nefertiti's* dining salon, and the gentle vibration of engines hummed beneath our feet as the ship cut through the tawny waters of the Nile.

Beyond the polished windows, life continued as it had for millennia—women balancing water jugs on their heads, farmers coaxing oxen through fields, children running along the banks, waving. Though our floating palace of European luxury was a new addition.

I paused at the salon's entrance, surveying the room. After a restless night contemplating Lord Ashford's casual mention of the Brotherhood of the Blue Flame, I'd risen early, determined to catalog our fellow passengers with greater care.

The room buzzed with conversation and the delicate symphony of silverware against fine china. Stewards circulated with trays of poached eggs, kippers, and toast points alongside Egyptian flatbread and preserved dates—the Empire's culinary mashup in miniature.

Annie appeared at my elbow, looking refreshed despite the early hour. "Good morning, Dr. Bell. You're up with the sun."

"Sleep proved elusive," I admitted. "Too many questions."

"About the auction? Or about sharing adjoining rooms with Mr. Quinn?" Her eyes slitted with mischief.

"The door remained firmly locked, thank you very much."

"Pity," Annie said. "I was hoping for a breakthrough in your excavation of emotional barriers."

"The only thing being excavated is your employment if you continue," I said, but couldn't maintain my stern expression.

Quinn materialized beside us, looking well-rested.

"Good morning, my devoted fiancée." His voice pitched loud enough for nearby passengers to hear. Against my ear, he murmured, "You've dark circles under your eyes. Were you up all night pondering Lord Ashford's Brotherhood comment?"

"Among other things," I said. "We should—"

"Dr. Bell!" A commanding voice cut across the salon. A woman with prematurely silver hair arranged in an elaborate Gibson Girl style waved enthusiastically from a corner table. "You simply must join us! We're discussing the mathematical properties of the Temple of Karnak."

Quinn's hand touched my arm. "Shall we?"

I didn't flinch this time—progress in our charade, I supposed—and allowed him to guide me toward the table.

Three people occupied the corner table: the silver-haired woman with the intense gaze of someone who might corner you at a dinner party, a nervous-looking man who appeared to be her son (with the haunted expression of someone who has been cornered at every dinner party of his life), and a severe woman with ashy blonde hair and thick spectacles, who seemed to be taking notes.

"Dr. Cordelia Waverly," the silver-haired woman introduced herself, extending a hand adorned with multiple rings featuring heavy gemstones. "Love your work, Dr. Bell! This is my son, Marcus, and my new research assistant, Fraulein Greta Becker."

Marcus nodded with the pained expression of someone perpetually embarrassed by his mother's enthusiasm.

"I am quite fortunate in Fraulein Becker," Dr. Waverly said, with a languid smile. "My previous assistant could not travel. Reliable help is nearly impossible to secure on short notice."

Fraulein Becker acknowledged the compliment, such as it was, with a stiff nod.

"The sacred ratios breathe through every stone of Karnak," Dr. Waverly continued without prompting. "The ancients encoded harmonic frequencies into the very architecture! The spacing between columns isn't arbitrary—it's mathematical poetry."

"Mother," Marcus interrupted with a tight smile, "perhaps not everyone at breakfast wishes to hear about numerical mysticism."

I quickly searched for nicknames for these two, in an attempt to remember all my new shipmates.

Dr. Waverly could only be *Mysticism & Mathematics.*

And her son—*Mother's Embarrassed Shadow.* Sorry, Marcus.

Dr. Waverly waved him off. "Nonsense! Dr. Bell understands the importance of such matters. The Brotherhood has always valued scholars who see beyond mere artifacts to the knowledge they contain."

My attention sharpened. "The Brotherhood?"

"Of scholars," she added quickly, glancing at her son. "The academic community, naturally."

I felt Quinn's posture shift subtly beside me, his body angling toward Dr. Waverly with new interest.

Mrs. Pemberton, the Manchester widow with the collector husband, approached our table, still holding her oversized beaded reticule like protection against unseen dangers. Her anxious gaze darted between faces as though expecting someone to leap up and accuse her of something terrible.

Behind her walked Lady Penelope Fairfax—the American heiress married into her British title—looking immaculate in a morning dress of pale mint green that probably cost more than my entire academic salary for the year. She moved with the practiced grace of someone who had been taught deportment by wielding books on her head since childhood.

*Social Butterfly... with Teeth.*

"Good morning," Mrs. Pemberton said, her voice pitched higher than necessary. "Mind if we join you?"

I pictured Mrs. Pemberton writing a query about social etiquette to her local advice columnist. *Signed, Anxious in Manchester.*

Quinn pulled out chairs for the newcomers with practiced gallantry.

A tall, distinguished gentleman with steel-gray hair and a military bearing approached our expanding group. "Colonel Reginald Hartwell," he announced, taking a seat without waiting for an invitation. "Delighted to make your acquaintance, Dr. Bell. I've followed your work with interest."

This one was easy. *Military Man* would be quite sufficient.

Annie discreetly withdrew to a neighboring table, positioning herself close enough to overhear while giving us space to work. I noted Inspector Hassan sitting alone at a table near the windows, checking his pocket watch.

Fraulein Becker cleared her throat. "Ze pigmentation analysis in your monograph, Dr. Bell—" her Germanic accent seemed to thicken as she spoke, "—ze techniques for differentiating pigments. Most impressive." Her accent was so pronounced as to be almost comical.

*We'll call her Spectacles & Ink Stains.*

"Thank you. Although I've found chemical testing is more reliable than visual examination alone."

"One wonders about the authenticity of certain auction pieces," Mrs. Pemberton interjected, lowering her voice conspiratorially. "My late husband collected Egyptian artifacts with blue pigmentation. Beautiful pieces, though I've often questioned their provenance since his passing." She tested her tea with excessive caution before sipping.

"The strategic application of ancient knowledge, Dr. Bell —that's where the true value lies," Colonel Hartwell said, fixing me with a penetrating stare. "These harmonic principles

Dr. Waverly mentions could have practical applications beyond academia, wouldn't you agree?"

The conversation was taking a strange turn. I glanced at Quinn, who gave an almost imperceptible shrug, confirming he'd noticed too.

"I prefer to focus on historical accuracy rather than modern applications," I said carefully.

"Tell me, Mrs. Quinn," Mrs. Pemberton said, demolishing my professional identity with a single phrase, "will you continue your little archaeological hobby after marriage? My husband always said a wife's intellectual pursuits must give way to household management. Though he found Carter's business with Tutankhamun quite fascinating—wouldn't you agree? Though some question his methodology."

My stomach clenched at the casual erasure of my credentials, that hollow feeling I knew too well from academic conferences where I was introduced as 'Armand Bell's daughter' rather than by my publications.

"It's Dr. Bell, actually. And archaeology isn't my hobby, it's my profession. The distinction between hobby and vocation isn't merely semantic—it's the difference between dabbling and dedication."

"Of course, of course," she patted my hand sympathetically, as though I were clinging to a childish fantasy. "But surely once there are children—"

"My fiancée will continue revolutionizing our understanding of ancient Egypt," Quinn interrupted smoothly, "with my enthusiastic support. Though I confess she's banned me from organizing her research notes after the Great Papyrus Incident of 1923."

Colonel Hartwell chuckled. "Wise man, knowing when to retreat. What was this incident?"

"Classified information," I said primly. "Suffice to say it nearly caused an international incident involving the British Museum, three Oxford professors, and a very confused camel."

Quinn's surprised laugh warmed me more than it should have.

"You must tell everyone of your proposal." Lady Penelope touched my hand charmingly. "Such an amusing story."

Quinn and I exchanged glances.

"Nothing extraordinary, I'm afraid."

"How long have you two known each other?" Colonel Hartwell pressed.

"Three years," I said.

"Two years," Quinn said simultaneously.

An awkward silence fell.

Dr. Waverly finally cleared her throat. "How extraordinary that an engaged couple cannot agree on the duration of their acquaintance."

"Three years professionally," I amended, heat creeping up my neck, "though we've only been… personally acquainted for two."

"Darling counts from our first meeting," Quinn said, draping his arm around my shoulders. "I count from when she finally acknowledged my existence beyond being 'that irritating man who keeps moving my reference books.'"

"I never called you irritating," I protested. "At least not to your face."

No one as much as smiled. Tough crowd.

"The first time you spoke directly to me," Quinn continued, eyes twinkling, "was to inform me I had shelved Petrie's reports in the wrong chronological order. Most romantic moment of my life."

This prompted genuine laughter, diffusing the tension.

"Mr. Quinn," Dr. Waverly leaned forward eagerly, fingering the lapis lazuli pendant at her throat, "what's your opinion on Clarissa's hypothesis about lapis lazuli being reserved for texts containing specialized knowledge?"

Quinn didn't miss a beat. "I've always admired how she connects pigmentation choices to content importance. Her work comparing the chemical signatures of blues used in astronomical texts versus decorative pieces is groundbreaking. Though she's too modest about it."

I stared at him, genuinely surprised.

"She's brilliant at finding patterns others miss," Quinn continued, his eyes meeting mine with unexpected warmth. "Whether it's trace elements in pigments or mathematical sequences in temple layouts. It's what makes her work so valuable."

The genuine admiration in his voice caught me off guard, and I found myself momentarily speechless.

Inspector Hassan approached our table, his expression concerned rather than his usual stern mask.

"Excuse me," he said, "has anyone seen Faraj this morning? He was supposed to meet me at dawn to begin cataloging the auction items."

The silent pause as my table companions stared up at Hassan carried a chill. I glanced across each expression and saw a common thread: each of them seemed displeased at Hassan's presence.

"The young man who was with you yesterday?" Mrs. Pemberton asked. "I haven't seen him since last evening's reception."

"Perhaps he overslept." Lady Penelope delicately patted her lips with a linen napkin.

Hassan shook his head. "Faraj is always punctual. This is unlike him."

"I saw someone on deck very early this morning." The ship's steward paused as he cleared nearby dishes. "Around four o'clock, when I was preparing the morning service. I assumed it was a crew member."

I noticed Mrs. Pemberton's hand trembling slightly as she set down her teacup.

"Did you see who it was?" Hassan asked sharply.

"No, sir. Just a figure by the railing. It was still dark."

Hassan's professional demeanor cracked slightly, concern bleeding through. "He's not in his cabin. I've already checked."

A thin man with even thinner brown hair and wire-rimmed spectacles approached our table, carrying a worn leather case. His gray eyes assessed our group with a cataloging gaze that reminded me of my own.

"Mr. Mullen," Hassan acknowledged him with a nod.

"Dr. Bell," Mullen said in precise, measured tones, "I wonder if I might consult with you about certain anomalies I've observed in the auction catalog? Professional integrity demands I seek a second opinion on authentication matters."

I glanced at Hassan.

He was clearly distracted but waved a hand. "I insisted Mr. Mullen join us for this journey, to review the auction legitimacy. He's had experience in such things."

"I see—"

"I need to check the cargo hold. Faraj mentioned inspecting some crates last night."

Hassan's hand moved unconsciously to check his service revolver, a gesture I recognized from Quinn's similar habit.

"I'll help you look," Quinn offered, standing. "I'm sure he's just lost track of time examining artifacts."

Something in Hassan's expression suggested he feared worse. The cargo hold contained the valuable auction pieces—if Faraj had discovered something problematic...

I rose as well. "I'll come too."

Mullen looked disappointed but nodded. "We can discuss authentication later. Finding your assistant takes priority, Inspector."

Annie caught my eye as I passed, raising her eyebrows in silent question. I gave her a slight nod, and she immediately understood, returning to her letter to maintain appearances. I noticed "Dearest Freddie" at the top of the page and a sketch of the *Nefertiti* in the margin. Her correspondence with Lady Blackwood's footman had grown quite dedicated since our adventure there. At least one of us was making genuine romantic progress.

We followed Hassan through the ship's elegant corridors and down a narrow staircase toward the lower decks. The polished woods and plush carpeting gave way to more utilitarian surroundings. The engine vibration grew stronger beneath our feet, and the air became warmer, tinged with the scent of oil and river water.

"Did Faraj come down here alone?" I asked quietly.

"He's thorough," Hassan replied. "He mentioned wanting to check the crating methods for the more fragile pieces. The boy has a future in conservation if he—" He stopped abruptly.

We turned a corner and saw it immediately—the heavy door to the cargo hold stood ajar rather than locked as it should be, a sliver of darkness beckoning from beyond.

Hassan quickened his pace, alarm now evident in his movements.

Quinn's hand moved subtly toward his jacket.

As we approached the partially open door, Hassan's footsteps faltered.

A distinctive metallic scent reached my nostrils, stirring memories of another investigation, another body. My sense of smell—unusually acute even among archaeologists trained to detect subtle chemical changes in ancient materials—registered the unmistakable copper-penny tang.

Blood—fresh and abundant—waiting just beyond the threshold.

# CHAPTER SIX

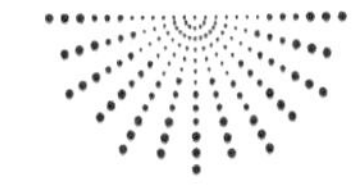

The cargo hold presented a stark contrast to the polished elegance of the upper decks—all functional utility and industrial purpose.

Hassan's sharp intake of breath confirmed what we all feared.

In the glow of the cargo hold's single electric bulb, Faraj lay crumpled between two wooden crates, his head at an unnatural angle against the corner of a heavy wooden container. Deep crimson blood pooled against the dark wood of the floor, shocking in its violence against the ship's refined pretensions. The rhythmic creaking of the ship's timbers continued unabated—life moving forward despite death.

"Nobody move." Quinn's arm shot out like a gate barrier, blocking my instinctive step forward as his eyes swept the scene for disturbances in the dust. "We need to preserve what we can of the scene."

I squared my shoulders against the wave of nausea and forced myself to remain still.

Hassan stood frozen in the doorway, his composure faltering as he took in the extent of the head trauma.

"Faraj." The name escaped as barely more than breath. He pulled a pristine white handkerchief from his pocket, the starched fabric crisp against the violent red staining his assistant's clothing. His hands clenched at his sides, professional protocol clearly warring with human grief.

"I can see the wound from here." I leaned against a stack of crates for stability, studying what was visible without disturbing anything. "Head trauma along his temple. But the amount of blood and the location of the wound..."

Something seemed off. I didn't know much about head wounds, but this one didn't seem like it would have killed him. Even if he'd tripped and fallen, would the blow to his head have been fatal?

"Someone must have struck him," Hassan observed, pointing to the blood on the edge of the wooden container. "Someone with enough strength to send him backward into this crate."

Faraj's notebook lay beside him, spattered in blood, his pencil still clutched in stiffened fingers. From our position at the threshold, I could make out neat Arabic script interspersed with mathematical calculations and sketched hieroglyphs, now marred with dark stains.

"He was cataloging pieces when he was attacked." I leaned forward slightly while keeping my feet planted. "I can see question marks next to what appear to be catalog numbers, and there's something specific about pigmentation that caught his attention."

Quinn examined the nearby crates from the doorway, his practiced eye taking in details without contaminating evidence. One wooden container sat slightly askew from the others, its lid not quite flush with the sides.

"That crate's been forced open recently." Quinn knelt, fingertips hovering above the fresh wood shavings scattered around the damaged lid. "Fresh splinters around the edge. Someone used considerable force."

Hassan's professional mask settled back into place, though his eyes remained haunted. "We'll need to document everything before we disturb anything. But first..." He carefully stepped around the blood and used his handkerchief to reach for the notebook.

"Hassan," I said gently, "we should photograph the scene first, if possible, before moving anything. I know you want to preserve Faraj's work, but—"

"You're right," he said, his hand stopping mid-reach. "Faraj would want us to do this properly. The ship's steward mentioned having a camera for passenger photographs. We'll document everything first." He sighed. "Faraj had an exceptional eye for authenticity. If he suspected forgeries..."

"Or if he discovered something someone wanted kept secret," I finished quietly.

"He joined my team straight from university," Hassan said quietly. "Brilliant mind. Refused positions at the British Museum to stay in Egypt—said our heritage belonged in Egyptian hands." His voice faltered slightly before he regained control.

The cargo hold felt suddenly oppressive, its electric lighting casting harsh shadows that transformed innocent wooden crates into potential hiding places for secrets worth killing for. The swaying lanterns cast shifting shadows across the cramped space, highlighting the single narrow door that served as both entrance and exit—an uncomfortable reminder that we were effectively trapped in this floating box of secrets. The gentle rocking of the ship seemed incongruous with the scene.

Quinn straightened from his examination of the disturbed crate. "We need to inform the Captain immediately. And secure this area—"

"What exactly is going on here?"

We all turned to find Captain Mason standing in the doorway, his weathered face cycling from confusion to alarm as he took in the scene.

"Captain," Hassan said, rising with dignity intact despite the circumstances. "I'm afraid we have a serious situation. My assistant has been killed."

Mason stepped closer, his naval training overriding his obvious distress as he methodically examined the scene. His eyes tracked from the blood spatter to Faraj's unnatural position, to the damaged crate corner, his expression growing more grim with each detail.

"Good God. This wasn't an accident." It wasn't a question.

"Captain—" Quinn began.

"A murder. On my ship." He was quiet for a long moment, consulting his watch . "We're four hours from the nearest port with adequate facilities, eight hours from anywhere with proper authorities." His gaze moved to Hassan. "Inspector, I assume you'll want to be part of this investigation?"

"If possible, yes."

"And you two—" Mason looked between Quinn and me, "—I don't suppose this is coincidental, given your... reputation for being present at crime scenes, Dr. Bell?"

I straightened. "Captain, I can assure you we had nothing to do with—"

"No, no," he waved off my protest. "I mean your expertise. If there's been a murder aboard my ship, I'd prefer it solved by competent investigators rather than creating a diplomatic incident by bungling the response."

Hassan bristled. "I can assure you, the Egyptian authorities—"

"Inspector, my passengers include some very influential people who expect discretion. Lord Ashford alone could destroy the cruise line's reputation with wealthy British clients."

Hassan nodded slowly. "And you do not mention, a precipitous return to Cairo would require explanations to Egyptian customs authorities about why a ship carrying antiquities would have a murder aboard."

*Not to mention the likelihood of artifacts that were stolen or purchased on the black market.*

Mason's jaw tightened. "As I said, discretion." He half-bowed. "I have every confidence you can conduct a discrete investigation. We will maintain passenger confidence, avoid diplomatic complications, and potentially solve this matter before reaching Luxor, where there are adequate British administrative facilities."

"That's assuming we can identify the killer without further incidents," Quinn pointed out.

"Indeed." Mason's eyes were steely. "Which is why I'm placing this investigation under Inspector Hassan's official authority, with Dr. Bell and Mr. Quinn as consulting experts. I'll provide full cooperation from my crew, but I want this resolved quickly and quietly."

He pulled out his watch again, checking the time with the precision of a man accustomed to rigid schedules. "We maintain normal cruise activities. I'll inform the passengers that your assistant took ill and is under medical care, Inspector."

Hassan nodded once.

Captain Mason cleared his throat. "In the meantime, I'll bring Dr. Henley down—he is our ship's physician and handles passenger medical needs. He'll need to examine..." He gestured toward Faraj's body. "Though I suspect his experience is more with seasickness and digestive complaints than... this sort of thing."

"That's fine," Hassan said. "We need an official medical assessment, even if preliminary. Dr. Henley can at least document the obvious trauma and estimated time of death."

"I'll speak with him privately," the Captain continued. "Tell him we have a medical emergency that requires absolute discretion. He's been with the cruise line for eight years—he understands the importance of protecting passenger confidence."

I gestured toward the notebook and the disturbed crate. "The evidence suggests Faraj discovered something significant about the auction pieces. Someone may have killed him to prevent him from reporting his findings."

Quinn nodded grimly. "We need to contain the situation, Captain. If we announce a murder, the guilty party will either panic and flee, or find a way to dispose of evidence."

"Secure this cargo hold," Hassan instructed. "No one enters without our permission. As you suggest, we will act as though nothing unusual has happened. Tell passengers that Faraj took ill and is resting."

Quinn nodded. "And Captain, we'll need access to passenger manifest information and any observations your crew might have made about unusual behavior last night."

I studied Faraj's notebook again, committing the visible details to memory. "I'll also need to examine those auction pieces properly. If Faraj died for what he discovered, we need to understand what that was."

"And how do we explain examining auction items when the auction isn't until later in the cruise?" the Captain asked.

"Leave that to me," I said. "I'm here as an archaeological expert. It would be natural for me to show professional curiosity about the pieces."

Hassan carefully closed Faraj's notebook, wrapping it in his handkerchief. "I'll preserve this as evidence. His observations may be crucial to understanding what happened."

Mason nodded. "I want regular updates on your investigation. The moment you identify the killer, we'll contain him until we can reach authorities at the next port."

"Faraj was a good man," Hassan said quietly, his composure finally cracking. "He wanted to protect Egypt's heritage, ensure our artifacts weren't stolen or misrepresented. He didn't deserve this."

Quinn's hand found my shoulder as we climbed back toward the passenger decks. "Are you alright?"

"I'm angry," I admitted. "Faraj was young, dedicated, trying to do the right thing. Someone killed him to protect their criminal activities."

"And we're going to find out who," Quinn said with quiet conviction.

# CHAPTER SEVEN

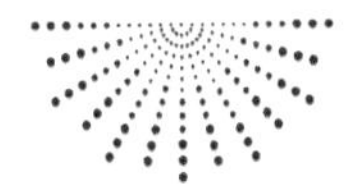

The narrow corridor leading to Faraj's cabin felt oppressive.

Hassan walked ahead of us, his shoulders rigid beneath his dark uniform, each step measured with the deliberate control of a man holding grief at bay.

The distant afternoon call to prayer drifted across the water from a riverside mosque, the muezzin's voice carrying faintly through the ship's hull. Hassan paused momentarily at the sound, his shoulders squaring as if drawing strength from the familiar ritual.

The cabin door stood slightly ajar, and Hassan pushed it open with the back of his hand, avoiding the handle. The space beyond was spartanly furnished but meticulously organized— books arranged by subject, a small desk cleared except for a several notebooks, a brass inkwell, three precisely aligned pens, and a cold cup of tea that still carried the faint scent of cardamom.

A small prayer rug lay perfectly aligned toward Mecca in the corner, its worn fibers speaking of daily use. The ceiling beams hung low enough that Quinn had to duck slightly as he entered, emphasizing the contrast between these utilitarian quarters and our spacious passenger cabins above. Through the single porthole, I glimpsed a felucca gliding past on the river, the boatman's silhouette a dark smudge against the afternoon light.

"Faraj kept meticulous records," Hassan said, his voice tight. "If he discovered something about those artifacts, there will be evidence." He straightened the stack of notebooks on the desk, aligning them perfectly with the edge. "He was brilliant. Youngest assistant I've ever trained, but he could translate hieroglyphs faster than scholars with decades of experience."

A half-finished letter lay on his desk, the midnight-blue ink dry enough not to smudge under my finger. It began with an affectionate greeting to his mother, promising to send money at the month's end. Beside it lay a newspaper folded open to an article about Sa'd Zaghlul and the Wafd nationalist party's latest confrontation with British authorities. The margins of his notebooks revealed annotations in three languages—Arabic flowing into French and then English with seamless fluidity. His intellect radiated from every corner of the small space.

Quinn examined a small magnifying glass from Faraj's desk, turning it over in his hands. "You mentioned he was like a son to you."

Hassan's composure slipped for just a moment, his hands clenching at his sides. "His father died when he was fifteen. I found him working as a translator for tourist guides, teaching himself hieroglyphs from French archaeological texts." He touched the photograph with a gentleness that made my throat tighten unexpectedly. "He sent money to his mother every month. Never missed a payment, never complained about the responsibility."

The grief in his voice made me look away, feeling like an intruder on his private pain. I cleared my throat before speaking.

"He was comparing excavation techniques," I observed, recognizing the diagrams in one notebook. "Carter's recent work must have inspired him."

"He attended the public exhibition in Cairo," Hassan

replied, professional interest momentarily overcoming his sorrow.

"What was he investigating yesterday?" Quinn's tone was carefully neutral. "You mentioned concerns about the auction catalog."

Hassan's dark eyes sharpened, suspicion reasserting itself. "Discrepancies in provenance documentation. Several pieces that didn't match their listed acquisition dates." He paused, studying Quinn with uncomfortable intensity. "Speaking of discrepancies, I find it curious how your engagement has suddenly materialized just as this cruise began."

My shoulders tensed, and I touched my false engagement ring, turning it around my finger. The word "discrepancies" hung in the air like an accusation.

Before I could respond, Quinn moved from the doorway with fluid grace. His arm settled around my waist—a gesture that appeared protective but positioned him to block Hassan's view of my face. His hand rested with familiarity in that space at the small of my back, the warmth of his palm steadying through the light fabric of my dress. The practiced intimacy of the movement surprised me, how natural it felt.

"Clarissa prefers to keep personal matters private until she's certain of her decisions," Quinn said smoothly. "Given her previous... disappointments in Cairo's expatriate community, I hardly blame her for discretion."

Disappointments. That was one way to describe Richard's spectacular transformation from devoted suitor to my father's antiquities acquisition agent. I added *Creative Euphemisms for Romantic Disasters* to Quinn's growing list of useful skills.

The reference to my ex-fiancé Richard was perfectly calculated—enough truth to sting, enough implication to suggest romantic history without requiring elaborate lies. I leaned into Quinn's embrace, partly for authenticity and partly because his steady warmth grounded me.

My fingers found Quinn's hand where it rested on my hip. "Benedict has been remarkably patient with my schedule." I hoped my voice conveyed appropriate affection rather than investigative panic. "Archaeological expeditions aren't particularly conducive to courtship."

"No," Hassan agreed, but his tone remained skeptical. "Shall we continue our search? Time grows short before I must seal this room officially."

We worked in careful choreography after that—Hassan methodically documenting Faraj's belongings while Quinn and I examined notebooks and papers. The methodical pace familiar to any archaeological cataloging session seemed excruciatingly slow under these circumstances, but evidence destroyed was evidence lost forever.

The mathematical calculations in Faraj's work were sophisticated beyond anything I'd expected from someone so young. His notebook's margins were filled with references to recent theories about tomb proportions. Astronomical charts covered with precise calculations, hieroglyphic translations that revealed advanced knowledge of ancient surveying techniques, and page after page of questions about specific artifacts.

I paused at a diagram comparing the acoustical properties of various temple chambers, recalling similar research I'd encountered at Oxford. Archaeological work and detective work, I realized, required the same fundamental skills—patient observation, pattern recognition, and the ability to reconstruct narratives from fragmentary evidence.

Faraj had been working with ratios, though I couldn't understand why a young Egyptologist would be connecting temple sound properties with artifact authentication.

"He was also investigating the blue pigmentation," I continued, pulling out one of Faraj's notebooks and tracing the chemical formulas with my finger. "These are tests for distinguishing lapis lazuli from Egyptian blue—the same methods I use for authentication."

The blue ink of his notes seemed to absorb rather than reflect the lamplight, the chemical equations meticulous and precise. I recognized the methods immediately—copper calcium silicate versus sodium aluminum silicate with sulfur. The synthetic Egyptian blue versus the genuine imported lapis lazuli from Afghanistan, the latter worth more than gold in ancient times and reserved for royalty and divine representations.

Hassan looked up from cataloging Faraj's personal effects. "What's this?"

Through our adventures in Cairo and Luxor, we'd thus far kept our investigation of the blue pigments under wraps, even from Hassan. The lapis lazuli that was somehow a key to everything...

My thoughts trailed off, seeing a pattern in Faraj's notes.

"What is it?" Quinn asked, reading my expression with the intuitive accuracy.

"He was tracking specific pieces—all with lapis. Look at these catalog numbers." I pointed to a series of entries marked with question marks and calculations. "These aren't random acquisitions. They're connected somehow."

Hassan moved closer, his suspicion temporarily overcome. "Connected how?"

Before I could answer, footsteps echoed in the corridor outside. Hassan immediately moved to block the doorway, his body language shifting into protective mode. A crew member appeared, speaking rapid Arabic I couldn't follow but that made Hassan's expression darken.

"What is it?"

"They've found something else," Hassan said grimly. "Faraj's jacket, hidden in the cargo hold behind crates we hadn't examined yet."

The return to the cargo hold felt like descending into the underworld. The oppressive atmosphere seemed heavier now, weighted with knowledge and loss. Hassan's oil lamp cast writhing shadows as we navigated between wooden crates toward a corner I hadn't noticed during our initial investigation.

The jacket hung from a nail driven into the ship's hull, positioned behind a stack of ceramic storage jars that would have concealed it from casual observation.

Hassan crossed to the jacket.

I took the opportunity to better search Faraj. Something still seemed off about his head injury.

I bent to the body quickly, scanning the wound, his arms and hands, his face.

*His neck.*

I straightened and turned to Quinn and Hassan without mentioning what I'd seen.

"Here," Hassan said quietly, withdrawing a folded paper from the inner breast pocket. "Mathematical calculations... and this."

He held up a small sketch torn from a notebook page. Even in the flickering lamplight, the symbol was unmistakable—a blue flame identical to the one on my invitation, but surrounded by geometric patterns that made my breath catch.

"Those are harmonic ratios," I whispered, recognizing the mathematical relationships from acoustic architecture texts. "Some scholars believe that ancient temples used these specific proportions—phi ratios, sacred geometries—to create resonant frequencies during religious ceremonies."

"To what end?"

I shrugged. "It's only speculation. But perhaps to amplify voices, create echoing effects, even produce harmonic frequencies that supposedly enhanced spiritual experiences."

Quinn leaned closer, studying the sketch. "So, this isn't just academic theory?"

"Not theory. But not accepted science, either." The implications were fascinating. "If someone understood these principles and had the right architectural setting—"

"They could recreate the effects," Hassan finished. "I've seen similar calculations in restoration projects at Dendera. The temple's acoustic properties were so precise that priests' voices could be heard clearly throughout the entire complex. But implementing such design requires extraordinary mathematical sophistication. And why would Faraj be investigating this? What does ancient acoustics have to do with stolen artifacts?"

The question hung in the air. I stared at the blue flame

symbol surrounded by its mathematics, pieces of a larger puzzle clicking into place. "Unless... unless the artifacts themselves are part of the equation. If these pieces were designed to work together, to create some kind of harmonic sequence..."

Hassan's intelligent gaze hadn't missed my theorizing He watched our analysis with growing suspicion, his professional objectivity warring with personal grief. "You seem remarkably well-informed about these symbols, Dr. Bell. Both of you."

The accusation in his voice was unmistakable. My hand went to my throat. I realized how our expertise must appear to someone investigating his assistant's murder. We knew too much, understood too quickly, arrived too conveniently.

Quinn's eyes met mine, appearing deeper in the shadowy cabin, a silent message passing between us.

"Hassan," I began, but he held up his hand.

"I think it's time we had a more formal conversation about your presence on this cruise," he said, his tone carrying the weight of official authority. "Both of you. Separately."

The threat was clear—divide and interrogate, the standard technique for uncovering deception. My heart hammered against my ribs as I realized our careful charade was crumbling.

Quinn's hand found mine, his fingers intertwining with a possessiveness that felt entirely too real. "Inspector, surely you don't suspect—"

"My initial reaction to Faraj's death must have clouded my judgment. I suspect everyone at this point, Mr. Quinn. Including the conveniently engaged couple who happen to possess expert knowledge about the exact subjects my assistant was investigating before his death."

The oil lamp flickered, casting our shadows in patterns against the cargo hold walls. In the half-light, Hassan looked less like a grieving mentor and more like the experienced investigator he was—someone who had seen enough deception to recognize it even when wrapped in expensive clothes and university credentials.

"We'll begin with formal interviews this afternoon," Hassan continued, tucking Faraj's sketch into his official documentation. "Until then, I suggest you both consider very carefully what you haven't yet told me about your reasons for being aboard this vessel."

He turned to leave, then paused at the cargo hold entrance. "And Dr. Bell? Your fiancé might want to remember that authentic couples don't need to rehearse their shared memories quite so obviously."

# CHAPTER EIGHT

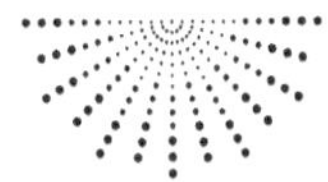

Hassan's makeshift investigation room was an unused cabin on a lower deck.

A single chair faced the porthole, positioned with the deliberate calculation of an experienced interrogator.

"Please sit, Dr. Bell."

I settled into the seat, acutely aware that harsh afternoon sunlight revealed more than words ever could.

"Let's begin with your expertise." Hassan remained standing, creating the power dynamic all good interrogators establish. "You've published extensively on pigments in Egyptian artifacts."

"Yes. My doctoral thesis examined New Kingdom ceremonial vessels specifically." I kept my voice steady, though discussing my academic work felt surreal given our current circumstances. "The recent discoveries in Carter's excavation have raised fascinating questions about authentication methods for ancient pigments."

"A rather specific area of expertise." His tone remained neutral, but his eyes narrowed. "Coincidentally, one of the subjects Faraj was investigating before his death."

The prickling sensation at the back of my neck intensified, and the cool metal of my engagement ring felt suddenly accusatory against my heated skin. "Many scholars study pigmentation. It's hardly unique."

"Perhaps. But not many arrive with sudden marital engagements and convenient invitations precisely when Faraj begins tracking suspicious patterns." Hassan withdrew a folder from his papers, his movements sharp with barely controlled frustration. "Another generation of Europeans mapping our treasures," he murmured, so quietly I almost missed it. Then, louder: "These are copies of correspondence between Faraj and scholars in Alexandria. He'd identified systematic anomalies in artifact provenance, particularly pieces containing lapis lazuli pigment."

My throat tightened as I examined the letters. Faraj's investigations had gone further than we realized. He'd been tracking the same pattern Quinn and I had discovered in Cairo—artifacts with genuine lapis lazuli being systematically removed from museum collections, sometimes replaced with forgeries containing synthetic Egyptian blue.

My heartbeat thundered in my ears. Faraj had discovered Operation Indigo independently.

"Dr. Bell, I've worked in antiquities long enough to recognize when someone is investigating rather than merely studying." Hassan leaned forward, hands flat on the table. "Why are you really on this cruise?"

The alibi I'd prepared felt thinner than papyrus and twice as flammable.

"We are following a pattern of artifact theft," I admitted, calculating how much truth might satisfy him without revealing Quinn's intelligence connections. "A systematic targeting of pieces with specific mathematical and astronomical properties."

"We?" His eyebrow lifted. "You and your... fiancé?"

I nodded, conscious of my engagement ring catching the sunlight. The hieroglyphic inscription felt suddenly accusatory.

"And your engagement's convenient timing? I find it curious how the notorious bachelor Mr. Quinn suddenly proposed just before this cruise. Not to mention your obvious... antagonism... toward each other when I last saw you just over a month ago in Luxor."

"Our relationship is... complicated." My teeth caught my lower lip. "Benedict and I have known each other professionally. Our personal relationship evolved from that."

"How recently?" Hassan's voice was soft but insistent.

"That's rather personal." I shifted in my chair, my discomfort authentic.

"Murder investigations tend to be personal, Dr. Bell." Hassan's grief slipped through his professional veneer.

The raw pain in his voice made my chest ache. I swallowed hard, weighing loyalty to Quinn against the moral imperative to help Hassan find justice for Faraj.

"I believe Faraj discovered what we've been tracking—a conspiracy to collect artifacts containing ancient mathematical and astronomical knowledge. We suspect there is a government-sanctioned operation underway, but I don't know who is involved, or their ultimate purpose."

Hassan studied me, measuring the truth in my words. "And by 'government' you mean the British Empire, yes?"

I swallowed. "Yes."

"And Mr. Quinn? What is his expertise in this matter?"

I hesitated, uncertain how to describe Quinn's role. "He has extensive connections in the antiquities trade. He recognizes patterns of theft and forgery."

"Indeed." Hassan set down his pen, the soft click echoing in the confined space like a judgment being rendered. "I'll be speaking with him separately, of course. Let's hope your stories align more convincingly than your public displays of affection."

Heat flooded my cheeks. "Is there anything else?"

"For now, no. But I'll be watching both of you very closely." He gathered his papers. "One last question, Dr. Bell. If you're truly investigating artifact theft, why not approach me directly? I am, after all, the official representative of Egyptian Antiquities Service."

The question hung between us, reasonable and damning.

"Trust is complicated when you don't know who's involved," I replied softly. "We couldn't risk alerting the wrong people."

"And now Faraj is dead." His voice carried controlled grief. "Perhaps your caution cost more than you anticipated."

The accusation hit like a physical blow. I stood on unsteady legs, desperate for fresh air and distance from the guilt his words had planted.

"I'm sorry for your loss," I managed. "Truly."

Hassan nodded once, dismissal clear in his posture. "Tell Mr. Quinn I'll see him in thirty minutes."

After his own interrogation with Hassan, Quinn had found me on the observation deck, and we'd quickly compared notes. Hassan had questioned him extensively about his background and antiquities expertise, pressing for details about our relationship that revealed how thin our cover story truly was.

"You might consider aligning your chronology with mine in future," I chastised.

"You're the one who amended it under duress."

"You contradicted me first."

He exhaled, lower now, more serious. "If they begin to suspect we're not what we claim to be," he said quietly, "they'll stop speaking freely around us. We'll be outsiders again. And right now, proximity is the only advantage we have."

"True."

But the major revelation I had for Quinn was what I'd seen on closer inspection of Faraj's body. While Hassan was assuming he'd been overpowered and violently struck by another man, I had seen the puncture mark on Faraj's neck. A needle mark that told us that anyone who could have gotten close to Faraj could have been the murderer.

No one from this cruise was beyond suspicion.

"We need that auction catalog." Quinn stared across the

river to the grassy bank passing by. "If Faraj identified specific artifacts, we need to know which ones."

"How do you suggest we get it? The auction materials weren't in Faraj's cabin."

"We start with official channels."

The *Nefertiti* boasted modern wireless equipment, a luxury not yet common on Nile steamers, so we made our way to the purser's office, which served dually as a wireless room. The crackling equipment and tangle of copper wires were a reminder that we weren't entirely cut off from the world—though it felt increasingly isolated with each passing hour. The narrow space made our conversation feel inherently confrontational.

The purser himself was a thin Englishman with the perfect blend of servility and authority required for his position.

"Mr. Quinn, Dr. Bell." He nodded, clearly aware of every passenger's identity and status. "How may I assist you?"

Quinn leaned forward slightly, his posture conveying privileged expectation. "We'd like to review the auction catalog for the upcoming events. As I understand it, there are several pieces of particular interest to my fiancée's research."

The purser's expression remained pleasant, but his posture stiffened. "I do apologize, sir, but the catalogs have been distributed exclusively to registered bidders. Professor Montague was most explicit about this restriction."

"Surely an exception could be made," I interjected, trying to project scholarly innocence rather than investigative intent. "My work on pigmentation techniques—"

"Most impressive, I'm sure, Dr. Bell." The purser's smile never reached his eyes. "However, I'm not authorized to distribute additional materials. Perhaps when Professor Montague joins us at Abydos, you might discuss it with him directly." His tone indicated the conversation was concluded. "Will there be anything else?"

Quinn and I retreated to a quiet corner of the observation deck, processing this new information.

I drummed my fingers against the railing. "So, only registered bidders received copies. I'm beginning to wonder why I'm here at all."

"Then we identify which passengers have them." Quinn's strategy shifted seamlessly. "Lord Ashford certainly. Likely the Waverlys and the Fairfax woman."

"Colonel Hartwell too," I added. "He mentioned investments in several pieces."

Quinn nodded. "Afternoon tea and evening dinner should provide opportunities to approach them."

I grimaced. "More engagement performance?"

His expression softened. "Think of it as fieldwork, Dr. Bell. Anthropological study of social customs."

The comparison startled a laugh from me. "A study of engagement rituals across class boundaries?"

"Precisely." His eyes crinkled at the corners. "Consider it research for your next scholarly publication."

Afternoon tea aboard the *Nefertiti* was a meticulous recreation of English social ritual, incongruously set against the backdrop of Egyptian riverbanks sliding past. White linen tablecloths and silver service created an oasis of colonial civilization, while the open deck doors allowed warm desert air to filter through the salon.

I wore my drop-waist pale pink linen dress—one of the few appropriate items Annie had insisted on packing while muttering about "proper ladies needing proper frocks."

The afternoon tea ritual unfolding before us was indeed a masterpiece of social anthropology. Other passengers were watching our table while pretending intense interest in their cucumber sandwiches, and I could practically feel their collective assessment of Quinn's and my performance.

Lord Ashford spotted us immediately, rising from his table with practiced grace. "Dr. Bell! Mr. Quinn! You must join us."

His circle included Lady Penelope— *Social Butterfly with Teeth*—and our *Military Man* Colonel Hartwell, their conversation pausing as we approached. Ashford pulled out a chair beside his own, clearly intended for me.

"You look absolutely radiant today," he said, blue eyes

twinkling with practiced charm. "The Egyptian air agrees with you."

"Thank you, Lord Ashford." I settled into the offered seat, acutely aware of how the warm afternoon air from the open deck doors made the salon feel intimate despite its size.

Quinn claimed the seat opposite rather than beside me, creating a subtle tension in our supposed engagement performance. His expression remained pleasant, but something in his posture had shifted—a territorial awareness that seemed more instinctive than performed.

"I was just telling Lady Penelope about my private collection," Ashford continued, leaning slightly toward me. "Several pieces featuring the blue pigmentation you've so brilliantly written about. Perhaps you might advise me on their authenticity? I could arrange a private viewing in my cabin this evening."

The invitation hung in the air, its impropriety thinly veiled by scholarly pretense. Lord Ashford's attempts at seduction were about as subtle as the Great Pyramid—impressive in scope, ancient in technique, and requiring an enormous amount of sand to make them work properly.

"How fascinating," Quinn interjected before I could respond. His tone remained cordial, but his eyes had hardened to chips of obsidian. "I'm sure any authentication would benefit from my expertise as well. Clarissa and I often work as a team on such matters." His hand reached across the table to cover mine, his thumb brushing over the engagement ring. "Don't we, darling?"

The endearment sounded foreign from his lips—too formal, too deliberate. I turned my hand to squeeze his, partly for authenticity and partly in warning not to overplay the jealous fiancé role.

"Benedict is remarkably knowledgeable about provenance documentation," I offered, noticing Lady Penelope's carefully hidden smile behind her teacup. "Though I confess, Lord Ashford, I'm more interested in how you became involved with the Brotherhood of the Blue Flame." I nodded at his lapel pin.

Ashford fingered the blue pin with casual pride. "Family

tradition, stretching back generations. We've always been patrons of historical research, particularly concerning ancient wisdom traditions. Rather keen on the mathematical principles, actually—absolutely topping discoveries in the recent King Tut excavations."

"Wisdom traditions?" I kept my tone curious rather than skeptical. "Such as?"

"Harmonic principles, mathematical ratios encoded in temple architecture, astronomical alignments." He warmed to the topic, clearly enjoying the chance to display knowledge to a female academic. "The ancients understood frequency and vibration in ways modern science is only beginning to rediscover. My grandfather was particularly fascinated by temple acoustics—how certain chambers could amplify specific tones."

Colonel Hartwell cleared his throat. "Perhaps not the appropriate setting for such technical discussions, Ashford."

"Nonsense," Ashford waved away the caution. "Dr. Bell is an expert! I'm sure she's encountered the mathematical principles in her research." He leaned closer, voice dropping conspiratorially. "I'd be delighted to show you some documentation in my private collection. Several scrolls with acoustical diagrams that might interest you."

So many opportunities for private viewings. I should be flattered.

Quinn's grip on my hand tightened imperceptibly. "I believe we're already committed this evening, aren't we, Clarissa?" His eyes met mine, communicating more than his words. "The Captain's dinner?"

"Of course," I improvised. "Though perhaps another time, Lord Ashford. I am curious about these acoustical properties."

Lady Penelope set down her teacup with an elegant *clink*. "Do share your wedding plans, you two."

The question was innocent enough, but her piercing gaze suggested deeper curiosity. I felt Quinn tense beside me, aware that our timeline was being tested.

"Our engagement is quite recent," I managed, hoping my

smile appeared genuine rather than strained. "Benedict surprised me just before we departed Cairo. We haven't had a chance to plan."

Quinn leaned against me. "But I can assure, I am quite eager to make this amazing woman my wife."

Something in his tone made my cheeks warm. Was this all performance? The boundary between pretense and truth suddenly seemed less distinct.

"Clarissa prefers intellectual passion to roses and champagne," he explained, his expression softening as he looked at me. "I fell in love with her mind first. Everything else followed."

The conviction in his voice startled me. For a moment, I almost believed him myself.

"How perfectly suited," Lady Penelope observed. "Though I confess surprise, Mr. Quinn. The Yorkshire estate has been without a mistress for so long, I'd begun to think you preferred bachelorhood."

Yorkshire estate?

I turned to Quinn.

An uncharacteristic flush was creeping up his neck.

"The right person changes one's priorities," Quinn replied.

But his quick glance of assessment, measuring my reaction to this rather significant disclosure about his apparently extensive personal resources, was telling.

The information hit me like a pottery shard to the forehead. Not only was Quinn an antiquities dealer-turned-intelligence-officer with mysterious government connections, but now it seemed he was also landed gentry with ancestral property?

And what of his story about growing up too poor to afford medication for his dying mother?

I maintained my smile while adding *Landowner* to my rapidly expanding file of *Things I Didn't Know About My Pretend Fiancé*—a file beginning to rival the British Museum's Egyptian collection in both size and mysterious contents.

Lord Ashford, clearly displeased by this romantic interlude, steered the conversation back to antiquities.

And Quinn very smoothly sent the conversation toward the auction.

"I'm not officially registered." He shrugged. "This was a last-minute trip, to accompany Clarissa. "But I'm curious about the catalog. I understand the offerings are quite select."

"Indeed." Ashford perked up, opportunity restored. "I'd be happy to show you my copy this evening. Perhaps after dinner?"

I caught Quinn's eye, our mission objective suddenly within reach. "That would be wonderful. Perhaps around nine?"

Quinn's expression remained pleasant, but I sensed his displeasure at my acceptance of Ashford's invitation. The remainder of tea passed in polite conversation about the upcoming Abydos excursion, but the undercurrent of tension between Quinn and me remained palpable.

An hour later, as we excused ourselves to prepare for dinner, I caught sight of Mrs. Pemberton—*Anxious in Manchester*—watching our table with undisguised anxiety. When our eyes met, she quickly looked away, hands trembling slightly as she gathered her things to leave. But as we passed her table, she whispered urgently, "The harmonic principles— they're more dangerous than you know." Before I could respond, she hurried away, leaving me to wonder what mathematical properties could inspire such fear in a middle-aged British matron.

I was eager to press Quinn for some personal information, but the Yorkshire estate revelation would have to wait. We had a catalog to acquire, a murder to solve, and a conspiracy to unravel.

Though I now also had a growing suspicion that Quinn's secrets ran deeper than I had imagined—which, considering the breadth of his mysterious background, was saying quite a bit.

# CHAPTER NINE

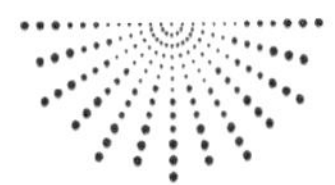

Once again, white-gloved stewards circulated through the dining salon with silver platters of roast duck and delicate vegetable terrines, the chandelier light catching on crystal stemware and polished silverware.

I had just arranged my napkin across my lap when the salon doors burst open.

One of the junior stewards stumbled in, his uniform disheveled and his eyes wide. "There's been a murder!" he blurted, voice cracking. "The Egyptian assistant—in the cargo hold!"

Conversations halted mid-sentence. A serving spoon froze halfway to Colonel Hartwell's plate.

Quinn leaned toward me. "That's the same steward I was telling you about earlier—the one who mentioned seeing Faraj in animated conversation with Lady Penelope."

Apparently, it had happened near the aft deck, but he couldn't hear what was said.

"What is the meaning of this?" Captain Mason emerged from a side door, his face darkening with controlled fury.

Inspector Hassan was at his side in an instant, speaking in rapid Arabic I couldn't follow, but the meaning was clear—the young steward had just destroyed any hope of a discreet investigation.

Mrs. Pemberton's fork clattered against fine china as her hand flew to her throat. "Murder? On our vessel?" Her voice emerged as a strangled whisper, her complexion assuming the approximate shade of library paste.

I tried to catalog everyone's reactions at once and filed Mrs. Pemberton's reaction under *Excessive but Potentially Genuine Terror.*

"How perfectly dreadful," Lady Penelope remarked, dabbing her lips with her napkin. Her sapphire eyes, however, surveyed the room with calculating coolness.

Dr. Cordelia Waverly clutched her son's arm. "The Egyptian boy who was listing the artifacts? But what about the auction?"

Marcus closed his eyes briefly, as though praying for patience. "Mother, a man is dead."

Lord Ashford leaned forward, blue eyes glittering with poorly concealed excitement. "I say, trapped on a boat with a killer. Rather dramatic, isn't it?"

I updated Ashford's file from *Harmlessly Frivolous* to *Ghoulishly Macabre.* Most people didn't greet news of murder with enthusiasm.

"I never spoke to him," Mrs. Pemberton announced to no one, clutching her napkin to her chest like a talisman. "I want that officially noted."

The ship's gentle rocking caused the chandeliers to sway slightly, casting shifting shadows across worried faces—in that dancing light, everyone looked suspicious.

"Ladies and gentlemen." Captain Mason's strident voice silenced the dining salon. His starched white uniform gleamed under the crystal chandeliers, his cap tucked under one arm. "I'm afraid it is true that we've had a death. And considering recent... circumstances, I regret to inform you that shore excursions to Abydos tomorrow must be restricted."

The collective intake of breath around the salon was a peculiar mix of anticipation and dread.

Lord Ashford was the first to break the silence. "Completely unacceptable," he declared, setting down his wine glass. "I've specific research interests at the temple that cannot be postponed."

I glanced across at Quinn, whose expression remained neutral despite the tension thrumming beneath the surface.

Cordelia Waverly—*Mysticism & Mathematics*—the silver-haired American classics professor, joined the protest. Her voice quavered with genuine distress. "Captain, you don't understand the significance—"

"I understand perfectly, madam," Captain Mason replied, his Portsmouth accent becoming more pronounced under stress. "However, the health and safety of all passengers must take priority."

Colonel Hartwell rose slightly from his chair, spine stiff. "I've traveled six thousand miles specifically for these archaeological sites, Captain. Surely some accommodation can be arranged."

So. We had *Entitled Objection* (Ashford), *Scholarly Indignation* (Waverly), and *Military Authority Challenge* (Hartwell). The pattern was fascinating—each protest based on their personal investment, yet all circled around the same destination.

Hassan stood silently at Captain Mason's shoulder. His dark eyes surveyed the dining salon, lingering momentarily on each passenger.

"The decision has been made in consultation with Inspector Hassan here, of the Egyptian Antiquities Service," Captain Mason continued.

"This is Egyptian high-handedness," Marcus Waverly muttered, though loudly enough to be heard. His mother placed a restraining hand on his arm.

I leaned toward Quinn. "We need to intervene before this escalates," I whispered. "Hassan can't alienate everyone if we're to continue investigating."

Quinn nodded once. He stood with practiced grace,

drawing all eyes to him. "Captain, might I suggest a private word?"

The two of us, along with Hassan, followed Captain Mason into his quarters. The wood-paneled room smelled of pipe tobacco and beeswax polish, with nautical charts spread across a mahogany desk. Through the windows, the Nile glittered darkly under the emerging stars.

"This is becoming untenable," Captain Mason said, pacing the small space. "I cannot have my passengers in open rebellion, yet you insist on restricting shore access."

Hassan remained stoic. "A young man is dead. The crime scene must be preserved."

"Perhaps a compromise?" I suggested. "Limited and supervised excursions in groups, remaining in public areas only?"

"With crew members assigned to each group," Quinn added. "It would allow basic tourism while maintaining observation."

Hassan's eyebrow lifted slightly. "You seem remarkably invested in facilitating temple access, Mr. Quinn. One might wonder why."

"Merely practical, Inspector," Quinn replied smoothly. "Keeping passengers confined will only heighten tension and create antagonism toward your investigation."

Captain Mason nodded slowly. "He's right. Better to maintain the appearance of normalcy while limiting opportunity for... interference."

We returned to the dining area with the news, and the relief around the tables was palpable. Though I noticed Lady Penelope Fairfax watching us with shrewd assessment. Those sapphire eyes missed nothing, despite her seemingly frivolous demeanor. She raised her champagne glass slightly in my direction.

"Well played," she murmured as we passed her table.

I was beginning to suspect Lady Penelope saw through our performance entirely. Given that my last attempt at amateur theatrics had involved a disastrous Oxford production of *Hamlet* where I'd forgotten my lines and improvised with passages from my thesis on faience glazing, followed by a line or two from a Gilbert and Sullivan song, her suspicion was entirely plausible.

Quinn and I returned to our seats. I leaned toward him. "Should we still go to Lord Ashton's cabin, to view his auction catalog this evening? It's our best opportunity to identify what Faraj discovered."

Quinn's jaw tightened almost imperceptibly. "Perhaps you prefer to visit his cabin alone? His interest in you appears to extend beyond scholarly collaboration."

"Jealousy isn't necessary for our cover, Quinn." I whispered, surprised by his reaction.

His dark eyes met mine. "Who said anything about our cover?"

Across the table, Mr. Mullen cleared his throat quietly. "May I ask who compiled the provenance citations for Lot Twelve?"

"Perhaps now is not the time to discuss business." Lord Ashford tilted his head as though sympathetic. "Given the news we've just had."

Hassan scowled. "Mr. Mullen is quite thorough in his assessments. We would not wish for any irregularities to compromise the proceedings."

The subtle tension between them rippled across the table.

But no one offered an answer to Mullen's question, and the rest of dinner passed quietly, the mood appropriately subdued. Clusters of conversations happened in whispers, and I gained little information on any of our fellow passengers.

We allowed Lord Ashton a few minutes after dinner, before heading to his cabin.

He swept the door open and looked only at me.

"Clarissa! I failed to mention at dinner that you look absolutely ravishing this evening!" He took my hand before I could avoid the contact. His lips brushed my knuckles, lingering a moment too long.

Quinn pushed his way into the room. "You didn't fail to mention, Ashford."

I laughed. "Benedict, you are misremembering. That was at *tea* this afternoon, and the comment then was 'radiant,' I believe."

Ashford winked. "Well, forgive my repetition. The Egyptian air has given you a positively goddess-like glow."

Quinn stepped forward. "The catalog, Ashford?"

"All business tonight, eh?" Ashford's blue eyes sparkled with mischief as he reluctantly released my hand. "Very well."

The room was exactly what I'd expected—opulent and excessive, with the slightly tacky trappings of the rich. It smelled of expensive cologne and leather-bound books, with an undertone of the Nile's muddy waters drifting through the open porthole. I noticed subtle blue flame motifs engraved on his cigarette case and cufflinks—belonging to the Brotherhood was clearly a status symbol for Lord Ashford, worn as proudly as his Cambridge rowing colors.

Ashford retrieved a booklet from his desk. "The collection is quite extraordinary." He directed his comments primarily to me despite Quinn's presence. "Several pieces feature the pigmentation techniques you've so brilliantly analyzed in your publications."

I accepted the catalog, acutely aware of both men's attention as I opened it.

The pages were heavy stock, with detailed photographs and descriptions of each artifact. An architect's measuring rod, a tablet, and a beautiful musical sistrum. I turned more pages, noting details of a resonance bowl used in temple rituals and other tools used by builders. My fingers drummed against the catalog's edge in frustration. The lighting on the photographs was exemplary, but it was impossible to tell how many items contained blue pigment, let alone the lapis lazuli we were watching for.

"These are all from the same time period," I noted, turning pages with growing interest. "New Kingdom, Eighteenth Dynasty."

Quinn leaned close enough that his breath warmed my ear,

and his arm brushed mine as he pointed to a particular notation. Lapis lazuli. "Note the authentication marks."

"Oh yes," Ashford leaned closer, his shoulder pressing against mine. "These pieces aren't merely decorative—they're functional components. The ancients understood that certain mathematical ratios, when physically manifested, could create resonance patterns."

His hand covered mine as he turned to a specific page, displaying a tablet covered with astronomical markings. Ashford's flirtation technique appeared to have been learned from the same manual that taught Victorian gentlemen how to collect butterflies—lots of hovering, excessive enthusiasm, and a troubling desire to pin down the specimen.

"This one is particularly fascinating. The spacing of these symbols corresponds precisely to the acoustic chambers at Abydos—the same mathematical ratios that create the temple's famous echoes."

I knew he was right about the acoustics; I'd read the recent survey reports.

"I'd be delighted to show you personally tomorrow. There's a *wonderfully private* alcove where the sound properties are remarkable." The way he emphasized 'wonderfully private' brought heat to my face—not from attraction, but from annoyance at his transparent manipulation.

Quinn's patience visibly snapped. "I believe Dr. Bell will be accompanying me tomorrow, Ashford." His tone held none of the urbane charm he typically maintained. "And perhaps you could refrain from pawing my fiancée while I'm standing beside her."

"No need to be territorial, old boy," he said with a smirk. "Intellectual admiration only."

"Your hand is still on hers," Quinn pointed out, each word precisely measured.

I extracted my hand from beneath Ashford's, clearing my throat. "These mathematical ratios—they appear in multiple artifacts?"

My attempt to redirect the conversation worked partially.

Ashford reluctantly returned to scholarly discussion, though his eyes frequently drifted to my face rather than the catalog.

"Each piece contains elements of the same mathematical sequence," he explained. "When properly arranged, they form a coherent system—rather like a musical scale, but for resonance rather than melody."

Despite the catalog's comprehensive documentation, I couldn't immediately identify what had alarmed Faraj enough to get him killed. Each piece was valuable, certainly, but nothing seemed uniquely significant.

"Who is selling these artifacts?" Quinn asked, his composure restored though his posture remained tense.

"Various collectors." Ashford waved vaguely. "The Brotherhood has... resources."

"And who exactly belongs to this Brotherhood?" I asked.

Ashford's smile turned secretive. "More than you might expect, Dr. Bell. People of vision who appreciate ancient wisdom." He glanced meaningfully at Quinn. "Your fiancé might be more familiar with our membership than he admits."

Quinn's expression remained impassive, but I felt him tense beside me.

"I'd best return Dr. Bell to her cabin," Quinn said, standing abruptly. "Thank you for sharing the catalog."

Ashford rose with aristocratic grace. "Perhaps you'll reconsider my offer of a private tour tomorrow, Clarissa. There are aspects of the temple that would... *resonate* with your research interests." A smile quirked at his lips, a bit leering, it seemed to me.

"My fiancée is quite capable of determining her own schedule," Quinn replied before I could answer, his voice carrying an edge. "Good evening, Ashford."

I allowed Quinn to guide me from the cabin, the catalog's contents swimming in my mind. Outside in the corridor, the ship's engines vibrated through the floorboards as we walked in tense silence.

"That was unnecessary," I finally said when we reached a

quiet stretch of deck. "I can handle Ashford's flirtation without your intervention."

Quinn leaned against the railing, moonlight silvering his profile. "It wasn't entirely for show, Clarissa."

"What do you mean?"

"All that business about a private tour. And watching him touch you—" He stopped himself, drawing a measured breath. "It was unprofessional of me. I apologize."

The admission hung between us, complicated and genuine. I found myself studying his face, searching for the line between performance and truth.

I still wanted to talk about the Yorkshire news, but it didn't seem the right time.

"Don't worry," I finally said. "I have a policy against 'resonating' with anyone who uses archaeological terminology as innuendo."

He laughed, but looked away.

"Did you notice that every passenger seemed disturbed by the potential cancellation of Abydos?" I asked, allowing us both retreat from the emotional precipice.

Quinn nodded, accepting the change of subject.

"This isn't a coincidence, Quinn. Whatever this Blue Brotherhood is and its connection to Operation Indigo, Faraj's murder, these specific artifacts..." A bead of nervous perspiration traced down my spine despite the evening breeze.

"What are you thinking?"

"This isn't a cruise," I said quietly. "It's a conspiracy convention."

# CHAPTER TEN

I spent half the night poring over what little we'd gleaned from Lord Ashford's auction catalog, my Morocco leather field notebook now filled with observations that remained frustratingly disconnected.

"You haven't slept, have you?" Annie's voice carried gentle reproach as she entered with a tea tray. "I can always tell. Your hair assumes a particularly wild quality when you've been running your hands through it all night."

"There's something here," I muttered, tapping my pencil against a sketch of one artifact—a lapis-adorned calculation device with astronomical markings. "They're all connected, but I can't see the pattern."

*Archaeological Mysteries, subcategory: Potentially Solved by Adequate Sleep and Better Lighting.* Neither seemed likely to be available.

Annie set down the tray and moved to the window, drawing back the curtains fully. Beyond the glass, the landscape had changed dramatically since yesterday—the lush cultivation along the riverbanks had given way to starker terrain, with sandstone cliffs rising in the distance.

"We'll be arriving at Abydos within the hour," she said, pouring tea with practiced efficiency. "The captain announced it just after dawn. Most passengers are already gathering on deck."

I accepted the cup gratefully, the strong black tea cutting through my mental fog. "Has Quinn been seen this morning?"

Annie's expression shifted to something like amusement. "Your *fiancé* was observed in conversation with the ship's wireless officer at first light." Her emphasis on "fiancé" carried a wealth of innuendo. "He asked me to inform you that he'd meet you on deck when you're ready."

"Thank you," I replied, ignoring her tone.

"The salmon-colored day dress would be appropriate for temple exploring," she continued, moving to the wardrobe. "Though perhaps you'd prefer something less conspicuous today? You do seem to attract a remarkable amount of attention in that color."

I looked up from my notes. "What do you mean?"

"Only that Lord Ashford's gaze already seems to follow you rather persistently, so perhaps you'd rather not draw more eyes." She laid out the dress anyway. "And Mr. Quinn seems particularly attentive to Ashford's infatuation."

I sighed and shook off her accusation. "This is an investigation, Annie. Not a romantic escapade."

"Of course," she agreed, her expression infuriatingly serene. "Which explains why you were holding hands on the observation deck until well past midnight."

"We were maintaining our cover," I protested, though the memory of Quinn's fingers entwined with mine sent an unwelcome flutter through my chest.

"If you insist." She turned to leave, pausing at the door. "Though I must say, Dr. Bell, for someone so skilled at cataloging ancient artifacts, you seem remarkably determined to miscategorize your own feelings."

Before I could formulate a suitable retort, she was gone.

I dressed quickly, my mind returning to the auction. What was the true connection of these pieces? I tucked my notebook into my satchel, added my magnifying glass and measuring tools, and headed for the deck.

The *Nefertiti* hummed with anticipation as we approached Abydos. Passengers lined the railings, pointing toward the distant temple complex just visible on the horizon. I found Quinn at the bow, his profile etched against the desert landscape as he conversed quietly with the purser.

"Good morning," I said, joining him at the railing.

Quinn turned, his eyes warming slightly. "You look..." he paused, seeming to recalculate his words. "Prepared for archaeological exploration."

"As opposed to?"

*Romantic entanglement, which apparently requires an entirely different sort of equipment I haven't yet cataloged?*

"As opposed to the lady who spent most of the night making notations in her journal instead of sleeping." His voice dropped to ensure privacy. "Did you find anything useful?"

"Nothing conclusive." I extracted my notebook and opened it to my sketches. "But I keep returning to this mathematical sequence that appears on multiple artifacts. It's not just decorative—it's functional."

Quinn studied my drawing, his shoulder pressing against mine. The contact felt steadying somehow. "What kind of function?"

"That's what I can't determine from catalog photographs alone. But based on what Ashford said about acoustic properties..." I tapped the page. "Ancient Egyptians understood that certain mathematical relationships created specific acoustic effects in enclosed spaces. But to think that they created temples specifically for that purpose..."

"It would imply an even more advanced science than we have attributed to them," Quinn murmured.

"Exactly." I glanced around, noting several passengers watching us with varying degrees of interest. "Any luck with your wireless?"

Quinn understood my reference to his contact with his handler, via the ship's Marconi wireless equipment. "Limited. My colleague expressed concern about the blue flame insignia.

Apparently, it's appeared in other contexts recently, including certain offices in Whitehall."

The implications sent a chill through me despite the warming morning air. "Infiltration?"

Quinn nodded almost imperceptibly. "Wheels within wheels, it seems."

Our conversation was interrupted by Captain Mason's announcement that we would be docking momentarily. The crew bustled about, preparing for our arrival, while Hassan gathered the first shore excursion group near the gangplank. His expression remained professionally detached, though I noticed his eyes lingering on each passenger with careful assessment.

"We'll be in the first group," Quinn said, guiding me toward Hassan. "Along with the Waverlys, Lord Ashford, and Colonel Hartwell. Hassan is keeping his suspects together." Quinn smiled at the group ahead, all charm. "Easier to observe," he said through his smile.

Lord Ashford spotted us immediately, his aristocratic features brightening. "Ah, the lovely couple! I was hoping you'd join our expedition." He offered me his arm, deliberately ignoring Quinn. "I'd be delighted to show you those acoustic chambers I mentioned."

"Dr. Bell will be remaining with me," Quinn stated, his tone pleasant but firm. "Archaeological exploration being a shared interest of ours."

Ashford's eyebrows rose slightly. "How fortunate she has such an... attentive fiancé."

Dr. Cordelia interjected before the tension could escalate. "The temple alignments are extraordinary this time of year." Her silver hair gleamed in the sunlight as she clutched her notebook with scholarly enthusiasm.

Her son Marcus was absent. Apparently, he'd attached himself to the group that did not include his mother.

Colonel Hartwell approached our group, his posture ramrod straight despite the casual setting. "First tour group assembled and ready, Captain," he announced unnecessarily, with a quick salute.

Hassan's expression revealed nothing as he led us down the gangplank, but I caught the subtle tightening of his shoulders as Lord Ashford continued his enthusiastic discourse on "harmonic chambers" and "resonance frequencies."

The path to the temple of Abydos wound through a small modern village, where locals watched our procession with the weary tolerance of those accustomed to foreign visitors. The ancient limestone structure gradually emerged from behind modern buildings, its massive columns rising like sentinels against the cerulean sky.

"The Temple of Seti I," Hassan announced, resuming his official guide persona. "One of Egypt's most significant religious sites, dating to approximately 1290 BC."

As we entered the temple proper, the temperature dropped noticeably, the thick stone walls providing blessed relief from the desert sun. The ancient incense still seemed to linger in the stone's pores, carrying whispers of ceremonies conducted millennia ago. The Hypostyle Hall spread before us, its columns decorated with exquisitely preserved reliefs and hieroglyphs illuminated by shafts of brilliant sunlight that cut sharp geometric patterns across the dim interior. My hands unconsciously gripped my notebook tighter as I noticed how sound behaved strangely here—whispers seemed to carry further than expected, echoing in ways that made me acutely aware of who might overhear what.

"Note how the hall is constructed," Hassan continued, his voice automatically dropping to a reverential tone. "Seven chapels dedicated to different deities, with Seti I offering sacrifices to each."

While other passengers clustered around Hassan, I felt Quinn's hand at my elbow, gently guiding me slightly away from the group.

"Our three fellow passengers have been exchanging glances since we arrived," he murmured, his lips close to my ear.

"Hartwell, Waverly, and Ashford. They're waiting for something."

I followed his gaze discreetly. Indeed, the Colonel had positioned himself near a specific column, while Ashford seemed to be checking his pocket watch with unusual frequency. Dr. Waverly had drifted to a seemingly random wall panel, but her attention remained focused on her companions rather than the hieroglyphs before her.

Lord Ashford lingered near a particular column, his hand resting casually against a hieroglyphic panel. Our eyes met briefly, and the smile that crossed his features sent a chill through me despite the desert heat.

"I wonder if they are measuring the sunlight," I realized, noting the angle of light moving slowly across the decorated walls. "Waiting for a specific illumination pattern."

Before Quinn could respond, Hassan's voice rose slightly. "Please remain with the group. These temples contain structural vulnerabilities that can be dangerous to the unwary."

His warning carried professional authority, but I caught the undercurrent of suspicion as his gaze swept over our scattered companions. Lord Ashford merely smiled, bowing slightly in acknowledgment before turning to drift away.

"I'm going to follow Ashford," Quinn whispered. "Stay close to Hassan."

Before I could protest, he'd moved in Lord Ashford's' direction. I suppressed a flare of annoyance at his protective instinct and turned my attention to the hieroglyphs near where Dr. Waverly had been standing.

"Colonel Hartwell," she called softly, her voice barely carrying over the echoing footsteps of the other tourists. "The upper corridor. We must see it."

The Colonel approached with his characteristic military bearing, though I noticed his eyes held the same fervent gleam that had marked our earlier conversations about "practical applications" of ancient knowledge.

I joined them, knowing the location where this was leading and suspecting the interpretation that might follow.

Dr. Waverly led us toward a narrow stone stairway that accessed the temple's upper levels. "Most tourists never venture here," she explained, her voice dropping to a whisper. "But this is where the real evidence lies."

The upper corridor was dimmer than the main halls below, its stone ceiling lower and more intimate. Several sections showed concerning cracks where millennia of sandstorms had worn the limestone, and I noticed loose stones near the walkway's edge that overlooked the main hall far below. The precarious nature of these ancient walkways always made me nervous —one careless step could prove fatal.

Dr. Waverly stopped before a specific lintel—a carved stone beam spanning the passageway overhead.

"Here." She pointed to the hieroglyphs with trembling fingers. "The panel that narrow-minded archaeologists dismiss so readily."

Colonel Hartwell stood on his toes, his weathered face creasing in concentration. "Good God," he breathed. "That formation there—it's remarkably like the rotary mechanism in de la Cierva's autogyro designs. I've seen the technical drawings from Madrid."

"Precisely!" Dr. Waverly's voice carried triumphant vindication. "And here—" she indicated another section where the overlapping hieroglyphs created curious curved forms "—this configuration suggests a flying apparatus of some kind. Not the simple levers and ramps our textbooks describe, but something far more sophisticated."

Colonel Hartwell craned his neck to examine the carved surface above us.

The reliefs were indeed unusual—where overlapping hieroglyphs had been carved one atop another, the composite shapes formed curious configurations that could, with sufficient imagination, resemble mechanical devices.

"Extraordinary," Colonel Hartwell murmured, his weathered face creasing in concentration.

"Indeed! And on this specific lintel, in this upper corridor where only initiated priests would walk. The placement is deliberate." Dr. Waverly's voice carried triumphant vindication. "These aren't religious symbols at all, but technical schematics rendered in symbolic shorthand."

Colonel Hartwell nodded grimly. "I've seen similar engineering notations in military technical manuals. Simplified diagrams that convey complex mechanical principles to initiated readers." He glanced around the temple chamber with new appreciation. "If the Egyptians possessed such knowledge, imagine the strategic applications."

"The knowledge wasn't lost through ignorance," Dr. Waverly added, lowering her voice conspiratorially. "It was deliberately suppressed. Hidden away by later dynasties who inherited only fragments and feared what they couldn't fully understand."

"The implications are staggering," the Colonel was saying, clearly unable to conceal his excitement. "If ancient engineers possessed rotary flight capabilities—even primitive ones— think of the reconnaissance advantages. The strategic superiority. But do you believe these... devices... could be reconstructed from the hieroglyphic instructions?"

"With the right mathematical keys, absolutely," Dr. Waverly nodded. "The harmonic principles we mentioned earlier—they're not just acoustic. They represent a unified science of mechanical resonance. The ancient Egyptians understood that all motion, all power, derives from vibrational frequencies properly applied."

The Colonel grunted. "Modern aviation engineers are discovering the same principles. Rotational lift, gyroscopic stability—de la Cierva's autogyros prove that controlled rotary flight is entirely feasible with sufficient understanding of aerodynamic harmonics."

I couldn't help myself...

"Surely, you're not suggesting that ancient Egyptians achieved powered flight? The metallurgy alone would have been impossible with Bronze Age technology."

Dr. Waverly's eyes held the fervent gleam of absolute

conviction. "You're thinking in terms of modern materials, Dr. Bell. But what if they possessed different methods entirely? Sound-based propulsion? Harmonic levitation? The temple acoustics we've discussed suggest they understood vibrational principles far beyond our current science."

"The evidence is accumulating," Colonel Hartwell added with certainty. "These hieroglyphs, the mathematical ratios in temple construction, the acoustic properties we've observed— they all point to a sophisticated technological civilization that deliberately obscured its achievements in religious symbolism."

It was time to bring some scholarly sense to this conversation.

"The original inscription bore Seti I's royal titles." I drew upon years of Oxford training to provide the established archaeological interpretation. "When Ramesses II had his own names carved over portions of his father's work—a common practice—the overlapping hieroglyphs created these composite shapes as the painted plaster fill eroded over nearly three millennia. The process is well-documented in other temple sites throughout Egypt."

Dr. Waverly turned a kindly, though condescending eye on me. "Of course that is what they have *told* you. The 'official' explanation." Her tone suggested she found it woefully inadequate. "But consider the implications of your own words, Dr. Bell. Why would Ramesses II choose this location to overlay his father's inscriptions? Why not simply create new wall space elsewhere in this vast temple?" She smiled. "No, they are deliberate encoding. Technical schematics rendered in hieroglyphic shorthand, hidden in plain sight within religious inscriptions."

I followed them back down to the main chapel, finding their absolute certainty unsettling.

*Suspicious Academic Specimens, subcategory: Potentially Dangerous When Exposed to Sunlight and Ancient Architecture.* These weren't uneducated mystics, but respected professionals convinced they were uncovering suppressed historical truth— which somehow made their theories even more alarming.

I was still formulating a response that would suitably dismantle their fanciful interpretations when a shout echoed through the temple chambers, followed by the crash of metal striking stone.

# CHAPTER ELEVEN

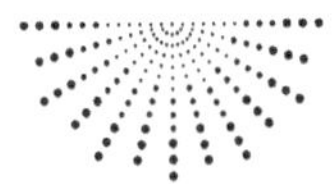

The screech of twisted metal echoed through the sacred chamber, a jarring modern sound that seemed to violate the eternal stillness watched over by carved falcon-headed gods.

I glanced up to see a massive limestone block, no longer supported by the collapsed framework, shift ominously in its setting, centuries-old mortar crumbling at its edges.

I had just enough time to register the danger—and file it under *Archaeological Hazards, Subcategory: Ironic Death by Ancient Architecture*—before strong hands seized my shoulders, yanking me backward as the massive limestone block crashed to the floor, exactly where I had been standing.

The impact would have flattened me instantly, not merely injured me.

The impact sent clouds of limestone dust billowing through the chamber—ancient stone particles that carried the scent of millennia mixed with the metallic tang of twisted scaffolding.

Dust motes danced in shafts of sunlight streaming through the entrance as I collided with Quinn's chest, his arms instinctively tightening around me. The groaning echo of stressed metal gradually faded into the vast silence of the chamber.

"Are you alright?" His voice was tense against my ear, his heart hammering against my shoulder blades.

I nodded, too startled to speak.

Hassan was trotting toward us. "The scaffolding in the eastern chapel has collapsed," he called. "Someone disturbed the support braces."

The Egyptian Department of Antiquities had installed these metal supports following Pierre Lacau's new conservation protocols—a systematic approach to preserving monuments threatened by increased tourism after the Tutankhamun discoveries. The framework required expert placement; disturbing even one brace could trigger a catastrophic cascade.

"We must evacuate immediately." Hassan gestured toward the entrance with swift authority, his trained eye already assessing potential structural weaknesses in the remaining scaffolding. "Please proceed calmly toward the entrance."

I glanced at the Colonel and Cordelia. "Where is Lord Ashford?"

"He's returned to the ship already," the Colonel nodded. "Said he'd had enough of the heat."

"This scaffolding was deliberately sabotaged," Hassan said quietly, for our ears alone. "Someone loosened the support braces. The question is whether you were the intended target, Dr. Bell, or merely in an unfortunate position."

Had someone just tried to kill me?

Quinn's arm remained around my waist, ostensibly supporting me but positioning himself between me and the rest of the passengers now gathering at a safe distance. "I believe we can rule out coincidence," he replied, his voice carrying the dangerous edge I'd heard only during our most perilous moments together. "Particularly given recent events."

Hassan nodded grimly. "We return to the ship. Now."

As our group moved hurriedly toward the exit, Fraulein Becker observed me with unsettling intensity. Her dark eyes, magnified behind those thick glasses, betrayed neither concern nor surprise at my near miss with death, as if she'd expected to find me either safely evacuated or conspicuously absent from the group entirely.

Something about her gaze sparked a memory—a flicker of recognition that I couldn't quite place. Had I encountered that assessment somewhere else?

My contemplation was interrupted by excited voices at the temple entrance. A small group of Europeans milled about—a woman in a fashionable dropped-waist dress adjusting her T-bar shoes with obvious discomfort, and a red-faced gentleman in a pith helmet consulting his pocket watch while muttering about "native inefficiency" and the disruption to his touring schedule.

"Dr. Bell!" A familiar voice called out, and my heart leapt with unexpected relief.

Professor Montague strode toward us. His tweed jacket seemed incongruous against the desert landscape, his beard neatly trimmed and his expression warm with genuine pleasure at seeing me.

"My dear girl," he continued, taking my hands in his. "What extraordinary timing! I'd planned to be aboard the ship before it departed Abydos, but am glad to find you here."

I would never admit it, but I was overwhelmed by the comfort of seeing a trusted friend after the near brush with limestone.

"Professor," I managed, returning his smile. "So good to see you again."

"There's been an accident in the temple," Hassan informed Montague, his tone professional but measured. "A stone collapse that nearly injured Dr. Bell."

"Good heavens!" Montague's concerned gaze swept over me. "Are you hurt, my dear?"

"I'm fine. Thank you." Close enough to the truth.

He turned to Quinn, extending his hand. "And Mr. Quinn. I trust you have been well since we parted ways in Luxor?"

As Quinn reluctantly shook the offered hand, I caught the

subtle tension in his jaw—a tell I'd learned to recognize when he was concealing strong emotion.

Was it my brush with death, or Montague's arrival? Surely he understood what it meant for our investigation? Here was someone we could finally trust, a respected academic with connections throughout the archaeological community.

Montague's expression grew serious. "These old temples can be treacherous, but..." He glanced around at the assembled passengers, lowering his voice. "Perhaps we might continue this discussion aboard the vessel? I understand you've had other concerning... incidents."

As our group made its way back toward the *Nefertiti*, with Montague walking between Quinn and me, I felt a surge of hope. Surely Montague could help us unravel the details of the Brotherhood, given that the invitation he'd sent me carried the blue flame symbol.

"Professor, I wanted to ask you about the blue flame—"

"Clarissa," Quinn interrupted, his voice carrying a warning edge. "Perhaps we should save detailed discussions for more private settings."

I frowned at his tone, but Montague merely smiled. "Your fiancé is wise to be cautious. Walls have ears, particularly among those interested in ancient acoustics."

I blinked. "How did you know about our engagement?"

"News travels quickly in archaeological circles." Montague shrugged. "Though I must admit, I was rather surprised, Clarissa. When we last spoke in Luxor, you seemed wholly dedicated to your academic pursuits."

"Circumstances change," I said carefully, matching Montague's light tone while my mind raced. How exactly had he learned of our supposed engagement? We'd created the cover story only days ago, and I hadn't communicated with him since leaving Cairo. Had he been in communication with someone on the ship?

"And how is dear Lady Blackwood, Professor Montague?" I smiled conspiratorially. His affection for our Luxor hostess, despite the murders and mayhem that had occurred there, had been obvious.

"I'm afraid my work at the museum in Alexandria has kept me busy these past weeks, and I've not seen her at all."

We arrived at the gangplank where Captain Mason awaited our return, his expression troubled as Hassan briefly reported the temple incident.

"Professor Montague," Captain Mason nodded, though his eyes reflected the wariness of a man who'd seen enough trouble in the last three days to last a lifetime. "Welcome aboard. Your cabin is ready for you."

As we ascended to the main deck, I noticed Lady Penelope watching our arrival with particular attention, her eyes narrowing slightly when they fell on Montague. For just a moment, her carefully maintained façade of frivolous aristocracy slipped, revealing something harder beneath.

Lord Ashford approached immediately, his charm turned to maximum effect. "Professor Montague! You join us at last. I look forward to cigars and stimulating conversation."

Montague bowed in Ashford's direction, but allowed himself to be led away by the purser.

Before Ashford could engage us in conversation, Quinn drew me toward a quieter section of the deck, his expression uncharacteristically troubled.

"I don't like this." He ran a hand through his hair, his usual composure cracked by the day's events.

"Certainly, you don't suspect Montague of anything? After all his help with that business in Luxor?" My protest weakened toward the end, however, and I heard the uncertainty creeping into my voice.

"He knew about our engagement when no one outside this ship should have that information," Quinn countered. "Not to mention his immediate rapport with Ashford. And the mention of acoustics."

I considered this, reluctantly acknowledging the logic. "He did have the blue flame on the invitation he sent me..."

"Perhaps everything we thought we knew about this case

may be wrong," Quinn finished grimly. "Including who's involved."

I glanced across the deck where Montague had reappeared and was now engaged in animated conversation with Dr. Waverly, both academics gesturing enthusiastically about some scholarly point.

"What exactly are we even accusing him of? A symbol on a piece of stationery and surprising knowledge of our relationship?"

"*Alleged* relationship."

I rolled my eyes, conceding the point. But in truth, my slip of the tongue had been unintentional, and I feared I was beginning to believe my own performance.

His hand found mine briefly, the touch reassuring in its warmth against my dust-covered fingers. "Fine. But until we know for certain, trust no one outside this partnership."

# CHAPTER TWELVE

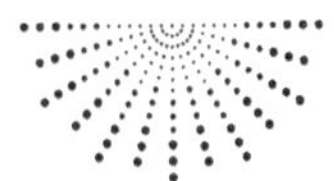

The ship's salon had transformed with evening's arrival, lamplight filtering through silk shades creating intimate conversation spaces throughout the elegant room.

Evening jasmine from the shoreline drifted through the open windows, its sweet fragrance belying the tension crackling beneath polite conversation.

The gentle sound of Nile water against the hull provided a rhythmic backdrop to the murmur of passengers in their evening attire—ladies in drop-waist frocks with long pearl strands, gentlemen in white dinner jackets appropriate for the desert climate.

I sat with Annie at a small table near the windows, watching Professor Montague charm Inspector Hassan with scholarly enthusiasm while Quinn observed from across the room, positioned where he could monitor both the conversation and potential exits.

"The Professor certainly knows how to make himself indispensable," Annie murmured, folding her napkin in her lap.

She was right. Montague had seamlessly inserted himself into Hassan's investigation, offering insights with the confidence of a man accustomed to authority. His voice carried clearly in the intimate space as he gestured toward the auction catalog spread between them.

"Inspector, I'd be delighted to assist with your investigation," Montague was saying, his familiar scholarly warmth making my chest tighten with conflicted loyalties.

"How thoughtful of you to offer, Professor," I said across the space between us. "I'm sure you did not anticipate these sorts of complications when you arranged this gathering."

"Arranged?" Montague's eyebrows drew together in confusion. "My dear Clarissa, I am merely an invited guest, as yourself."

I frowned. The salon's warm lighting suddenly felt deceptive, casting shadows that seemed to shift. "But you sent me an invitation."

He shook his head, with a smiling glance at Hassan. "I assure you, it was not I who invited you. Though of course I'm delighted you are here."

I set my teacup down with more force than intended, the china rattling against its saucer. "That's impossible."

"When did you receive this invitation?" Montague asked gently.

"A week ago. During my lecture at the Continental-Savoy." My voice sounded hollow. "It bore a distinctive blue flame emblem."

Something flickered across Montague's features—recognition mixed with concern. "And it purported to be from me?"

"I need to retrieve it," I said, rising from my chair. "You'll see your name is clearly mentioned."

Annie started to follow, but I waved her back. "I'll only be a moment."

The corridor to our cabin felt longer than usual, my footsteps echoing against the polished wood. Inside my room, I pulled the invitation from my writing desk drawer, where I'd kept it alongside my archaeological notes. The blue flame insignia seemed to gleam more ominously in the dim cabin light.

When I returned to the salon, the conversation had

continued without me. Montague was discussing authentication methods with Hassan.

"Here," I said, placing the invitation on the table between us. "You'll find your involvement quite explicit."

Montague lifted the heavy paper with the delicate handling of a scholar examining ancient papyrus, adjusting his spectacles with practiced movements.

"'Join Professor Nigel Montague and distinguished guests for an exclusive examination of recently acquired artifacts,'" he read aloud slowly. "How curious."

"Curious?" My voice sharpened. "Your name is right there."

"Yes, I can see that I am mentioned, but it does not actually say that it is from me. It's unsigned. And my invitation was quite similar, missing the mention of my own name of course."

"Who sent yours?"

Montague gave an elegant shrug. "All very mysterious, isn't it?"

If the invitation wasn't from him, then was he connected to the Brotherhood of the Blue Flame at all? Thus far, only Lord Ashford seemed part of it. Did he send the invitations?

The forced smile I gave Montague didn't reach my eyes, though I doubted he noticed in the forgiving lamplight. "I am quite certain my dig site director, Dr. Bradford, said that you contacted him directly."

"It must have been someone using my name."

"Who would—?"

"Who indeed? Perhaps it is just as it says... whomever wanted you here wished to avail themselves of your authentication expertise." He glanced around the salon at the guests clustered at tables.

As if summoned by the mention of authentication concerns, Mr. Mullen approached our group with his leather tools case clutched against his chest. His usually meticulous appearance showed signs of strain—ink-stained fingers suggesting hours bent over documents with magnifying glass, rumpled waistcoat, the haunted expression of a man whose professional integrity had been violated.

"Inspector Hassan," Mullen said quietly, "I must speak with you privately about what I've discovered. The irregularities go far beyond simple misattribution."

Hassan gestured to an empty chair. "Please, Mr. Mullen. Professor Montague has offered his own talents. Perhaps you could share your concerns with our group."

Mullen glanced nervously around the salon before sliding into the chair, his body shifted as if he might need a quick exit. "I'm not certain the salon is the ideal location to discuss..."

Hassan studied Mullen's anxious demeanor with professional interest. "Mr. Mullen, these gentlemen and Miss Bell are assisting with my investigation. Please, share your concerns openly."

Mullen's grip tightened on his leather case. "Inspector, I really must insist on privacy—"

"Mr. Mullen." Hassan's voice carried the authority of his office. "A man is dead. Whatever irregularities you've discovered may be connected. I require your full cooperation."

Mullen glanced around our group—Montague watching with scholarly interest, Quinn maintaining his collector's facade, myself leaning forward with what I hoped appeared to be professional curiosity rather than desperate need for answers.

"Very well." Mullen's voice dropped to barely above a whisper as he opened the brass clasps of his leather case. "The auction catalog contains fundamental irregularities that suggest the entire enterprise may be fraudulent."

"What sort of irregularities?" Hassan asked.

Mullen withdrew a small notebook from among his authentication tools—magnifying glasses and calibrated measuring devices that caught the lamplight. His meticulous handwriting covered every page. "First, no reserve prices have been established for any lot."

He turned to me, as if I were uninformed of the antiquities trade. "In legitimate auctions, minimum bids are set to protect sellers' interests. The absence of reserves suggests the organizers have no intention of protecting the pieces' value."

Montague leaned back in his chair. "Perhaps they wish to ensure active bidding?"

"No, Professor," Mullen shook his head firmly. "More concerning—I can find no authorization from any established auction house. Christie's, Sotheby's, even smaller European houses—none have documentation of this sale. The catalog bears no auction house seal or certification."

Quinn maintained his role perfectly, frowning like a concerned collector. "Surely there must be some legal framework—"

"That's precisely the problem," Mullen interrupted, his professional composure cracking. "No legal framework exists. No terms of sale, no transfer of ownership protocols, no insurance documentation. It's as if someone simply gathered valuable artifacts and printed an elegant catalog without any intention of conducting legitimate commerce."

Hassan made notes in his own book. "What do you conclude from these observations?"

Mullen's hands trembled slightly as he closed his notebook. "I suspect the auction itself is a fabrication, Inspector. The question is why someone would go to such elaborate lengths to create the illusion of a sale when no actual transaction is intended."

The salon fell silent except for the gentle sound of water against the hull and the distant murmur of other passengers maintaining their evening's civilized facade. I found myself unconsciously twirling the engagement ring Quinn had given me.

"Most troubling," Montague murmured thoughtfully. "Again, we are faced with the question... who has orchestrated all of this?"

Hassan nodded grimly. "Mr. Mullen, I strongly advise you to remain vigilant. Share your findings with no one beyond this group."

Mullen clutched his leather case tighter. "Of course,

Inspector. Though I fear I may have already said too much to certain passengers who expressed scholarly interest in my work."

"Which passengers?" I asked.

"Fraulein Becker, primarily. She's been most helpful with the cataloging process." Mullen's voice carried an undertone of unease.

"We should circulate among the other guests," I suggested, rising from my chair. "Perhaps casual conversation will reveal more about who truly organized this gathering."

Hassan nodded. "An excellent idea. But be discrete. We cannot afford to alert our quarry."

The next hour passed in a careful dance of social conversation. Quinn and I moved through the salon like a newly engaged couple enjoying an evening's entertainment, but our attention remained sharply focused on gathering intelligence.

I found myself drawn into conversation with Mrs. Pemberton, who seemed increasingly agitated as the evening progressed. When I mentioned the mysterious invitations, her teacup rattled against its saucer.

"Oh yes, the invitations," she whispered, glancing nervously around the room. "My husband received similar correspondence before his death. Blue flame emblems, promises of rare knowledge..." She trailed off, her eyes darting toward where Fraulein Becker sat alone, engrossed in her book.

Meanwhile, Quinn engaged Colonel Hartwell in discussion about the practical applications of ancient engineering.

"Fascinating how sound can be weaponized," Hartwell mused, unaware that Quinn was cataloging every revealing comment.

Lady Penelope proved equally enlightening, though in subtler ways. When I complimented her extensive knowledge of Egyptian artifacts, she smiled with calculated sweetness.

"One learns so much from careful observation," she said, her gaze lingering on Montague's animated discussion with Dr. Waverly. "Sometimes the most interesting discoveries come from watching who speaks to whom, and when."

As the evening wound down, several passengers began retiring to their cabins. Quinn and I maintained our engaged couple performance, walking arm-in-arm from the salon, while Hassan disappeared toward his own quarters with Mullen's concerning revelations clearly weighing heavily on his mind.

"We still need to have that conversation about this 'Yorkshire estate.'" I leaned into his shoulder. "Lord Quinn."

He chuckled. "Trust me, there is absolutely no title involved. Only money. But it's a story for another day."

"But—"

"Clarissa." Quinn's voice carried the low urgency reserved for genuine danger as we paused outside the salon doors, the jasmine-scented evening air now seeming deceptive rather than romantic. The sound of civilized conversation behind us masked deadly intentions, while ahead the dark Nile stretched toward Dendera's approaching lights. "Whoever sent that invitation and arranged this so-called 'auction' has been manipulating events from the beginning. They wanted you here for a specific reason, and I suspect you aren't safe until we discover what that is."

Through the salon's windows, I caught Hassan watching our exchange with the sharp attention of a man trained to read relationships. It appears our natural partnership—the way Quinn anticipated my thoughts, how I unconsciously sought his protection—was convincing him our engagement was genuine. At least something about this evening was working according to plan.

# CHAPTER THIRTEEN

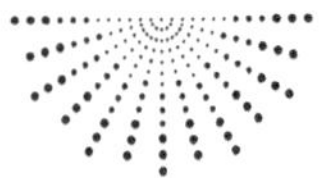

The familiar scratch of my pencil against paper as I made notes at my table in the breakfast salon felt comforting after the scaffolding incident. My left shoulder still ached where Quinn had wrenched me away from the falling stones.

"Cataloging passengers again?" Annie set down her teacup. "Mrs. Pemberton keeps glancing this way as if she expects you to spontaneously combust."

"More than cataloging." I straightened my shoulders. "I'm beginning to notice some rather illuminating patterns."

My supposed concentration on my notes had apparently rendered me invisible, and our principal suspects had been chatting freely.

I'd overheard Mrs. Pemberton ask Dr. Waverly "How is your mother's arthritis?" before catching herself with obvious embarrassment. Colonel Hartwell had casually mentioned to Marcus about "that Vienna authentication going smoothly," while Lady Penelope referenced something Lord Ashford had said "at last month's salon." Even Fraulein Becker had haughtily corrected someone's story about Egyptian burial customs with details strangely specific for a teacher's assistant.

I followed Annie's gaze to where the nervous Manchester widow sat alone at a corner table, her fingers worrying the edge of her serviette. Dark circles shadowed her eyes, and she'd barely touched the elaborate breakfast spread.

"She's been like that since Abydos," I murmured. "Notice how she avoids eye contact."

The observation proved prophetic. Lord Ashford approached her table with his characteristic swagger, blue flame insignia glinting on his lapel, and Mrs. Pemberton visibly shrank. She mumbled something about an urgent letter to write and fled toward the deck, leaving her breakfast untouched.

"How illuminating." Quinn slid into the chair beside me. His presence brought the familiar scent of sandalwood and leather, along with the subtle tension that had marked our interactions since Professor Montague's unexpected appearance yesterday.

"Learn anything useful from your morning reconnaissance?" I asked, not looking up from my notes.

"Nothing worth reporting. You?"

I briefed him quietly on my observations.

Quinn frowned. "You think they all knew each other before this trip?"

"Perhaps. We need to track down that steward who overhead the conversation between Penelope and Faraj. Perhaps they also knew each other."

"I'm afraid he's not aboard anymore," Annie said.

"Not aboard?"

"He asked to be put ashore at the last stop. Said he'd had enough of this voyage."

I sighed. "Well, regardless, someone orchestrated this entire voyage to bring specific people together."

"With you as the centerpiece," Quinn said grimly. "The question remains: who's conducting this particular orchestra?"

Our conversation was interrupted by Mrs. Pemberton's hesitant approach. She'd returned from the deck and now stood beside our table with the desperate air of someone who'd summoned considerable courage.

"Dr. Bell," she began, her accent thick with anxiety, "might I... that is, could we possibly speak privately?"

I glanced at Quinn, who gave an almost imperceptible shrug. "Of course, Mrs. Pemberton. Shall we take some air on deck?"

The forward deck provided relative privacy, though I noticed Fraulein Becker positioned at the rail with a book—close enough to observe, if not overhear. Mrs. Pemberton seemed unaware of our audience, her attention consumed by whatever internal struggle had driven her to seek me out.

"My husband," she began without preamble, her hands trembling violently on the rail, "corresponded with collectors about the Brotherhood of the Blue Flame activities before his death. I found the letters after the funeral." She glanced over her shoulder toward the breakfast tables before continuing.

My pulse quickened, but I kept my voice gentle. "What sort of correspondence?"

"They wrote about these 'harmonic resonance' theories." She opened her reticule, withdrawing a folded letter. "Albert became frightened by what they were suggesting. He wanted to withdraw from their... experiments, but they wouldn't let him."

Fraulein Becker's book snapped shut with a sharp crack, and she materialized beside us. She physically stepped between Mrs. Pemberton and me, blocking any retreat.

"Perhaps," Fraulein Becker said in her precise German accent, her spectacles nearly opaque with the glare of the morning sun, "Frau Pemberton would join me for morning constitutional? The exercise aids digestion, yes?"

Mrs. Pemberton startled like a rabbit catching scent of a fox, hastily refolding the letter with shaking fingers.

"I... yes, of course. Dr. Bell, perhaps we could continue our discussion later?"

"Certainly," I replied, though I suspected no such opportunity would arise.

As the two women walked away—Fraulein Becker's hand firmly guiding Mrs. Pemberton's elbow—I felt like a tomb robber who'd accidentally triggered every trap at once.

I mentally arranged our fellow passengers like a museum display: *Conspiracy Hierarchy, Dynasty XX, Recent Acquisition.* Lord Ashford would be the ceremonial centerpiece—all flash and religious significance. Colonel Hartwell, the practical military implements. Mrs. Pemberton, unfortunately, appeared to be damaged goods headed for storage.

Quinn appeared beside me, having observed the interaction from the salon doorway. "Interesting timing."

"Mrs. Pemberton was about to reveal something crucial." Frustration sharpened my voice. "That letter—"

"May still be retrievable. But first, let's consider what we've learned."

He was right. We retreated to my cabin, where the morning light revealed the details I'd been assembling. Spread across my writing desk were sketches from the temple visit, passenger observations, and the mathematical sequences I'd identified in Faraj's notes.

"The real question is, are the artifacts supposedly up for auction even on this ship? If the catalog is a fake and the auction is a cover for something else, perhaps the items don't even exist."

Quinn traced a finger over one of my papers. "They exist. I've come across a couple of them in my past dealings and have heard about others. But whether they are on this ship..." He shrugged.

"Well, if they do exist , then these pieces aren't a random collection of auction items. And if Mullen is correct and there is no auction, then my guess is someone is trying to bring them all back together for some reason. If they are on the ship."

"Our mysterious auctioneer? Or the Brotherhood?"

"Or someone using the Brotherhood as a cover." I tapped my pencil against the desk. "Notice how different passengers demonstrate varying levels of fascination with all this acoustic language? Ashford seems genuinely enthused about ancient wisdom. Colonel Hartwell believes he's chasing military research. And Dr. Waverly seems to think she's advancing human spiritual evolution."

"While others, like Mrs. Pemberton, appear terrified."

"Exactly. I think we may have true believers, useful tools, and reluctant participants being coerced into cooperation."

Quinn moved to the connecting door between our cabins, testing the lock I'd kept firmly secured. "What about Fraulein Becker's intervention just now?"

"Calculated. She's been observing Mrs. Pemberton's increasing agitation since Faraj's murder. The moment Mrs. Pemberton approached me with evidence, Fraulein Becker acted to prevent disclosure."

"Evidence suggests our severe academic friend is more than she appears."

A soft knock interrupted our discussion. Annie entered, her usual cheerful demeanor showed signs of strain.

"The passengers are gathering for departure to the Temple of Hathor." She glanced at my morning dress with concern. "Captain Mason requests all shore parties assemble within the hour."

"Excellent." Something in Annie's manner suggested complications. "Is everything quite alright?"

"It's probably nothing," Annie said slowly, "but I just had a strange interaction with Mrs. Pemberton."

"Tell me."

"She tried to slip me a note for you, but Fraulein Becker intercepted her. The German woman claimed she'd deliver it personally."

"Naturally." My jaw clenched. "Did you see the note's contents?"

"Only a glimpse. Something about her husband."

Quinn and I exchanged glances. Mrs. Pemberton had attempted multiple approaches, each thwarted by increasingly aggressive intervention.

"We need to reach her during the temple visit," I said, gathering my archaeological equipment. "Away from Fraulein Becker's observation."

"Agreed."

I had a sudden inspiration. "Annie, please let Captain Mason know that we will join the Dendera party in a short time, at the Temple of Hathor. Tell him..." I glanced at Quinn. "That we need a little private time together as a couple." The words nearly lodged in my throat.

Annie's eyebrows had the good sense to remain in place, but her lips betrayed her. "Of course, Miss Bell. I'll be happy to pass that along."

She paused in the open doorway, as Lord Ashford appeared in the corridor.

He leaned around her to give me a little wave.

"Delighted you're joining today's expedition," he said, though his smile didn't reach his eyes. "The Temple of Hathor offers remarkable acoustic properties. I'm told certain chambers amplify whispers across impossible distances." His usual insouciant charm seemed forced.

"Indeed," I replied carefully. The phenomenon was well-known to any serious Egyptologist. "Have you visited before?"

"Several times. The ceiling maps there show Cleopatra's cartouche alongside Roman astronomical calculations—a perfect fusion of ancient wisdom and imperial power." His gaze flicked between Quinn and me with calculating intensity. "I trust you'll find the experience... enlightening."

"I'm sure we will." I left the curt response hanging.

He nodded and moved on, but not before his eyes lingered on my engagement ring.

Annie retreated to the hall and closed the door to my cabin with another smirk. Asking for 'private time as a couple' was mortifying enough without her expression suggesting she expected to hear furniture being rearranged.

Quinn took a step closer, grinning. "Not sure what this 'private time' is about, but count me in."

The man could make reading the telephone directory sound like a marriage proposal. My senses sparked despite my better judgment, but I flattened a palm against his chest, feeling his heart beating beneath the fine cotton of his shirt.

"Don't get any ideas. I just thought with everyone ashore, it might be the perfect chance to find out if the artifacts are here."

"Ah." Quinn's voice dropped into disappointment.

He had to have known the message I gave Annie was a ruse. Didn't he?

I pulled away and gathered my papers into a neat pile. "We just need to wait a few minutes, until we're sure they've left."

"Hmm. What could we do to pass the time?"

I laughed, despite myself. "Again with getting ideas. How about we discuss that Yorkshire estate I've been hearing so much about.?"

The comment sounded casual, but we both knew it wasn't. Injecting the mention of his continued deceptions into what could have been an intimate moment was deliberate on my side. From his expression, it was noted on his.

He turned away, running his fingers along the edge of my writing desk where my notes lay scattered. His jaw worked as if he were wrestling with something more substantial than mere evasiveness.

"I haven't been there in a long time."

"I thought you grew up in poverty. Both your parents have passed away—"

"I didn't say that."

I huffed. "That story you told me, then? How your family lost everything when you were young? You said your father died, and then your mother fell ill. You tried to sell your grandfather's Roman coin to buy medicine but were cheated by a crooked antiquities dealer."

"First off, I'm certain I never said my father died. Because he didn't. He simply... left. You assumed he was dead."

I thought back, but couldn't recall his exact words. "Fine, perhaps I misunderstood. But how does the boy with no money for his mother's medicine end up an aristocrat in Yorkshire?"

"I'm not aristocracy, Clarissa. Never claimed to be. The Langham family—old Yorkshire lineage, fifteen generations—fell on rather desperate times after the war. Lost two sons, couldn't maintain the estate. I purchased Calderstone Hall from them at considerably less than market value, allowing them to retreat to their London house with dignity intact." His voice carried genuine conflict between honesty and operational necessity, his forehead furrowed as if wrestling with something more substantial than mere evasiveness. "They needed a buyer who would preserve the property rather than tear it down for development."

"And the money? Even at bargain prices, that estate must have cost a fortune."

He picked up one of my pottery sketches, studying the sherd classifications with unnecessary attention. "It did. Some of that money came from... consulting work for the government. Authentication services, recovering stolen artifacts, occasionally preventing valuable pieces from falling into the wrong hands." He set the sketch down carefully. "Not always through channels you'd approve of."

I scowled. "And?"

"And what?"

"You know what I'm asking, Benedict Quinn. Was the money earned legitimately? Or through dealing in black market antiquities?"

It was an old argument, but still valid. He knew how I felt about the illegal trade in history.

He sighed. "Some compromises are necessary—"

I held up a hand. "Say no more. National security and all that. Must ensure that Great Britain remains in control, right?"

"Clarissa—" he reached for me.

I backed away.

"It's not like that. Not that simple, at least. I needed a cover—"

"I'm sure it's far too complicated for me to understand." I glanced through my porthole. "Looks like the tender boat is taking everyone ashore. Let's focus on more important things."

I breezed past him, into the corridor before he could pull me back—into conversation, or into the cabin that was far too private for my rapidly dissolving professional composure.

Behind me, I heard Quinn's frustrated sigh mixing with the distant sounds of our co-conspirators preparing for whatever waited at Hathor's Temple.

# CHAPTER FOURTEEN

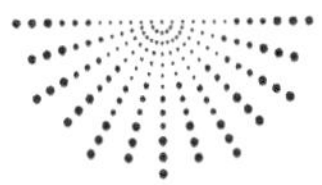

We moved swiftly through the ship's corridors. The search for evidence of the auction items felt dangerous in a way that crawling through ancient tombs never did.

The narrow stairwell leading below decks creaked beneath our weight. I tried not to think about Faraj's body being discovered in this same space just days ago. The crate he'd fallen against had been labeled as ship's supplies. Could it have been something else?"

"These artifacts had better not be down here," I whispered. "They should be secured somewhere temperature-controlled, away from engine vibration."

The ship shifted and I nearly stumbled.

Quinn placed a steadying hand on my shoulder as the ship rocked gently against its mooring.

The cargo hold sprawled in shadowed sections, neatly organized crates stacked along bulkheads. We moved systematically through each row, checking manifests and searching for anything bearing the blue flame insignia.

Some labels were in French, others English. Quinn translated any in Arabic.

Most bore predictable labels—"Kitchen Supplies," "Linen

Storage," "Medical Equipment"—all the mundane necessities of luxury river travel.

"Not seeing anything suspicious so far." I ran my fingers along a crate marked "Champagne—Reims."

"Keep looking. If I were smuggling priceless antiquities, I wouldn't label them 'Stolen Egyptian Artifacts—Handle with Care.'" Quinn's whisper carried a hint of amusement.

I rolled my eyes. "Thank you for that insight, Mr. Quinn. I had planned to stop at the first crate marked 'Illegal Contraband.'"

His soft chuckle warmed something in my chest that I promptly ignored. We continued our methodical search, moving deeper into the hold where the air grew heavier with the scents of engine oil and river water.

"Wait," Quinn paused, examining a stack of crates near the bulkhead. "Notice anything odd about these?"

I joined him, careful not to brush against his arm, though the narrow space made it difficult. The crates appeared ordinary—wooden, well-constructed, with shipping labels.

"They're... newer than the others?" I ventured.

"And look at the labeling pattern." Quinn pointed to several boxes marked with innocuous descriptions: "Research Materials," "Academic Publications," "Laboratory Specimens."

"Academic materials wouldn't normally be stored in a cargo hold," I agreed, studying the labels more carefully. "They'd be in passengers' cabins or the ship's library."

"Exactly. And notice this?" His finger traced a small mark in the corner of each label—not the Brotherhood's blue flame, but a simple three-digit number that varied slightly from crate to crate.

I leaned closer, my shoulder brushing his chest as I squinted in the dim light. "Cataloging codes?"

"Or something simpler—cabin numbers." Quinn moved to a nearby toolbox and retrieved a pry bar. "Shall we take a look?"

"Breaking into private property? How shocking, m'lord." I

feigned scandalized propriety while simultaneously examining the lock mechanism on the nearest crate.

"I told you, I'm not—" He huffed and shook his head. Then wedged the bar under the lid of a crate marked "Museum Catalogs."

The wood creaked in protest before surrendering with a sharp crack that sounded alarmingly loud in the confined space. We both froze, listening for footsteps above, but heard only the creaking of the ship.

"Well," I whispered after a moment, "we've committed to crime now. Let's at least make it worthwhile."

Quinn carefully lifted the lid, revealing a bed of straw packing. I reached in, brushing aside the protective material, and gasped softly as my fingers touched something smooth and cool.

"It's the architect's measuring rod," I breathed, carefully lifting the segmented wooden artifact with its distinctive lapis lazuli inlay. "Look at these mathematical notations—exactly as described in the auction catalog."

Quinn peered at the three-digit number on the crate's label, then consulted a small notebook from his pocket. "You're right about the numbers—152 corresponds to Colonel Hartwell's cabin assignment."

"He mentioned military applications of ancient engineering yesterday," I recalled. "Said something about sound being weaponized."

We carefully repacked the rod and moved to the next suspicious crate. This one, labeled "Manuscript Research—Alexandria University," opened to reveal the calculation tablet I'd seen photographed.

"This belongs to Mrs. Pemberton," Quinn said, matching the digits to my notes. "She inherited it from her husband."

"The one she's terrified about," I added, examining the beautiful limestone tablet with its lapis mathematical notations. "These aren't just decorative patterns—they're advanced calculations."

We continued our illicit inventory, finding Lady Penelope's

sistrum in a crate marked "Astronomical Charts—Private Collection" and Cordelia Waverly's resonance bowl hidden among "Archaeological Survey Equipment."

"They're all here," I whispered, excitement building despite the danger. "The entire collection described in the auction catalog."

"And they all belong to specific passengers," Quinn added, "who have some sort of connection with each other."

As we reached for the final crate simultaneously, our hands collided. Quinn's fingers wrapped instinctively around mine, warm and solid in the cool hold.

"Sorry," we both said at once, neither of us immediately pulling away.

The ship chose that moment to rock against its mooring, sending me off balance. Quinn caught me by the waist, steadying me against his chest with reflexive grace.

"Careful, archaeologist," he murmured, his voice dropping to that dangerous timbre that made my pulse quicken.

"Professional hazard," I managed, attempting to sound unaffected while my body betrayed me with an inconvenient flush of warmth. "Archaeologists are always falling into things."

"Is that what we're calling this?" His smile held a challenge.

I cleared my throat and stepped back, nodding toward the unopened crate. "Let's finish what we started."

"By all means." His eyes held mine a moment longer before returning to the task.

The final crate, labeled "Reference Materials—Private Collection," contained what appeared to be a miniature architectural model with blue-pigmented interior surfaces.

"I've no idea what that is." I shrugged. "What cabin?"

Quinn studied it. "This corresponds to cabin 12—Fraulein Becker's."

"That can't be right." I frowned. "She's Waverly's research assistant, not a collector."

"Perhaps she's more than she appears." Quinn carefully replaced the model. "Like someone fiancée I know."

I shot him a look as we resealed the crate. "Very amusing."

"I find our arrangement increasingly so." He helped me to my feet as we finished securing the evidence of our trespassing. "For instance, the way you blush when I stand too close."

"That's indignation, not embarrassment," I countered, dusting off my hands. "And we should leave before someone comes looking for us."

"As you wish." He gestured toward the stairs with exaggerated gallantry. "After you, my dear fiancée."

I rolled my eyes, and his quiet laughter followed me up the stairs as we hurried back to the main deck. The tender boats were returning empty from their first trip dropping off passengers at Dendera—our investigation had ended just in time, as we could now join the rest of the group.

"Shall we agree on a next step?" Quinn asked as we smoothly transitioned into our public roles, his hand settling lightly at the small of my back.

"We need to speak with Mrs. Pemberton before Fraulein Becker intervenes again," I said quietly. "And figure out what connects these artifacts—why someone would go to such lengths to have our new friends gather themselves, and their precious artifacts, all in one place."

# CHAPTER FIFTEEN

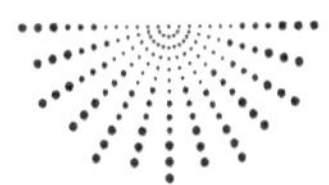

The honey-gold stones of Dendera's Temple of Hathor glowed like ancient amber in the morning sun, their carved surfaces seeming to pulse with warmth despite the early hour. I stood with our shore party inside the temple, watching sunlight dance across hieroglyphs that had witnessed three millennia of human ambition and folly.

"Magnificent preservation," Professor Montague murmured. "The acoustic properties alone make this visit invaluable."

Hassan supervised our group with the weary efficiency of a man accustomed to managing tourists who confused enthusiasm with expertise.

Mullen clutched his leather case against his chest, his usual meticulous appearance showing fresh signs of strain—ink-stained cuffs, a waistcoat that had seen too many anxious adjustments.

"The temple complex demonstrates sophisticated understanding of sound engineering," Montague continued, leading us through the outer courtyard. "Notice how the colonnade creates natural resonance chambers."

I exchanged glances with Quinn, who maintained his

collector's facade while observing Montague's commentary with sharp attention. The professor's knowledge was remarkably detailed about the mysterious sound-related references.

"Have you studied Dendera's acoustics extensively?" I asked.

"One develops appreciation for such matters," Montague replied.

Cordelia Waverly stepped closer to our group, her silver hair gleaming beneath a wide sun hat. "Professor Montague, surely you agree these acoustic effects were intentional? The ancients encoded sacred frequencies into architectural proportions?"

"Undoubtedly."

Mullen gave a perturbed sigh.

I glanced at him. Did he share my skepticism over the intentionality behind the famous "whisper effect"?

He looked my way, but then quickly the other direction, as if he had no desire to share a mutual rolling-of-the-eyes moment.

"Shall we explore the inner chambers?" Montague suggested, gesturing toward shadowed corridors that promised cooler temperatures.

Our group moved deeper into the temple complex, footsteps echoing against stone floors worn smooth by countless pilgrims. Colonel Hartwell positioned himself near Dr. Waverly.

Waverly's gray eyes flashed with evangelical fervor. "Dr. Bell, mainstream archaeology systematically ignores evidence that threatens conventional timelines."

"What sort of evidence?" Quinn asked. "Anything that would increase the value of certain pieces, perhaps?" He waggled his eyebrows, as if Hartwell understood his collector's greed.

Ashford joined our conversation. "The Brotherhood has spent decades researching how ancient civilizations harnessed vibrational frequencies for practical applications."

"Such as?" I pressed, genuinely curious about the depth of their delusion.

"Consciousness expansion, matter manipulation, communication across vast distances." Ashford's casual tone made these claims sound like discussing weather patterns. "The ancients didn't disappear their knowledge—they encoded it into architectural ratios and ritual objects, waiting for worthy inheritors."

Lady Penelope had been observing our discussion from a strategic position near carved wall reliefs. "How fascinating that such knowledge would surface now, when collectors with appropriate resources can appreciate its significance."

Her comment carried implications that made my chest tighten. The auction, the cruise, the carefully assembled passenger list—were we the people intended to appreciate the significance?

"Lady Fairfax raises an excellent point." Montague guided us toward a deeper chamber where stone walls created intimate acoustic spaces. "Perhaps we should further test these harmonic principles with practical demonstration."

He positioned himself in an alcove carved with Hathor's distinctive cow-eared features, gesturing for our group to gather in the opposite chamber. The arrangement separated us by thirty feet of solid stone corridor, making normal conversation impossible.

"Can you hear me clearly?" Montague's voice reached us with startling clarity, as if he stood among our group rather than hidden in distant stonework.

"Remarkable," breathed Dr. Waverly. "The vibrational alignment is perfect."

"Your turn, Mr. Quinn" Ashford called cheerfully. "Whisper sweet nothings to your fiancée. Let's see if romance carries across ancient stones."

I flushed as other passengers positioned themselves to observe our performance.

I was about to object, but Quinn's lips quirked into a smile.

"Happy to oblige," he said, moving across the space.

"The night I proposed..." he began, his voice low and intimate, as though meant only for me, yet played for the sake of an audience. "Standing beneath Cairo stars, do you remember what you told me?"

The assembled audience looked to me, in various states of amusement.

I wasn't as quick with improvisation as my fabricated fiancé.

"Uh..."

"You said that archaeology has taught you something important—that some treasures are worth any risk."

Quinn's eyes met mine across the chamber, with an intensity that felt genuine .

I swallowed hard and smiled. "And you laughed and said I was being absurdly romantic for an archaeologist. Then you kissed me before I'd even said yes."

The invented intimacy hung in the warm air between us, made more unsettling by how easily the fictional memory emerged from our lips.

Around us, our fellow passengers smiled indulgently.

"How charming," Lady Penelope tipped her head in my direction.

True to his word, Lord Ashford found a private moment with me, as we wandered the temple.

Ashford leaned close to the wall, fingertips hovering just above the carved face of Hathor, as though he feared direct contact might disturb something unseen.

"Do you hear it?" he asked quietly.

I frowned. "Hear what?"

"The silence," Ashford said. "It isn't empty. It's waiting."

I smiled. "That's poetry, not science."

"It's both," he replied calmly. "Hathor was not merely worshipped here. She was invoked through sound. Chant, rhythm, vibration. Her priests understood that the temple itself was part of the ritual—that these chambers were vessels, designed to contain resonance."

"You're suggesting the architecture itself has a function beyond shelter."

"I'm suggesting," he said, "that it was an instrument."

He gestured toward the darkened corridor behind us.

"Stone does not absorb sound. It reflects it. Preserves it. Certain tones, given the proper space, will sustain themselves. Amplify. Interact. The ancients knew this, even if they described it in spiritual rather than mathematical terms."

I glanced toward the shadowed passage, uneasy despite myself. "And you believe bringing the artifacts here would... what? Make them louder?"

"No," Ashford said softly. "Not louder. Aligned."

He turned, his expression intent now.

"Each artifact was created within its own harmonic context—its own ratio of form, material, and symbolic purpose. Separated, they are inert. But gathered here—within a structure dedicated to the goddess of vibration itself—they may reestablish their original relationship. Their original frequency."

I gave him another smile, this one less skeptical. Perhaps I'd learn more from this strange group by playing along. "You make it sound as though they might awaken."

Ashford returned the smile, faint and unreadable.

"Perhaps," he said, "they already have. We're simply standing too far away to hear it."

As afternoon shadows lengthened across Dendera's golden stones, our group began the journey back to the *Nefertiti*. Quinn and I walked hand-in-hand, maintaining our performance while processing the day's revelations.

"Montague's knowledge is too specific," I said quietly. "Those acoustic demonstrations required detailed advance study."

"Agreed. And notice how our passengers coordinated their positioning throughout the temple. They're following predetermined plans, not casual exploration."

I twisted Quinn's ring against my thumb, in what was becoming a habit. The truth would emerge from darkness. But first, we had to survive whatever revelation waited in the shadows of the journey still to come.

As we boarded the ship, Quinn released my hand with what felt like reluctance. Or maybe I was imagining that.

# CHAPTER SIXTEEN

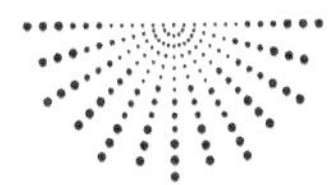

Soon after we returned from Hathor's Temple, Quinn disappeared toward the wireless room again, promising to report back anything he learned.

Left to myself at teatime, with everyone up on the main deck, I had a sudden burst of investigative inspiration.

Why not do a little snooping, to see if I could corroborate the suspected connections between our new friends?

I cornered Freddie in the galley.

"Mr. Williams," I'd said, pitching my voice low, "I wonder if you might assist me with a small matter."

His eyes had widened with eager helpfulness. "Anything, Miz Bell."

"I seem to have misplaced my cabin key, and with everyone busy serving tea, I'd hate to trouble the stewards." I'd arranged my features into what I hoped was appropriate distress. "Might there be a spare set somewhere? Or perhaps a master key...? Just temporarily, of course."

"Well..." He'd hesitated, eyes darting toward the busy crew. "There is the master set, but..."

I'd touched his sleeve lightly. "You've been so extraordinarily helpful throughout our journey. I do hope I can rely on your discretion in this small matter." I gave a little conspiratorial wink, which did the trick.

His chest puffed slightly. "Of course, Miz Bell. Wait here."

Three minutes later, an extra set of the ship's master keys had been pressed into my palm. Amazing how helpful romantic young men could be when properly motivated by a combination of flattery and the suggestion of shared secrets.

Minutes later, the master key, a weighty brass Bramah pattern, slid into Lady Penelope's cabin lock with a soft click that seemed thunderous in the hushed corridor. I paused, listening for footsteps or voices that might indicate someone abandoning their tea early, but heard only the distant strains of conversation, the rhythmic tapping of the ship's engine far below, and the familiar creaking of the hull.

The ship's clock chimed the half-hour somewhere above. Every minute increased my risk of discovery.

Lady Penelope's cabin reflected her carefully cultivated image of fashionable frivolity—silk scarves draped artfully over chair backs, expensive perfume bottles arranged on the dressing table (enough French scents to asphyxiate a small village), and jewelry cases that probably contained more wealth than said Egyptian village would see in a decade. The cloying sweetness of Guerlain's L'Heure Bleue hung in the air, mingling with the mustiness of old documents.

But it was the methodical organization beneath the feminine clutter that caught my attention. Her evening bag lay open on the writing desk, revealing not the usual collection of lipstick and calling cards, but a small leather notebook filled with dates and locations.

More significantly, nestled in a velvet-lined jewelry box between a strand of pearls and sapphire earrings, lay a small blue stone amulet carved in the distinctive eye-of-Horus design. The lapis lazuli was genuine—the deep blue coloration and gold flecking distinguished true Afghan lapis from Egyptian blue substitutes without requiring chemical testing.

My fingertips tingled with a sensation somewhere between academic excitement and primal dread as I lifted it for closer examination. What made my pulse quicken was the modern gold setting and the tiny engraved flame symbol on the reverse.

Brotherhood membership token.

Footsteps echoed suddenly in the corridor outside—heavy and measured, approaching with alarming speed.

I froze, then slipped behind the heavy velvet curtain separating the sleeping area from the sitting room, holding my breath as the footsteps paused outside the door. The brass handle jiggled slightly, then the steps continued onward. My heart hammered so loudly I feared it might give me away even through the thick fabric.

My hands trembled as I emerged and took quick notes, then sketched the amulet into the small notebook in my pocket.

Dr. Cordelia Waverly's cabin required more careful navigation, as her academic materials were scattered across every surface in organized chaos that reminded me uncomfortably of my own work habits. Each doorknob and drawer pull made my stomach clench tighter.

Mathematical journals lay open beside calculations about harmonic ratios, while letters from various "Brotherhood correspondents" carried terms like "Acoustic Research" and "Sacred Geometry Applications."

But the big discovery was waiting in plain sight, as though deliberately positioned for me to notice.

There on her bedside table, displayed like a talisman, sat an identical blue amulet. Same lapis lazuli, same gold setting, same flame symbol. The deep azure stone seemed to absorb the cabin's electric light rather than reflect it. There was no need to sketch it, as it was identical to Lady Penelope's piece.

On to Colonel Hartwell's cabin. Not surprisingly, it reflected military neatness—everything squared away, clothes hung at regulation intervals. Also not surprising: his amulet occupied a position of honor atop his writing desk.

If there'd been any thought that the amulets were simply matching pieces of jewelry belonging to the two women, that false notion was banished by the presence of the amulet in the Colonel's belongings.

Beside the amulet lay a stack of maps of Egypt marked with red ink annotations. The maps showed temple locations, river distances, and what looked like tactical assessments of archaeological sites. One document caught my eye—correspondence regarding tensions between British excavation teams and the newly established Egyptian Antiquities Service, with specific mentions of sites along our itinerary.

I filed these conspiratorial cabins under *Evidence: Incriminating but Complicated Due to Breaking and Entering.*

Three identical amulets. Three confirmed Brotherhood members with coordinated jewelry and shared objectives. Four, if one counted Lord Ashford and his many blue-flamed items. This wasn't a casual philosophical society—it was an organized network with specific goals and matching accessories.

The implications made my academic training rebel. These people might want to appear simply as wealthy collectors with eccentric theories about ancient wisdom. But they were part of something systematic, something that had already claimed Faraj's life.

Was Fraulein Becker part of all this? She seemed to always remain apart from the others, but that could simply be a cover. She certainly seemed eager to keep Mrs. Pemberton quiet.

Would I find amulets in those two women's cabins? In Mullen's or Montague's?

The ship's horn blared suddenly, signaling tea's end, and I heard the telltale shuffling of feet and voices growing louder in the corridors.

My heart leapt to my throat as I hastily locked Colonel Hartwell's cabin and pocketed the master key. There would be no time to check the remaining cabins—not without risking discovery.

I found Quinn on the steps between decks, frowning.

He turned when he saw me, and we headed up to the open air to talk.

"Handler?" I asked quietly.

"Troubling news." He kept his voice low. "The blue flame insignia has appeared in classified documents at the Foreign Office. Higher infiltration than we suspected."

A chill ran down my spine. "How high?"

"High enough to compromise Operation Indigo investigations. My superiors are questioning which departments can be trusted."

The implications were staggering. If Brotherhood influence extended into government intelligence services, then our investigation—and our safety—depended on resources that might already be compromised.

"We're more isolated than we thought," I murmured.

"Indeed. But we're not entirely alone. Hassan remains trustworthy, and we have each other."

The simple declaration carried weight that our false engagement couldn't fully explain.

"You won't believe what I've discovered—"

My revelation was interrupted by Mullen's approach to where Professor Montague stood near the stern rail. The authentication expert still clutched his leather case, his nervous energy visible even from our distant position.

"Looks like Mullen wants to discuss something with your mentor," Quinn observed.

I watched as Mullen engaged Montague in what appeared to be scholarly conversation. Montague listened with his characteristic patience, occasionally nodding as Mullen gestured toward his case. Then Montague placed a paternal hand on Mullen's shoulder, guiding him toward a more private corner of the deck.

Their body language shifted subtly—Mullen's posture becoming increasingly tense while Montague remained composed, almost consoling. Whatever discussion they were having required privacy from other passengers.

I quickly filled my partner in on what I'd discovered searching cabins.

He whistled, low and slow. "How far does this thing actually go?"

Quinn's handler's message had indeed raised concerns. If the Brotherhood's infiltration extended into intelligence departments, and even into Operation Indigo, then every communication, every plan, every trust could be compromised.

"We need to warn Hassan about the government infiltration," I said. "And we should document everything we've observed, in case—"

"In case we don't survive to testify," Quinn finished grimly. "Agreed."

Our planning was interrupted by Mrs. Pemberton's hesitant approach. She'd changed into evening attire, though her widow sensibilities kept her wardrobe conservative compared to other passengers' elegant displays.

"Dr. Bell," she began, then noticed Colonel Hartwell materialize beside her.

"Mrs. Pemberton," Hartwell's voice carried authority that brooked no argument. "I believe you mentioned wanting to review the evening's entertainment schedule?"

Her face drained of color. "Oh. Yes, of course. How thoughtful of you to—"

"Shall we?" Hartwell offered his arm with gentleman's courtesy that felt more like enforcement.

Mrs. Pemberton glanced desperately toward me before allowing herself to be escorted away.

"That wasn't coincidental," Quinn said.

"No. Is it just me, or is *everyone* conspiring together to ensure that our conversation doesn't happen?"

The sun had fully set by the time I knocked on Mrs. Pemberton's cabin door an hour later. No response came to my gentle inquiry, though light showed beneath the door frame.

"Mrs. Pemberton? Are you quite well?"

Silence.

I tried again, concerned. "It's Clarissa Bell. I wondered if you'd like some company for the evening?"

Still no response, though I heard what might have been movement within the cabin.

Returning to the deck, I found Quinn maintaining watch

over the evening's social activities. Passengers clustered around the salon's warm lighting, engaging in civilized conversation.

"She's not answering," I reported. "Either she's genuinely indisposed, or someone's made it clear that speaking with me would be... inadvisable."

"Given today's revelations about government infiltration and Brotherhood coordination," Quinn said, "I suspect the latter."

# CHAPTER SEVENTEEN

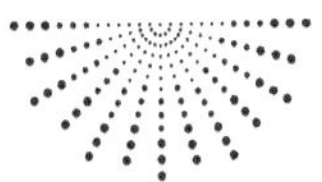

I stood at the rail with my morning coffee, watching tourist boats already crowding the water, eager pilgrims seeking pharaonic glory.

The Thomas Cook vessels were particularly distinctive—their crisp white awnings and uniformed guides suggesting the perfect balance of adventure and British propriety.

The contrast between ancient grandeur and modern commerce never failed to strike me—temple columns that had witnessed three millennia of human ambition now serving as backdrop for souvenir hawkers and camera-wielding tourists consulting their Baedeker guidebooks with reverent attention.

"Up early with the rest of the tourists?" Quinn joined me at the rail.

"Hoping to catch Mrs. Pemberton for a private word, before we all head out together."

In truth, I was a bit concerned for her, after last night's lack of response at her door.

But my fears were soon allayed. As if summoned by mention of her name, the widow herself appeared on deck, looking considerably more composed than during her previous attempts at conversation. Gone were the haunted circles beneath her eyes, replaced by the careful makeup of a lady preparing for public appearances.

"Dr. Bell," she smiled. "I do hope you slept well. I'm afraid I must apologize for my behavior yesterday—I'm afraid I was overtired and wasn't thinking clearly."

I studied her carefully. The nervous energy that had driven multiple attempts to reach me had vanished, replaced by an almost rehearsed normalcy. Though her fingers twisted at her mourning locket, eyes not meeting mine.

"Of course," I said gently. "I did stop by your room last evening—"

She waved away my comment, as though embarrassed. "My doctor has given me the nicest little pills to help me sleep. I'm certain I was dead to the world by the time you knocked."

Unfortunate turn of phrase aside, I wondered at her truthfulness. "If you'd still like that conversation—"

"No, no, I was probably being silly." Mrs. Pemberton's accent had softened, as if she'd been practicing more refined pronunciation. "Widowhood does strange things to one's imagination."

Quinn's slight frown suggested he shared my skepticism. Yesterday's desperate woman seeking urgent conference had been replaced by someone performing careful dismissal—a transformation that felt less like recovery and more like coaching.

"Well," I said, "should you change your mind—"

"How thoughtful of you, Dr. Bell. Now, I believe they're serving breakfast in the salon."

She departed with swift efficiency, leaving Quinn and me to exchange a raised-eyebrow look.

"Either those 'nice little pills' do more than help her sleep," Quinn murmured, "or someone convinced her that discretion serves better than disclosure."

Our speculation was interrupted by Annie's appearance on deck, her usual morning composure replaced by barely contained excitement.

"Clarissa," she began, then stopped herself with visible

effort. "I mean, Miss Bell, there's been the most extraordinary development."

"Oh?"

"I've just heard the ship will be taking on an additional steward here at Luxor. Someone quite... familiar." Annie's attempt at casual delivery failed entirely as a broad smile broke across her features.

As if on cue, a figure in ship's whites appeared from the crew quarters—tall, sandy-haired, and unmistakably Freddie Collins, Annie's romantic correspondent from Lady Blackwood's estate.

"Mornin', Miss Evanwood." He touched his cap with exaggerated ceremony, though his grin threatened to split his face in two. "Dr. Bell, Mr. Quinn. 'Ope you'll find the service up to snuff. Took a fair bit of sweet-talkin' to get meself signed on proper-like, but 'ere I am. Figured if ancient Egyptians could build pyramids to impress their sweethearts, least I could do was polish some brass on a fancy boat."

Annie's face had turned a delightful shade of pink. "However did you manage to arrange employment on this particular vessel?"

"Well, it's like this," Freddie said, his hands clasped behind his back in an attempt at professional deportment. "After your last letter mentioned this Nile cruise business, I got to thinkin' how it ain't right for a fellow to let his girl go sailin' off into Egyptian mysteries without proper... well, without someone keepin' an eye on things, like."

Annie's blush deepened. "Freddie, you didn't need to—"

"I did indeed. Went straight to Her Ladyship and explained the situation. Turns out Lady Blackwood knows the cruise line owners—some connection through the late earl's shipping interests. She said it was 'romantically enterprising' and wrote me a letter of introduction." He produced a folded paper from his pocket. "Apparently Lady Blackwood's word carries considerable weight in maritime circles, and Captain Mason just 'appened to have another crewman leave the ship early."

Quinn looked amused. "Enterprising indeed. Though I

suspect you'll find stewarding on a luxury cruise somewhat different from footman duties at a Luxor estate."

"'Ow hard can it be? Polish the brass, serve the tea, keep the toffs 'appy." Freddie's confidence faltered slightly. "Though I confess the uniform's a bit snug round the shoulders."

Annie composed herself with visible effort. "Well. I suppose... that is, it's quite... thoughtful of you to arrange employment nearby."

"Thoughtful," I murmured to Quinn. "That's one word for it."

I nodded to the two, who barely noticed us. "Well, we should prepare for the shore excursions. Hassan mentioned an early departure."

The morning's archaeological program proved extensive: the Colossi of Memnon, Karnak Temple, the Valley of the Kings including Tutankhamun's tomb, and Hatshepsut's magnificent terraced temple. Each site represented layers of Egyptian achievement, though I suspected our fellow passengers viewed them through rather different lenses.

Our journey required delightfully chaotic logistics—first docking on the east side of the Nile, then crossing the river by local felucca boats to reach the western desert sites, with boatmen calling cheerfully to one another in Arabic, navigating the muddy current with generations of inherited skill.

For the final miles into the necropolis, we mounted small donkeys, their patient eyes and plodding gaits a stark contrast to the gleaming motorcars that the wealthier, or less adventurous, visitors preferred. Our donkey-boys ran alongside, managing the animals while practicing multilingual negotiations: "Good donkey! Very fast! Baksheesh, madame? Baksheesh!"

At the Colossi of Memnon, Hassan gathered our group before the massive seated figures of Amenhotep III. The monoliths rose sixty feet against the desert sky, their weathered faces bearing the dignified resignation of monuments that had watched empires rise and fall while they remained.

Tourist parties clustered nearby, guides delivering well-rehearsed lectures about the statues' famous "singing" phenomenon—the dawn whistling sound that had once drawn Roman tourists just as reliably as it now attracted their modern counterparts.

I noticed the rapt attention our fellow passengers gave to this acoustic explanation, even though it was well-documented to have been caused simply by fissures in the stone.

We navigated next to Tutankhamun's tomb, where Howard Carter's meticulous cataloging work continued behind carefully guarded perimeters, while worldwide "Tutmania" had created an entirely new tourism economy.

I adjusted my wide-brimmed hat against the relentless sun, leaning closer to Quinn as my donkey matched pace with his. "Strange to be back again so soon."

The memory felt both distant and immediate. Two months ago, when we had visited this valley, Montague had seemed genuinely dedicated to solving the murder at Lady Blackwood's estate. Now doubts about his true allegiances crept like shadows across those memories. Had he been diverting attention from Lady Blackwood's involvement—or pursuing another agenda entirely?

"Extraordinary preservation," Mullen murmured as we descended into the antechamber, his professional appreciation momentarily overriding his recent paranoia.

"Indeed," I replied, hoping to draw him into conversation. "Your authentication expertise must find these intact contexts invaluable for comparative study."

But Mullen's moment of scholarly openness vanished as quickly as it had appeared. His eyes darted toward where Fraulein Becker stood examining the murals inside the burial chamber with her ever-present notebook, and his shoulders tensed.

"Yes, well. Everything appears quite... quite in order." His grip tightened on his leather case. "No irregularities worth discussing."

"Mr. Mullen," I pressed gently, "if you have concerns about the auction pieces—"

"Concerns?" His voice pitched higher. "No, no concerns whatsoever. Simply... professional observations of no particular significance."

Quinn stepped closer, his collector's facade in place. "Surely among fellow enthusiasts, you might share insights about authentication methods? I'd value expert guidance on identifying potential... inconsistencies."

Mullen's laugh sounded forced. "Mr. Quinn, I assure you, inconsistencies are rarely as significant as they initially appear. Often, what seems problematic proves perfectly... perfectly ordinary upon closer examination."

With that unconvincing reassurance, he hurried toward the tomb's exit, leaving Quinn and me to exchange frustrated glances in the golden glow of electric illumination.

I sighed. "It seems as though everyone who expresses concerns about this auction farce eventually changes their tune."

After the Valley of the Kings, hired motorcars transported us across the bridge back to the East Bank, providing blessed shade against the punishing midday sun. We arrived at the massive Karnak Temple complex as the afternoon light transformed the ancient sandstone to burnished gold.

The Karnak complex—with its forest of columns, sacred lake, and maze-like passages—provided perfect opportunities for both private conversation and surreptitious observation. As we entered the Great Hypostyle Hall, the temperature dropped perceptibly beneath the massive roof. The columns rose around us like stone trees, their tops lost in shadows. Each pillar could easily contain a dozen people, while hieroglyphs marched up their surfaces in endless processions of gods and pharaohs.

Lady Penelope tilted her head back, her pearl necklace catching the filtered light as she gazed upward through the forest of columns. "One feels quite insignificant among these architectural giants."

"It is quite the achievement," Quinn agreed, though I noticed his attention fixed on our fellow passengers rather than the ancient grandeur. "One might almost lose track of one's companions in such a maze."

Indeed, Dr. Waverly and Colonel Hartwell had already vanished among the columns, while Lord Ashford lingered near specific inscriptions with a focused intensity.

Hassan approached with his official clipboard and the slightly harried expression of a man trying to manage tourists while investigating murder. "The complex covers over two hundred acres," he announced. "We'll focus on the Hypostyle Hall and Sacred Lake, though visitors are welcome to explore independently within the designated areas."

Within moments, our group scattered like conspirators given the all-clear signal.

Momentarily free from his tour guide responsibilities, Hassan lingered near Quinn and me. He raised an eyebrow at our linked arms. "You make a harmonious couple, like Isis and Osiris."

"Let's hope our story ends differently," Quinn murmured. "I'm rather attached to all my body parts remaining in their original configuration."

I managed a laugh despite my concerns. "Ancient Egyptian marital metaphors aside, shall we explore the Sacred Lake area?"

We found Lady Penelope and Marcus Waverly near a quieter section of pillars, examining hieroglyphs with unexpected scholarly attention.

"Fascinating symbolism," I commented, approaching carefully.

Lady Penelope startled slightly, then composed her aristocratic features. "One develops an eye for these things when married to a collector. Edward was particularly drawn to musical motifs in Egyptian art." Her fingertips traced a carved sistrum instrument. "He always said certain artifacts seemed to resonate differently than others—physically, I mean, not just metaphorically."

"Have you studied archaeology, Lady Penelope?"

"Oh, merely as an educated gentlewoman's pursuit.

Though my late husband was quite passionate about ancient mathematics." Her tone carried carefully controlled bitterness. "He believed these monuments contained encoded knowledge that modern scholars systematically ignore or suppress."

Quinn's expression sharpened with interest. "Suppress? That seems rather... conspiratorial."

Lady Penelope's laugh held no humor. "Perhaps. Though when valuable artifacts disappear from collections and authentication records prove mysteriously unreliable, one begins to wonder whether academic oversight extends beyond mere scholarly disagreement and into something more dangerous."

The implication hung in the air like incense smoke. Was Lady Penelope yet another widow left with dangerous knowledge and unanswered questions?

"I heard you lost your husband recently. I'm sorry for your loss," I said gently.

"Thank you. Though I confess, Edward's death has left me with... curiosities... about his final research interests."

Before I could respond, she drifted away with the same unsettling silence, leaving Quinn and me to process her revelation.

"Is she investigating her husband's death? Or part of all this conspiracy?" Quinn asked.

We moved toward where Marcus still observed the lake.

"Magnificent setting for contemplation," Quinn said conversationally, settling onto the stone steps with the casual manner of a fellow gentleman seeking respite.

"Yes," Marcus replied, though his tone suggested contemplation wasn't bringing him peace. "Quite... overwhelming, really. All this ancient significance."

"Your mother seems particularly knowledgeable about the mathematical aspects," I observed, hoping to draw him into confidence.

Marcus's laugh sounded brittle. "Mother has... enthusiasms... that sometimes exceed practical considerations. I confess I don't always understand what she's gotten herself involved with."

The admission came with a glance toward where Dr. Waverly had wandered into the temple complex.

"Family business can be complicated." Quinn shrugged. "Particularly when it involves valuable collections and specialized knowledge."

"Indeed." Marcus's hands trembled slightly as he adjusted his spectacles. "Sometimes one finds oneself—participating—in arrangements that seemed perfectly reasonable initially but prove to have—complications—that weren't apparent at the outset."

I leaned forward with what I hoped appeared as sympathetic interest rather than investigative hunger. "Archaeological circles can be quite competitive, I've found. Particularly all those gray areas regarding authentication and provenance questions."

"Exactly. And I'm beginning to suspect those gray areas might be rather darker than I initially realized."

Before we could pursue this revelation further, Hassan's voice echoed through the complex, summoning our group for departure. Our fellow passengers emerged from their various alcoves and shadowed corners with the satisfied expressions of people who'd accomplished predetermined tasks.

As we made our way back toward the Nile and our waiting transportation, Quinn slipped his arm around my waist with what had become disturbingly natural ease.

"Productive afternoon, darling," he murmured, his breath warm against my ear in a way that sent shivers down my spine.

"Quite," I managed, hoping my voice sounded steady. "And I hope our time on the ship will continue to be... revealing."

His hand tightened slightly against my waist. "I can only hope you are referring to the dress you plan to wear tomorrow evening to the ship's formal evening of dinner and dance."

I pulled away, laughing. "I was referring to revealing *conversation*, Mr. Quinn. Not my evening wear."

"Pity."

# CHAPTER EIGHTEEN

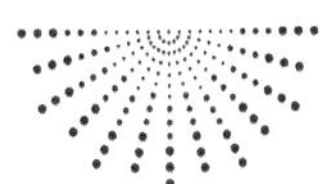

The departure from Luxor unfolded with the languid grace of a painting coming to life. Our steamship glided away from the Winter Palace Hotel's imposing facade while the morning sun transformed the Nile into molten bronze. I stood at the rail watching feluccas drift past like white-winged moths, their sails filling in the breeze.

"Penny for your thoughts," Quinn murmured, appearing beside me with two cups of coffee.

I accepted the porcelain cup, noting how the steam rose in perfect spirals—rather like the confusion in my chest whenever he materialized with thoughtful gestures. "I was thinking about temporal layers. How the river looks exactly as it did three thousand years ago, but we're viewing it through thoroughly modern eyes."

"Archaeological perspective on everything, I see." His smile held warmth that had nothing to do with the Egyptian sun. "Even lazy morning river journeys become dissertation material."

"It's called having an organized mind." I sipped the coffee, which was excellent. "Some people find it quite useful for solving murders."

"Among other things." His gaze lingered on my face in a way that made my pulse skitter.

Morning stretched into afternoon as we approached the notorious bottleneck at Esna. What should have been a brief river passage transformed into an hours-long ordeal as vessels queued like carriages in London traffic, waiting their turn through the single lock chamber built about fifteen years ago during the British modernization efforts.

Our steamship tied up alongside a crowded dahabiya while the lock master's whistle echoed across the water, signaling another tedious cycle. Colonel Hartwell provided enthusiastic commentary about hydraulic principles while Dr. Waverly muttered about "harmony disrupted by modern inefficiency." Even Fraulein Becker emerged from her scholarly solitude to observe the massive stone chamber slowly filling with thousands of gallons, raising the vessels ahead of us with mechanical deliberation.

"Remarkable how they've attempted to tame the river's natural flow," Lord Ashford commented, standing rather closer to me than strictly necessary as we watched crew members guide ropes along the wet stone edges. "Though one might question whether the cure isn't worse than the original navigation challenges."

"The ancients managed quite well without locks," I replied, stepping sideways to maintain appropriate distance.

By the time we finally rose through the chamber and continued south, the afternoon sun was already slanting toward evening, and I'd gained several hours' worth of behavioral observations that would prove useful for the night's planned investigation.

Hours later, the ship's salon had been transformed for our formal dance. Crystal chandeliers cast prisms across honey-colored wood paneling, while golden lotus patterns on the wall sconces threw geometric shadows across the polished floor.

A trio of hired musicians tuned instruments in the corner while stewards in white gloves arranged champagne flutes in perfect diamond formations atop linen-draped tables. Through the wide portholes, the twilight Nile had turned a deep purple-blue, contrasting with the glow of electric lights trying desperately to mimic the softer ambience of gaslight.

I'd chosen my charcoal black silk evening gown—the one Father insisted was "appropriately sophisticated for international society"—and found myself checking my reflection more carefully than usual.

"You look lovely, miss," Annie said, securing the last pearl hairpin. "Though I notice you've been distracted all afternoon."

"I've been thinking about investigative methodology." Which wasn't entirely untrue. I'd also been thinking about how Quinn's formal evening wear would complement his shoulders, but that fell under *Observations filed under Ignore Completely.*

"If you say so, miss. Will you be needing anything else this evening?"

"Just your discretion."

The salon-turned-ballroom buzzed with elegant conversation as passengers arrived in formal splendor. The ladies swept past in silk and beading while gentlemen adjusted white bow ties and checked pocket watches.

Captain Mason presided in his dinner jacket, stopping occasionally to announce the next dance with a small brass gong brought from the British colonial presence in India.

In a shadowed corner near the refreshment table, Hassan observed the proceedings with his usual grumpy expression, though I noticed his gaze lingered on me longer than seemed comfortable. His dark eyes followed my movements with unsettling attention, as though filing away discrepancies for future reference.

Quinn appeared looking devastatingly handsome in white tie and tails, his dark hair gleaming under the chandeliers.

I took a turn with Colonel Hartwell, and Quinn convinced an embarrassed Mrs. Pemberton to dance with him. Afterward, she fanned herself with a gloved hand and declared she'd had enough excitement for one day.

I watched her say goodnight to a few others, and felt Quinn approach from behind.

"Dr. Bell, I believe you owe me a dance."

"Do I?" I accepted his offered arm, noting how the fine wool of his jacket felt beneath my gloved fingers. "I don't recall making any such promises."

"It's implied in our arrangement." His eyes held mischief. "Engaged couples are expected to dance together. We wouldn't want to disappoint our audience."

Indeed, Lady Penelope and Lord Ashford watched with interest as he led me to the dance floor. The tiny orchestra struck up a waltz, and suddenly his hand was at my waist while mine rested on his shoulder. The required proximity of formal dancing created an intimacy our "engagement" had carefully avoided until now.

"You waltz surprisingly well for an archaeologist." He guided me through a perfect turn, his hand adjusting at my waist with practiced ease. The slight roughness of his palm against my gloved hand suggested work not entirely confined to office papers.

"And you navigate gracefully for an antiquities dealer." The black silk of my gown whispered against his formal trousers as we turned. A blend of women's French perfumes with men's Bay Rum cologne created an invisible cloud of expensive scents around us, yet I found myself distinctly aware of Quinn's particular scent. "Though I suppose both professions require attention to detail and careful timing."

"Among other skills." His fingers tightened slightly at my waist, creating sensations that had nothing to do with dance technique. "Such as reading situations accurately and adapting to unexpected developments."

"Like learning your fiancé has a surprise Yorkshire estate?" I kept my voice light despite the way his cologne was affecting my concentration.

"Ah." His smile turned rueful. "We're discussing honesty again."

"We're discussing the difference between necessary discretion and deliberate deception." The waltz required us to move closer as other couples swirled around us. "I've had quite enough of men who consider truth optional."

"Have you now." His voice dropped to the intimate register that made my pulse skip. "And what conclusion have you drawn about my relationship with honesty?"

"That you're entirely too comfortable with selective information sharing." Yet even as I said it, I found myself leaning slightly into his warmth. The contradiction between my words and actions was mortifying.

"Perhaps because some information comes with complications that extend beyond personal preference." His thumb brushed across my wrist, an oddly intimate gesture. "Though I admit to finding certain... truths... increasingly difficult to categorize as classified material."

The way he said "truths" while looking at my mouth made my breath catch. We'd stopped moving, standing perfectly still while other couples continued dancing around us. The space between us seemed to shrink with each heartbeat.

The ballroom had grown uncomfortably warm, or perhaps it was merely the proximity of his body to mine that created the sudden heat flaring across my skin.

"Clarissa." My name on his lips sounded different—less performance, more plea.

"Don't." But I didn't step away. Instead, I found myself studying the gold flecks in his dark eyes, noting how his pupils had dilated in the chandelier light. "This is exactly what we agreed wouldn't happen."

"Did we?" His free hand rose to touch my jaw, fingertips tracing the edge of lips. "Because I distinctly remember agreeing to convince people we were engaged. Difficult to do convincingly while maintaining complete emotional distance."

"There's convincing, and then there's..." I gestured helplessly between us. "This."

"This." He pulled me closer, close enough that I could feel the warmth radiating from his formal shirt front. "This feels considerably more honest than anything either of us has said in days."

"Quinn." My voice came out breathless despite my attempts at composure.

"Yes?"

"If you're going to kiss me, kindly do it properly. I refuse to spend the evening wondering what might have happened."

His smile was brilliant and entirely too satisfied. "Finally. A direct request I can fulfill without compromising anyone's security clearance."

But before his lips could meet mine, the orchestra concluded the waltz with a flourish that seemed to break whatever spell had captured us. We stepped apart as applause filled the ballroom, punctuated by the occasional clink of champagne glasses touching in toasts.

I stepped back, my throat suddenly dry. My body was staging an inconvenient rebellion against my brain's authority —a mutiny that seemed to intensify with each passing moment. I made a mental note to court-martial my hormones at the earliest opportunity.

"Well," I smoothed my gloves with hands that weren't entirely steady. "That was..."

"Educational." His eyes held promise of continuation. "Though I believe the lesson requires additional study."

"Perhaps." I accepted his offered arm as we moved toward the edge of the dance floor. "But not tonight. I believe I'll retire early. All this socializing is rather exhausting."

"Shall I escort you to your cabin?" The way he emphasized "escort" suggested activities beyond mere navigation.

"I'm not entirely certain whether your escort services would qualify as protection or as the primary danger to be avoided. Either way, I'll take my chances with the corridor ghosts." I adjusted the clasp on my evening bag, fingers confirming the solid outline of the master keys hidden inside. "You should stay and enjoy the dancing. I'm sure Lord Ashford would appreciate your company."

Quinn's expression suggested he knew I was planning something but couldn't determine what. "Clarissa…"

"Goodnight, darling." I rose on my toes to brush a kiss across his cheek—a gesture that appeared appropriately affectionate while positioning my lips near his ear. "Do try not to miss me too terribly."

Before he could respond, I swept toward the salon exit with what I hoped was an elegant departure.

Behind me, the hired musicians struck up a foxtrot while conversations resumed their elegant rhythm. Through the doorway to the viewing deck, I glimpsed couples stepping out between dances to see the moonlight reflecting on the Nile. The ship's lighting would switch from generator power to lanterns after ten o'clock, creating a more intimate atmosphere —perfect cover for what came next.

I'd left off searching cabins before I'd completed them all. I patted the master key, still in my evening bag.

Tonight, I intended to finish the job.

# CHAPTER NINETEEN

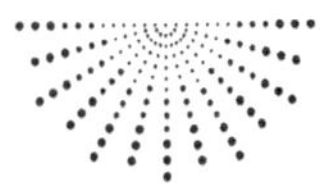

*D*ance music still drifted down from the salon, providing auditory cover, but the ship's gentle rocking against the Nile current created an unsettling sensation, as if the vessel itself objected to my illicit search.

It almost seemed pointless to search Lord Ashford's cabin, but I ducked in anyway, and found my fourth confirmation, though his amulet was casually tossed into a silver dish alongside cufflinks and collar studs, as if Brotherhood membership was merely another fashionable accessory. His approach to conspiracy appeared as cavalier as his attitude toward everything else.

Fraulein Becker's cabin was my next destination. I slipped down the corridor, needing to pass my own cabin, Quinn's, and then Mullen's stateroom. Mullen was no collector, and his concerns about the auction certainly ruled him out, so I wouldn't need to take the time there.

The orchestra above had transitioned to a waltz. Was Quinn dancing with someone else or would he also retire early, perhaps even to knock on my cabin door?

I hadn't told Quinn about tonight's search, and had to admit it was because I wanted to prove—perhaps to him, certainly to myself—that I could conduct this investigation independently. My academic reputation had always been questioned, my achievements attributed to wealth or connections. If I could unravel this conspiracy through my own efforts, perhaps I could finally silence the voice in my head that whispered the same doubts as my critics.

I reached Mullen's door, midway down the corridor.

Strange. It was ajar.

A chill ran across me, raising the hair on my arms. Mullen hadn't been at the dance, had he?

I stepped into the cabin. The room felt unusually cool compared to the warm corridor.

Was he asleep here in the darkness?

But then I saw him.

Mullen lay sprawled beside his writing desk, looking for all the world as if he *were* sleeping.

Documents were scattered across the floor around him in an almost perfect circular pattern, suggesting he had spun as he fell. Provenance certificates bearing Egyptian Museum stamps and British Museum verification codes formed a paper halo around his body.

I crouched beside him with the same care I'd use examining a delicate artifact, though my hands shook as I checked for vital signs I knew I wouldn't find. My knees locked in place, refusing commands to retreat while my lungs seemed to forget their purpose.

His skin was still warm. Whatever had happened here was recent. Probably within the last hour while I'd been waltzing with Quinn and exchanging witty repartee about archaeological methodology.

I pulled back his collar with the tip of my pencil, revealing the side of his neck. There—a tiny puncture mark, barely visible in the lamplight, the stark white of his collar contrasting sharply with the darkening bruise around the wound. The same detail we'd found on Faraj.

Two murders, two needle marks. This wasn't random violence or crimes of opportunity. Someone aboard this ship possessed the knowledge or equipment or charm to incapacitate victims before delivering the fatal dose, ensuring no struggle, no defensive wounds, no chance for the victim to cry out.

The authentication documents scattered around Mullen's body told their own story. And amidst the paperwork was a half-finished letter written in his precise handwriting:

*Dr. Bell, the convergence they plan at Aswan will—*

I picked up the letter, the paper trembling between my gloved fingers.

For some reason, it was the smell of his bay rum aftershave that threatened to overwhelm my composure.

Aswan. Perhaps not just the final temple stop on our cruise itinerary, but the ultimate destination for whatever the Brotherhood had been planning all along. Had the coordination I'd witnessed at Abydos, Dendera, and Karnak not been random scholarly interest, but preparation for something specific at the most remote temple complex on our route?

A convergence. The word echoed Dr. Waverly's discussions of harmonic frequencies and sacred geometry, Colonel Hartwell's military precision about timing and positioning, Lord Ashford's casual mentions of "bringing everything together."

Mullen had found some kind of proof. And Mullen was dead.

The guilt hit like a physical blow. While I'd been enjoying romantic tension and playing at investigation, a man had died trying to expose the very conspiracy we were meant to be unraveling. Mullen had possessed the evidence to stop whatever the Brotherhood was planning, and now that evidence was likely gone with him.

The blue amulets proved coordination. Mullen's murder proved desperation. And his final letter suggested that whatever the Brotherhood was planning would happen at Aswan— probably during our scheduled visit in just four days.

The orchestra music above shifted to something more dramatic, and I realized I'd been crouched beside a corpse for several minutes while cataloging evidence. The narrow space between Mullen's writing desk and his bed left barely enough room for his fallen body and my kneeling form. The practical urgency of my situation suddenly overwhelmed my scholarly instincts—I was alone in a dead man's cabin with stolen master keys and no reasonable explanation for my presence.

I had to get back to Quinn. Had to share this evidence with Hassan. Had to find some way to stop a conspiracy that was willing to commit murder to protect their archaeological delusions.

But as I reached for the cabin door, footsteps echoed in the corridor outside. Heavy, measured footsteps that suggested someone returning from the dance or making rounds to check on something—or someone.

My heart hammered against my ribs as I realized my position. Alone in a murdered man's cabin with stolen keys and criminal intentions, while a killer walked free among the elegant passengers dancing above. If I was discovered here, my investigation would end with accusations and confinement rather than solutions and justice.

The footsteps paused outside Mullen's door.

I held my breath, counting heartbeats while weighing options. The cabin's porthole was too small for escape, the door offered no alternative exit, and my evening wear was entirely unsuitable for desperate measures.

But once again, the footsteps continued past the door, fading toward the stairway that led to the upper decks. Whoever it was hadn't come for Mullen's cabin—at least, not yet.

I waited another eternal minute before cracking the door open and peering into the corridor. Empty. The dance music still provided cover, and the ship's familiar sounds masked any noise my departure might create.

As I slipped from Mullen's cabin, the full weight of discovery settled around my shoulders. Two men were dead. A coordinated conspiracy was operating among our fellow passengers. And somewhere above me, in a ballroom decorated with crystal and filled with elegant conversation, walked a killer who had just committed murder while maintaining perfect social alibis.

I needed to find Quinn immediately.

But first, I needed to scream.

The sound that emerged from my throat echoed through the corridor with all the horror and frustration of the evening's revelations—a cry that would bring running feet, concerned voices, and the end of any possibility for discrete investigation.

But Mullen deserved better than dying in silence while his killer danced to waltzes above.

The elegant cruise was over. The real investigation was about to begin.

# CHAPTER TWENTY

*W*ithin moments of the sharp, piercing note of my scream (one that would have made any soprano envious), the door at the end of the corridor burst open, followed by various passengers hurrying my direction.

The harsh electric bulbs cast elongated shadows against the narrow walls, turning each concerned passenger into a grotesque silhouette.

Led by Quinn. Of course.

"Good heavens, what—" Lord Ashford appeared from inside his cabin a few doors down, still adjusting his silk dressing gown, his usual languid charm replaced by alert concern.

"Clarissa!" Quinn materialized beside me with that unsettling speed of his, scanning the scene with professional thoroughness. "What are you—" He stopped mid-sentence as his gaze fell on Mullen's crumpled form sprawled across his cabin floor, documents scattered around him like academic confetti.

"Oh, dear God," breathed Dr. Waverly, pressing her hand to her throat. "Is he—?"

Hassan pushed through the growing crowd, his expression grim as he knelt beside Mullen's body. "Dead. Recently. Still warm."

Mrs. Pemberton's shriek could have shattered the ship's crystal. "Another murder! Oh, we're all going to die! Just like my husband said—the Brotherhood—"

"Mrs. Pemberton, please," Colonel Hartwell stepped forward, his eyes were sharp. "Hysteria helps no one."

"Clarissa?" Quinn's voice carried a dangerous edge as he positioned himself between me and the other passengers. "I thought you'd retired for the evening."

The disapproval in his tone made my spine stiffen. "I felt too anxious to sleep. I was... taking a walk..."

"Were you indeed?" His brown eyes held mine with uncomfortable intensity. "With a murderer on the loose?"

"Perhaps," Lady Penelope suggested with deceptive sweetness, "now isn't the time for romantic disputes?"

"Romantic?" Quinn turned that penetrating stare on her. "There is nothing romantic about murder—"

"Friends, please." Montague's voice cut through the chaos with paternal authority as he appeared in perfectly pressed evening wear. "A man is dead. Our personal concerns must wait."

Quinn's jaw tightened. "Yes, I find I am rather concerned about where my fiancée wanders at night. Alone and vulnerable."

The way he emphasized 'fiancée' made something flutter in my chest.

"Gentlemen," Captain Mason arrived with the authority of twenty-three years at sea, "I must ask everyone to return to their cabins immediately. This is a crime scene."

"Absolutely not." Hassan rose from examining Mullen's body, his voice carrying the weight of Egyptian governmental authority. "Two murders aboard this vessel in less than a week? I want everyone in one place, until police arrive."

"Police?" Mrs. Pemberton's voice climbed to a fevered pitch.

"Mrs. Pemberton." Fraulein Becker's voice cut through the hysteria like a Germanic scalpel. "Perhaps some chamomile tea would be beneficial?"

Mrs. Pemberton flinched at Becker's suggestion.

Within minutes, Captain Mason had herded our motley collection of suspects—because that's what we'd become, really —into the ship's main salon like a shepherd with particularly uncooperative sheep.

The distant splash of the paddle wheel against the Nile's surface provided a rhythm to our whispered arguments, like a metronome counting down our remaining time.

Hassan positioned himself strategically near the entrance while Captain Mason dispatched his steward with urgent instructions.

"Code three-seven," the Captain ordered, using the colonial emergency protocol that would summon both Egyptian police and British oversight.

The rest of us were left to wait in what could only be described as the most uncomfortable drawing room gathering in recent memory.

Lady Penelope arranged herself in a velvet chair with elegance, still managing to look perfectly composed despite her silk robe. "It's all absolutely dashed awful," she murmured, her clipped American tone cutting through the babble.

Lord Ashford slipped into the seat nearest mine, with what could only be described as predatory grace. "Dreadful business, this," he agreed, though his tone suggested he found it rather more stimulating than dreadful. "Two murders in six days. One begins to wonder if someone's collecting bodies."

"How macabre," Lady Penelope observed, adjusting her silk wrap. "Though I suppose we're rather a valuable lot, aren't we? All this expertise gathered in one place."

Mrs. Pemberton, meanwhile, had dissolved into what could generously be called a state of advanced nervous collapse. She perched on the edge of a settee like a bird preparing for flight, wringing her hands with such vigor I feared for her circulation.

"He knew," she whispered, her voice barely audible above the ship's gentle creaking. "Mullen, he... the frequencies... Albert tried to tell them..." Her words disintegrated into hiccupping sobs. "Oh God, I should have—when he asked me about the glyphs on the bowl—"

"Mrs. Pemberton," Colonel Hartwell's voice carried crisp authority. "Perhaps you should rest. This excitement—"

"Rest?" Her laugh held a distinctly unhinged quality. "How can anyone rest when they're picking us off one by one? First Faraj, now poor Mr. Mullen. I told Albert this would happen. I told him the Brotherhood—"

"The Brotherhood values discretion," Dr. Waverly interjected smoothly, her gray eyes fixed on Mrs. Pemberton with uncomfortable intensity. "Perhaps some water? You seem overwrought."

The way Mrs. Pemberton shrank back suggested 'overwrought' was the least of her concerns.

I found myself studying the assembled group. Mrs. Pemberton's terror felt authentic—the kind of bone-deep fear that came from knowledge rather than speculation. If I'd been choosing targets for elimination, Mrs. Pemberton's nervous chatter would have made her the obvious choice, not the man who seemed to have accepted whatever anomalies he'd found.

Which meant either I'd misjudged the killer's priorities, or Mullen possessed something particularly dangerous.

"Clarissa." Quinn's voice cut through my analytical reverie. "Might I have a word?"

The way he emphasized my name suggested I was about to receive what Annie would call 'a proper talking-to.' I followed him to a corner of the salon, acutely aware that every other passenger was watching our exchange with the avid interest of spectators at a tennis match.

"Where exactly were you tonight?" His voice carried the dangerous quiet that preceded volcanic eruptions. "Because I distinctly recall you mentioning retirement to your cabin."

I eyed the rest of the room. I was unsure if they could hear us, so I played along. "I told you, I couldn't sleep. I was taking a walk."

"A walk. Through ship corridors. At midnight." Each word

dropped like ice into warm champagne. "How remarkably adventurous of you."

"If you're suggesting—"

"I'm not suggesting anything." His whisper emerged through gritted teeth. "I'm stating that my allegedly devoted fiancée appears to have been conducting unauthorized investigations while claiming to be safely tucked in bed." His eyes held mine with uncomfortable intensity. "Engaged couples generally avoid such... creative interpretations of truth."

The irony was ludicrous. "Oh, how refreshing to hear you advocate for honesty in relationships."

"Meaning?"

"Meaning you're hardly in a position to lecture about secrets, darling." I smiled sweetly but whispered through gritted teeth. "Yorkshire estates, convenient delays in communication, mysterious handlers—shall I continue?"

A muscle in his jaw twitched. "That's entirely different."

"Is it? Because from where I'm standing, we both seem rather fond of compartmentalized information."

Lord Ashford's delighted chuckle drifted across the salon. "I say, Quinn, if you can't keep track of your lady, perhaps someone else should step in? I'd be delighted to ensure Miss Bell's evening safety. *Any* evening, as it happens."

The temperature in Quinn's vicinity dropped several degrees. "How generous."

"Think nothing of it, old man. Beautiful women require proper attention." Ashford's smile held enough mischief to spark a Quinn implosion. "Especially brilliant ones who appreciate... philosophical discussions."

I suppressed the urge to roll my eyes. I'd rather take an evening stroll with a hungry crocodile. At least its predatory intentions would be transparent.

Lady Penelope clapped her hands, as though appreciating a theater performance.

"Lady Penelope," I heard Dr. Waverly murmur, "perhaps we shouldn't encourage—"

"Oh, but it's terribly entertaining," she replied with a voice like honey over steel. "One so rarely sees genuine emotion these days. Most couples are dreadfully boring."

Genuine emotion. The phrase hit rather closer to home than comfortable.

Quinn stepped nearer, lowering his voice. "We'll discuss your nocturnal wanderings later."

If archaeology ever failed me, I could apparently pursue a promising career in enraging handsome men through the simple act of independent thinking. Perhaps there was a grant or scholarship for that.

"Ah, there's the 'Bene-dictator' I know and love."

I regretted the phrase the moment I uttered it, and couldn't meet his silent gaze.

His anger wasn't simply about control—I knew that. The tightness around his eyes betrayed fear, not possession. But understanding his concern didn't mean surrendering to it. Mullen had died trying to warn me; I couldn't abandon that responsibility simply because it made Quinn uncomfortable.

"Clarissa—"

I caught Quinn's arm. "There's no time for arguments. I need to search Mullen's cabin properly before the police arrive."

"I would have thought you'd already concluded your investigation, given your thorough evening constitutional." Quinn's fingers drummed a staccato rhythm against his leg.

"Quinn—"

His exasperated huff cut me off.

The obvious solution struck me. "Could you manage to keep this dreadful scene going? Something loud enough to occupy everyone's attention while I slip away?"

"A scene." His tone suggested I'd proposed ritualistic sacrifice.

"Jealous fiancé, public argument, wounded masculine pride—surely you could manage something suitably dramatic?"

"You want me to perform jealousy?"

"Well, you're certainly perfecting 'angry.' Perhaps channel more of that in Ashford's direction?"

Quinn's smile held dangerous promise. "Oh, I think I can manage something authentic enough."

He straightened his cufflinks and turned his back on me, striding back toward the assembled passengers with the measured pace of a man approaching a duel.

"Lord Ashford," his voice carried across the salon with crisp authority, "I believe we need to clarify something regarding my fiancée."

Ashford's eyebrows rose with delighted anticipation. "Do we indeed?"

"We do." Quinn positioned himself on the opposite side of Ashford, drawing all eyes to himself. "Clarissa and I are very much in love. I trust that fact is... clear?"

"Crystal clear, old man." Ashford's grin widened. "Though I must say, if you can't even provide adequate evening supervision—"

"Supervision?" Quinn's voice dropped, and several passengers leaned forward. "My fiancée does not require supervision."

"Well, she does seem to wander rather freely..."

"Perhaps," Quinn continued with smooth coldness, "you'd care to elaborate on that observation?"

The assembled passengers watched with the fascination of Romans at the Colosseum. Even Hassan paused in his note-taking to observe the developing drama.

"Benedict," I interjected with what I hoped sounded like embarrassed concern, "surely this isn't necessary—"

"Isn't it? Because I'm beginning to think we need to establish certain boundaries. Starting with this bounder."

He turned his attention back to Ashford.

While Quinn continued his masterful performance of masculine territorial display—complete with enough subtle threats to make Ashford back down while maintaining gentleman's honor —I slipped toward the salon exit with what I hoped appeared to be feminine retreat from unpleasant masculine posturing.

In reality, I was rather enjoying watching Quinn demolish Ashford's confidence with nothing more than precise vocabulary and strategic positioning. The man really was devastatingly effective when properly motivated.

The corridor outside Mullen's cabin remained mercifully empty. Within a few minutes, I found what I'd missed in the initial discovery chaos.

A leather portfolio, hidden beneath his mattress. I hesitated, my fingers trembling slightly. Was I becoming paranoid, seeing conspiracies where there might simply be academic rivalry? Perhaps Mullen's death was unrelated to his research—a robbery gone wrong, or personal vendetta.

Then I opened the portfolio and found documentation that made my breath catch. No, this wasn't paranoia. This was worse than I'd imagined.

Mullen's portfolio contained documents that redefined my understanding of our genteel floating house party.

Mullen had been maintaining surveillance notes on his fellow passengers with the thoroughness of a Scotland Yard detective. His observations made for uncomfortable reading:

*"Dr. Waverly—arrived with complete temple acoustic measurements, no indication how obtained."*

*"Colonel H.—refers to 'operational timeline' and 'activation protocols' in private conversations."*

*"Lady P.—asks specific questions about collection, suggests foreknowledge of auction contents."*

*"F. Becker—authentication expertise exceeds stated credentials, questions reveal insider knowledge."*

And most chilling: *"Montague arrival not coincidental—passengers defer to his authority despite claiming no prior contact."*

My hands trembled as I turned to Mullen's final entries, written in increasingly shaky script:

*"They're not collecting artifacts—they're assembling components. Mathematical sequence suggests acoustic amplification system. God help me, I think they mean to use them."*

*"Mrs. P. tried to warn me—husband discovered convergence*

*danger, died before he could prevent it. They plan to activate the complete collection."*

His final note, scrawled across the bottom margin: *"Must warn Dr. Bell—they know she can authenticate the mathematics. She's either recruitment target or elimination target."*

Elimination target.

The words struck me with the force of a temple column crashing down. Ice water seemed to replace the blood in my veins just as heavy footsteps echoed from the main deck above.

Police. Hassan's reinforcements had already arrived.

I pressed my ear to the cabin door, hearing Hassan's voice in the distance: "Two murders, Inspector. Yes, sir, we have detained all passengers pending your investigation."

Time to leave. Immediately.

# CHAPTER TWENTY-ONE

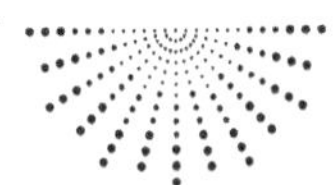

*I* slipped from Mullen's cabin, portfolio clutched against my chest, and managed three steps toward my own quarters before disaster struck in the form of Fraulein Becker emerging from the opposite direction.

She paused, glanced at me and then away. "Miss Bell. You seem distressed."

"Mr. Mullen's death was rather shocking." I hoped my voice conveyed appropriate feminine delicacy rather than criminal guilt.

"Indeed." Her gaze dropped to the leather portfolio in my arms.

"You appear to have retrieved something?" Her pale eyes fixed on Mullen's portfolio with the intensity of a hawk spotting prey.

My mind raced through plausible explanations while my pulse hammered against my collar. "My journal. I'd been taking notes during dinner about the temple acoustics we discussed." I clutched the leather case tighter. "Dr. Waverly's theories about harmonic frequencies were quite fascinating."

"Ah." She adjusted her thick spectacles, the gesture somehow managing to appear both nervous and predatory. "I did not observe you carrying a writing case at dinner."

The sound of approaching footsteps grew louder—Hassan's voice directing the police toward Mullen's cabin.

"I keep it in the salon's writing desk." The lie emerged easily. "For evening correspondence. One develops habits, you know."

"Indeed. Habits." Her gaze lingered on the portfolio's worn edges. "Such a... substantial journal for evening notes."

*Hathor's horns*, she was observant as a microscope.

"Well," I managed with desperate brightness, "I should return to my cabin. This has all been rather overwhelming."

"Quite." Fraulein Becker's smile held all the warmth of winter granite. "Though Captain Mason has been explicit about our presence in the Salon. I've only come to retrieve my glasses."

"You are already wearing them."

"Ah, yes. Shall we return, then?"

"Let me just slip my journal into my cabin."

I practically fled toward my stateroom, acutely aware of her pale eyes tracking me. My hands were shaking badly enough to make the key rattle against the lock.

When the portfolio was safe and my cabin locked again, I joined her in the corridor to return to the Salon.

We passed Hassan and two police officers on our way up. I did not miss Hassan's angry scowl in my direction.

I slipped back into the room just as Quinn was delivering what sounded like a beautifully crafted final declaration about the sanctity of engagement commitments and the unfortunate consequences of testing his patience.

"—trust that clarifies the situation adequately."

Lord Ashford had acquired the slightly stunned expression of someone who'd poked a sleeping lion and discovered it had rather more teeth than expected.

"Quite adequately," he managed. "My apologies for any... misunderstanding."

Quinn's smile held a satisfied menace. "No misunderstanding at all," he replied with silky politeness. "I simply believe in protecting what's mine."

The way he said *mine...*

Hassan's heavy footsteps announced his return before his grim expression confirmed our worst suspicions. The Egyptian official's face carried the weight of a man who'd discovered more than he'd bargained for.

"The police have secured Mr. Mullen's cabin," he announced without preamble. "However, there are additional... complications."

Captain Mason straightened in his chair. "Complications?"

"The autopsy findings regarding young Faraj." Hassan's voice carried the flatness of a man delivering unwelcome news. "What we hoped to be ruled an accidental death from a fall was not accidental at all. Poison. A toxin that killed him within minutes."

Mrs. Pemberton's strangled gasp echoed through the salon like a gunshot.

"Poison?" Dr. Waverly's academic curiosity warred visibly with horror. "What sort of—"

"Unknown," Hassan repeated firmly. "Which means we have a murderer among us who possesses specialized knowledge of chemistry or pharmacology." His gaze swept the assembled passengers. "The cruise schedule is hereby suspended pending complete investigation."

"Absolutely not." Lord Ashford rose to his feet with aristocratic indignation. "This is preposterous. One unfortunate incident—"

"Two murders," Hassan corrected with steel in his voice.

"Two alleged murders," Colonel Hartwell interjected, his military bearing somewhat ludicrous in his silk robe. "I served twenty-three years in His Majesty's forces, Inspector, and learned that preliminary findings often prove misleading upon proper examination."

"Are you questioning my professional competence, Colonel?"

The temperature in the salon plummeted several degrees.

Captain Mason cleared his throat diplomatically. "Gentlemen, perhaps we might consider the practical implications.

The cruise line's reputation, the passengers' comfort, the scheduled temple visits—"

"Temple visits?" Hassan's voice carried dangerous incredulity. "Captain, we have a killer aboard your vessel. One who has claimed two lives in six days."

"Which is precisely why," Dr. Waverly said with the passionate intensity I'd observed whenever she discussed ancient mathematics, "we cannot allow fear to prevent scholarly observation. The archaeological opportunities at Philae are irreplaceable. If we abandon our research because of... unfortunate coincidences..."

Her son Marcus shifted uncomfortably. "Mother, perhaps 'unfortunate coincidences' isn't quite—"

"Well, I suppose the boy has a point," Colonel Hartwell observed. "Two deaths suggest systematic elimination rather than coincidence. Which raises the question—who benefits from preventing this gathering?"

The implication hung in the air.

"I think," I interjected carefully, "we all have valid concerns about safety. However, abandoning the expedition entirely might not serve anyone's interests."

Quinn's eyes narrowed. "Meaning?"

"Meaning whoever orchestrated this gathering went to considerable effort to assemble specific people and artifacts. Disrupting those plans might simply force them to try again elsewhere." I studied the assembled faces. "Perhaps our safest course is proceeding under enhanced security, where Hassan can monitor everyone closely?"

Hassan grunted. "I will consider it, but I expect the authorities to have a different opinion, and be less concerned with tourism than with finding the truth."

"Naturally," Montague spoke for the first time since returning to the salon. "We're all committed to discovering the truth."

The way he emphasized the word made something cold settle in my stomach.

"Speaking of truth," Lady Penelope's sweet voice carried

unexpected steel, "might I ask how everyone came to know poor Mr. Mullen? Professionally, I mean."

The question landed like a stone into still water.

Dr. Waverly shifted in her chair. "He authenticated several pieces for our collection. Quite meticulous work."

"Yes, meticulously meticulous," Marcus added. "Perhaps too thorough, one might say."

"Too thorough?" I pinned Marcus with a look.

"He asked rather exhaustive questions about provenance documentation." Dr. Waverly shrugged elegantly. "More extensive than typically necessary for standard authentication work."

"Standard authentication," Montague murmured, "has become increasingly complex in recent years. So many... irregularities in the market."

"What sort of irregularities?" Hassan's voice carried official weight.

The silence stretched until Lord Ashford laughed with forced lightness. "Oh, the usual nonsense. Overzealous customs officials, diplomatic complications, paperwork delays. Nothing Mullen couldn't navigate with proper discretion."

"Proper discretion," Mrs. Pemberton whispered, her voice barely audible. "That's what Albert called it. Proper discretion."

Quinn cleared his throat. "Perhaps someone should explain why Mullen felt compelled to investigate these... irregularities?"

"Professional integrity," Montague suggested smoothly. "Mullen was concerned with maintaining standards."

"Standards," Hassan repeated slowly, "that apparently cost him his life."

The weight of that observation settled over our refined gathering.

"I think," Captain Mason announced with authority, "we've had quite enough speculation for tonight. Inspector Hassan, what are your requirements for securing the passengers?"

"Everyone returns to their cabins immediately. No corridor wandering, no private meetings, no unauthorized movement."

Hassan's gaze found mine with uncomfortable accuracy. "And I mean everyone."

As the passengers began dispersing toward their quarters, I caught fragments of whispered conversations:

Dr. Waverly to Marcus: "—must proceed as planned, regardless of complications—"

Colonel Hartwell to Ashford: "—timeline cannot be adjusted for police convenience—"

Lady Penelope to Mrs. Pemberton: "—careful what you say, dear. Some secrets are dangerous—"

Montague, surprisingly, approached me directly as I reached the salon exit.

"Clarissa, my dear, might I suggest extreme caution in your... investigative enthusiasms?" His paternal tone carried undertones I couldn't quite categorize. "Academic curiosity can sometimes lead scholars into situations beyond their expertise."

"What sort of situations?"

His smile held the warmth of winter moonlight. "The sort where brilliant young archaeologists find themselves... professionally compromised by association with irregular circumstances."

Quinn materialized at my shoulder with that uncanny ability of his. "Professor, are you threatening my fiancée?"

"Threatening?" Montague's chuckle sounded genuinely amused. "My dear Quinn, I'm trying to protect her. Clarissa has always been too intelligent for her own good."

"How thoughtful," Quinn replied with an undertone of menace. "However, Clarissa's protection is my responsibility now."

"Is it indeed?" Montague's eyes glittered with something that might have been amusement or calculation. "How wonderfully... conventional of you both."

Montague studied me for a moment longer than necessary, as though recalculating a formula he had once thought settled.

"You always resist ambitious hypotheses, Clarissa," he said

quietly. "I had hoped your experiences might broaden your perspective."

"Egypt has broadened many things," I replied evenly. "One cannot visit these sites without at least wondering whether we have misunderstood their purpose."

His gaze sharpened—not triumphant, not yet, but intrigued.

"I do not dismiss 'ambitious hypotheses,' Professor," I continued. "I simply prefer to see the proof before I declare it transcendence."

A faint smile ghosted across his mouth.

"Perhaps," he said, "you will."

With that cryptic observation, he glided toward his own cabin with the serene confidence of a man attending a garden party rather than fleeing a murder scene.

"I don't like him," Quinn murmured as we watched Montague disappear.

"He's just protective. Like a mentor."

"He's something, certainly." Quinn's tone suggested *mentor* ranked somewhere below *cobra* in his estimation.

We reached my cabin door, and Quinn circled my wrist with warm fingers.

"Clarissa, the connecting door—"

"Remains locked," I finished firmly, anticipating his suggestion.

He sighed. "Fine. However, given tonight's revelations about corridor wandering and unauthorized investigations, perhaps we should discuss security protocols."

"Security protocols?"

"Such as informing one's allegedly devoted fiancé before conducting midnight reconnaissance that might result in encountering murderers."

His voice carried genuine exasperation.

"Benedict—"

"Dr. Bell." His formal address stung more than expected. "I realize our arrangement is... unconventional. However, it would be professionally devastating if something happened to you during my watch."

"Professionally..." I repeated slowly.

"Extremely." His eyes held mine with uncomfortable intensity. "I'm quite fond of you, you know. Despite your unfortunate tendency toward spectacular risk-taking."

*Fond.*

Before I could formulate a response that wouldn't sound either pathetic or homicidal, Annie's voice carried clearly through my cabin door:

"Miss Clarissa? Is that you whispering in the corridor? Only I thought I heard—OH!"

The door flew open, revealing Annie in her nightgown with her hair already in curl papers, clutching a hairbrush like a weapon.

"Mr. Quinn! What are you doing lurking about at this hour?"

"Ensuring your mistress reaches her quarters safely," Quinn replied with admirable composure despite the circumstances. His voice dropped in that way that made my heartbeat misbehave. "Your mistress has a talent for finding trouble in the most unlikely places."

"Yes," Annie agreed with suspicious cheer, "she certainly does. Trouble seems to follow her everywhere. One might even say she attracts it."

The meaningful look she gave Quinn suggested we weren't discussing archaeological dangers exclusively.

"Precisely my concern." Quinn's smile held enough genuine warmth to melt Antarctic ice. "Someone should keep a closer eye on her."

"Someone should," Annie agreed sagely. "Someone very attentive and... committed to her welfare."

The subtext flowing between them was becoming ridiculous.

"If you're quite finished discussing my supervision requirements," I interjected with as much dignity as possible, "I'd like to retire."

"Of course." Quinn stepped back. "Sleep well, darling."

The endearment rolled off his tongue with casual intimacy that made my heart skip beats like a faulty gramophone.

I sent Annie to her own cabin, escaped into mine, and turned the key with relief that lasted exactly until I heard the soft click of the connecting door's lock being tested from the other side.

"Clarissa?" Quinn's voice carried through the wood with quiet urgency.

"Yes?"

"Whatever you discovered tonight—we'll discuss it properly tomorrow. Together."

Together. The word carried promises and threats in equal measure.

"Benedict?"

"Yes?"

"That was quite an effective jealousy performance."

A pause. Then: "Who said I was performing?"

I stared at the locked door connecting our cabins.

When exactly did my carefully categorized life develop such inconvenient complications?

Outside my porthole, the Nile whispered against the ship's hull with ancient patience, carrying us steadily toward whatever waited at our next port.

And somewhere in the darkness beyond my door, a killer walked free among passengers who'd gathered to reunite artifacts that Mullen had died trying to protect.

I stood with my forehead against the connecting door for a few minutes, thoughts flowing over all we knew, and all we didn't.

That's why I heard the soft click of Quinn's corridor door open and close once more.

Where on earth was *he* going?

# CHAPTER TWENTY-TWO

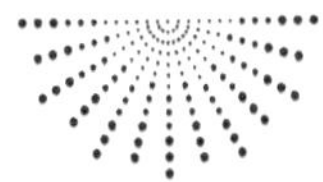

*I* froze, listening to Quinn's footsteps outside my hall door.

Where was he going at this hour, with a murderer loose on the ship?

I waited, irrationally hoping he was about to knock on my door.

And what would I do if that happened? My resolve to hold him at arm's length until I truly knew who he was had been weakening with each smile, each touch, each moment of genuine connection.

After a few moments, it became obvious he was not going to knock.

I eased my own door open. The corridor stretched empty before me, narrow and claustrophobic in the dim light, the patterned carpet runner absorbing the sound of my footsteps. I spotted the sleeve of his jacket disappearing through the door at the end. The ship's engines hummed below, a constant vibration like the anxiety building in my chest.

Curiosity, that eternally troublesome quality that had led me into numerous disasters, propelled me forward.

The upper deck lay mostly deserted at this hour, moonlight silvering the polished railings and casting long shadows across the wooden planks. I spotted Quinn's tall figure at the far end, his profile sharp against the night sky as he gazed upriver.

I slipped behind a lifeboat, watching as he checked his pocket watch with uncharacteristic impatience.

After several minutes, a small felucca appeared on the dark water, navigating silently toward our anchored vessel. The curved arc of the moon reflected in the rippling water, broken and reforming with each gentle wave. The boat's single occupant, wrapped in a dark *gallabiyah*, steered with practiced efficiency, allowing the current to carry him alongside the ship.

Quinn leaned over the railing, extending his hand. The boatman passed up a small envelope.

My breath caught.

Quinn was receiving communication from someone off the ship.

I watched as he broke the seal, read the contents with furrowed concentration, then extracted a pen and slip of paper from his jacket. He scribbled what appeared to be a reply, folded it precisely, inserted it back into the envelope, and handed it down to the waiting boatman.

The felucca pushed away, disappearing into the darkness as silently as it had appeared.

As Quinn turned to leave, I stepped from my hiding place. "Midnight correspondence? How fascinating."

He froze, his expression shifting from surprise to irritation faster than sand collapsing in an unstable excavation. "Clarissa. What are you doing here?"

"I could ask you the same thing." I crossed to him. "From your handler, I presume?"

His jaw tightened. "Intelligence work doesn't maintain banker's hours."

"And what exactly is your intelligence work requiring at this hour?"

"You know I can't—"

I moved with the suddenness that had served me well when retrieving artifacts from collapsing trenches. My fingers closed around the paper still clutched in his hand.

"Clarissa—"

But I'd already stepped back, unfolding the message with trembling fingers. The moonlight provided just enough illumination to read:

*QUINN -*
*CAIRO POLICE CONFIRM EVIDENCE OF PUNC-*
*TURE WOUND TO THE LATERAL NECK OF VICTIM.*

*OPERATION INDIGO APPEARS COMPROMISED*
*FROM WITHIN. EVIDENCE SUGGESTS HIGH-LEVEL*
*INFILTRATION. YOUR PRIMARY DIRECTIVE:*
*RETRIEVE ARTIFACT COLLECTION AND PREVENT*
*BROTHERHOOD AGENDA AT ANY COST.*

*QUESTION: ARE YOU COMPROMISED BY YOUR*
*ASSOCIATION WITH HER? CAN YOU COMPLETE*
*MISSION OBJECTIVES EVEN IF IT REQUIRES SACRI-*
*FICE? CONFIRM IMMEDIATELY.*

*- KINGSLEY*

The chilly night air crystallized in my lungs.

*Her.* Not Dr. Bell. Or even *your companion.*

Just *her*—dispensable, categorized, objectified. He was being asked if he could sacrifice me to complete his mission.

"What did you reply?" My voice emerged with remarkable steadiness considering my heart was performing excavations of its own, unearthing feelings I'd attempted to stratify and catalog away.

Quinn's expression hardened. "Give me that."

"No. What did you tell them?"

"That's classified."

"Classified." The word tasted bitter. "Just like your classified four-week absence? Your classified 'arrangement' with your handler? Your classified Yorkshire estate?" I waved the paper between us, my fingers trembling slightly. "This doesn't look classified. This looks rather like a question about whether I'm expendable."

Quinn tucked the pencil into his pocket. "You don't understand—"

"I understand perfectly. I'm a variable in your equation. A

potentially problematic one that might need elimination if I interfere with your primary objectives." I hugged myself protectively, arms crossed over my chest.

Quinn stepped closer, his voice dropping to that timbre that tonight felt dangerous.

"You're not trained for this, Clarissa. You're an archaeologist who thinks intelligence work is some extension of your detective games."

"Games?" Heat flooded my face. "Two people are dead."

"Exactly. Two people are dead, and you're wandering ship corridors alone, entering other passengers' cabins, confronting murderers—"

"I didn't confront—"

"You found Mullen's body, Clarissa! What if you'd interrupted his killer? What if you'd become the third victim? Did that occur to you during your midnight investigating?"

"Of course it occurred to me." I gripped the smooth polished wood of the ship's railing, cool under my white-knuckled fingers. "I'm reckless, not stupid."

"Yes! You are reckless! Brilliantly, catastrophically reckless. You dive into danger with the same enthusiasm most people reserve for champagne receptions."

"At least I'm honest about my methods." I held up the message. "Unlike some people."

"Intelligence work requires—"

"Deception? Manipulation? Calculating how expendable your 'fiancée' might be if she interferes with your precious mission?"

Quinn's face softened unexpectedly. "Is that really what you think?" He reached for my hand, his thumb brushing over the lapis lazuli ring he'd given me. "Clarissa, you're not—"

I pulled away. "Don't. You still haven't answered my question. What did you tell them?"

His expression shuttered. "My communications with my handler are—"

"Classified. Yes, so you've said." I folded the paper and

tucked it into my pocket. "I believe I'll keep this as a reminder of where we stand."

"Where we stand?" His voice held an edge that might have been anger or something else entirely. "We're standing on the deck of a ship with a murderer, surrounded by a conspiracy neither of us fully understands, with evidence suggesting British intelligence has been compromised at the highest levels. This isn't about us."

"There is no 'us,' Quinn. There's your mission and there's my investigation, which appear to intersect at the Brotherhood's auction. Beyond that..." I shrugged with a nonchalance I was far from feeling.

"Beyond that," he said quietly, "there's whatever makes you follow me across the ship at midnight because you're worried about where I'm going."

I had no ready retort for such inconvenient accuracy. Quinn's message scratched at my skin.

"Get some sleep, Dr. Bell." He touched my shoulder briefly, his fingers warm against the night chill. "We'll continue this discussion when you're not ready to throw me overboard."

I watched him walk away, his confident stride betraying nothing of our conversation, sandalwood cologne lingering in his wake.

He never did answer my question about his reply. All his talk of protection and concern, but when his handler asked if I was expendable... what had he said?

Sleep was clearly impossible. My cabin would only trap me with my thoughts.

I crossed through the salon to the opposite deck. The vast openness of the night sky made my troubles seem simultaneously immense and insignificant. The night air carried the metallic tang of the Nile mixed with the faint sweetness of night-blooming flowers along the shore, and the silver path of moonlight across dark water stretched like a road I couldn't follow, leading to answers just beyond my reach.

"Miss Clarissa?"

I started, turning to find Annie wrapped in a shawl, her

hair loose around her shoulders, the practical lavender scent of her soap familiar and comforting. "Annie! What are you doing wandering at this hour?"

"I might ask you the same." She settled beside me at the railing. The gentle splash of the Nile against the hull punctuated the quiet between us. "Though I suspect your reasons involve Mr. Quinn."

"I wasn't—" I began, then abandoned the useless protest. "That obvious?"

"Only to someone who's watched you categorize every emotion like it's a pottery fragment for the past year." She adjusted her shawl against the night breeze.

Despite everything, I felt my lips twitch. "Guilty."

"Let me guess: *Reactions to Benedict Quinn, sub-categorized by irritation level, cross-referenced with instances of physical proximity causing unprofessional sensations.*" She attempted to fix my wind-blown hair with increasingly frustration. "*With special notation for moments when his eyes do that crinkly thing.*"

I stared at her. "You're terrifying sometimes."

"I just pay attention." She smiled, wrapping her shawl tighter against the night breeze. "Unlike some brilliant archaeologists who can identify a pot from three thousand years ago but can't recognize when they've fallen in love."

"I have not fallen—" The denial died as Annie's eyebrow rose to a skeptical height. "It's complicated."

"Love usually is." She sighed, gazing out across the moonlit water. "Take me and Freddie. He's risked his position to be near me. It's romantic and it scares me, all at once."

"Why does it scare you?"

"What if he's thrown everything away for nothing? What if I'm not worth what he's sacrificed?" Her voice grew quiet. "The ship's purser already looks at us like we're doing something improper. And I'm not certain either of our families would think us suitable for each other. What if I choose wrong and ruin both our lives?"

I'd never heard Annie express such doubts. She always

seemed so practical, so certain. "I thought you were happy about Freddie's arrival."

"I am. And I'm worried. Both things can be true at once." She turned to me, her expression serious. "That's what you still haven't really learned about people, Miss Clarissa. We're messy and contradictory and confusing. Even to ourselves."

"I prefer things that can be properly classified," I muttered.

"I've noticed." Her smile softened the observation. "But feelings don't work that way. Especially regarding people we care about."

The gentle splash of the Nile against the hull punctuated the silence that followed.

Quinn certainly didn't fit any categories, with his contradictions, his secrets, the unreadable depths behind those expressive eyes.

"What if..." I began, then hesitated.

"What if what?"

"What if someone you thought you could trust turns out to be considering your... expendability?"

Annie's eyes widened. "Mr. Quinn would never—"

"You don't know that." I extracted the message from my pocket, the paper crackling between my fingers. "His handler asked if he could complete his mission even if it required... sacrificing me."

"And what did he answer?"

"I don't know. He wouldn't tell me."

Annie was quiet for a long moment. "Did you ask him, or did you accuse him?"

The question cut closer than comfortable. "I may have been somewhat... direct in my inquiry."

"Which means you attacked like one of those Egyptian cobras the guidebook warns about." She shook her head. "Men are strange creatures, Miss Clarissa. Sometimes they need gentler handling than ancient pottery."

"I prefer pottery. It doesn't lie about Yorkshire estates or receive mysterious midnight messages."

"No, but it doesn't look at you the way Mr. Quinn does,

either." She patted my hand again. "You know, just because you're brilliant at archaeology doesn't mean you can't also be brilliant at other things. You don't have to choose."

"Choose?"

"Between being Dr. Bell the archaeologist and Clarissa who might be falling in love. Between investigating murders and having feelings. Between being independent and being connected." She turned from the rail, the moonlight lighting the waves of her hair. "You're allowed to be more than one thing at once. We all are."

She left me with those unsettling words, her practical footsteps fading across the deck.

More than one thing at once. The concept felt foreign to my categorizing mind. Every artifact belonged in its proper classification: New Kingdom or Middle Kingdom, domestic or ceremonial, genuine or forgery. People were supposed to be similarly definable.

Yet here I stood, simultaneously furious with Quinn and worried about him. Both trusting and suspicious. My heart was performing its own excavation, digging up feelings. I was both Dr. Bell the professional and Clarissa the woman with entirely unprofessional feelings for a man who might or might not consider her expendable. The quiet intimacy of Annie's wisdom contrasted sharply with the loud betrayal still echoing in my mind.

I touched the fake engagement ring, its stone cool against my skin, while the Nile rocked the ship, waiting to take us south to Aswan and whatever "convergence" awaited.

The facts were clear: I couldn't trust Quinn completely. But I also couldn't solve this alone.

# CHAPTER TWENTY-THREE

The morning journey to Edfu began with chaos.

Children shrieked through streets of dust, donkey handlers bartered with wild gesticulations, and the air hummed with the perpetual symphony of a town that existed primarily to usher visitors toward its ancient treasure.

I twisted in my saddle, attempting to keep sight of Quinn while avoiding actual eye contact.

Montague rode ahead in animated conversation with Dr. Waverly, their donkeys plodding in synchronized indifference. Behind them, Colonel Hartwell maintained a watchful orbit around Mrs. Pemberton, whose gloved hands clutched her saddle pommel with the desperate grip of a drowning woman. Colonel Hartwell's jodhpurs and pith helmet marked him as Empire incarnate among our party, an advertisement for British authority that seemed to particularly irritate the Egyptian officials.

"Dr. Bell." Hassan adjusted the brim of his sun hat as he maneuvered his donkey alongside mine. "I cannot express my dissatisfaction with this arrangement strongly enough."

"Believe me, Inspector, I share your frustration."

Hassan's face was a study in controlled fury. Just hours ago, he'd been preparing to cancel all shore excursions when a police captain had arrived with a diplomatic miracle that smelled suspiciously of Brotherhood influence.

"With all due respect, Captain," Hassan had said to the policeman, "surely you agree that murder investigations supersede archaeological expeditions."

The police captain had shifted uncomfortably. "I'm afraid this comes directly from the Consul General's office, Inspector."

The resulting compromise was this ridiculous procession: suspected murderers and investigators alike, touring ancient monuments under police supervision like the world's most dangerous school outing.

"At least this way we can observe them," I offered as our donkeys picked their way through the market.

Ahead of us, the massive pylons of the Temple of Horus dominated the landscape, twin guardians covered in giant relief carvings of the falcon-headed god smiting his enemies. The walls told the ancient propaganda tale—Horus battling Seth for control of Egypt, order versus chaos rendered in limestone. I found myself sympathizing with both figures today—part righteous avenger, part agent of disruption.

As with everything in Egypt, the scale was deliberately intimidating, designed to humble worshippers approaching the divine presence. I currently felt less than humble—somewhere between seething and mortified, with a dash of professional determination keeping me functioning.

My companion was less concerned with ancient architecture than current suspects.

"I dislike diplomatic interference in my investigation," Hassan said. "And I especially dislike being told that a British cruise ship in Egyptian waters somehow exists in a jurisdictional limbo."

"Colonial bureaucracy at its finest," I replied, watching Quinn's straight back several riders ahead. His posture betrayed nothing, as if last night's revelation about potential sacrifice hadn't happened at all.

We moved from scorching brightness into the temple's embrace, my eyes adjusting painfully slowly. Massive columns rose around us in the hypostyle hall, their capitals blooming with lotus and papyrus designs in perfect geometry. The cool smoothness of stone against my palm steadied me during a moment of intellectual vertigo.

While tourists craned their necks in wonder, I was watching the Brotherhood members.

There it was again—the synchronized pocket-watch check that I'd observed at previous sites. Colonel Hartwell, Dr. Waverly, and Lord Ashford each consulted timepieces within seconds of each other, positioning themselves at precise angles to architectural features just as they had at Abydos and Dendera.

"Dr. Bell," Montague called, his voice carrying with unnatural clarity across the space. "Come observe this phenomenon."

I tensed. Quinn was already moving in that direction.

"The proportions of this chamber were designed for acoustic perfection, just as at Dendera." Montague tapped his walking stick against the stone floor at precise intervals, each tap reverberating through the chamber like an impromptu lecture demonstration. "Stand here and whisper something."

I positioned myself at the spot he indicated. "This seems rather theatrical," I murmured, barely audible.

Quinn, standing nearly twenty feet away, raised an eyebrow. "Perhaps less criticism and more constructive participation, darling?" His voice was quiet but carried perfectly to my position.

My shoulders tensed involuntarily, muscles tightening.

So, he could hear me. Fascinating acoustically, infuriating personally, as I really did not want to hear any false endearments this morning.

"The ancient architects," Montague continued, seemingly oblivious to our tension, "understood principles of sound propagation that we're only rediscovering now. Certain frequencies resonate particularly well within these stone chambers."

"The acoustic properties here are mathematically precise." Dr. Waverly tapped her walking stick against the stone floor at intervals, each tap reverberating through the chamber like an impromptu lecture demonstration. "The sacred proportions create harmony—sound waves traveling in perfect geometric patterns."

A tour guide's voice carried unexpectedly across the chamber, bouncing off perfectly angled walls to reach my ears with unnatural clarity.

I observed the other Brotherhood members recording measurements, noting specific hieroglyphic sequences, and testing acoustic properties by producing sounds at different positions. Whatever they were documenting, it followed the same methodical pattern I'd observed at previous temples.

I wandered to the start of the long tale of Horus avenging his father Osiris by defeating Seth, spread across the temple in a series of carved panels. The temple ceiling soared impossibly high above, making human conflicts seem petty yet inescapable within these ancient walls that had witnessed three thousand years of similar dramas.

"Remarkable, isn't it?" Lady Penelope appeared beside me, her lapis lazuli earrings catching the limited light. "So much drama. But drama is also so very easy to misinterpret."

I studied her carefully. Lady Penelope was either a vapid socialite, or a very good actress playing at one. The evidence remained frustratingly ambiguous.

"I find careful study and observation typically yields the truth," I replied.

"How delightful to maintain such certainty," she said with a smile that didn't reach her calculating eyes.

Before I could respond, she drifted away toward Colonel Hartwell, leaving me with the distinct impression I'd been both warned and mocked in the same conversation.

Mrs. Pemberton stood nearby. Good.

"Mrs. Pemberton, I wanted to ask—"

"Dr. Bell!" Colonel Hartwell materialized between us. "Mrs. Pemberton was just telling me how much better she's feeling today. Weren't you, my dear?"

Oh, good grief. This woman was minded closer than a toddler with a governess.

The widow nodded, clutching her handkerchief, her rehearsed smile as authentic as a plaster reproduction. "I've never felt better, truly. The Egyptian air is so refreshing."

He guided Mrs. Pemberton away with a hand firmly on her elbow, leaving me staring after them in frustration.

Annie appeared at my side, her practical presence a welcome relief from conspiratorial tensions.

"That woman wouldn't know a harvest scene from a bedroom fresco," she whispered, nodding toward Mrs. Pemberton, who was earnestly explaining a wall carving to another passenger. "She just told that gentleman that relief depicts 'traditional grain harvesting' when it's clearly... well, not agricultural in the slightest."

Even amid murder and international conspiracy, Annie's observations remained a lifeline to normalcy.

I glanced at the scene in question—a rather explicit depiction of fertility rites—and bit back inappropriate laughter. "Unless one counts the particularly enthusiastic propagation of royal bloodlines as agriculture. I suppose breeding pharaohs is technically a form of cultivation."

"Speaking of which," Annie murmured, "your fiancé keeps watching you when he thinks you're not looking."

I had no adequate filing system for the emotions that observation produced. Before I could formulate a response, our guide directed our attention to the temple's nilometer—a stairwell descending into darkness, its ancient markings recording the Nile's moods for millennia.

"The priests used these marks to calculate taxes," the guide explained. "Higher water meant better harvests and higher taxes. Lower water meant potential famine."

I noticed Fraulein Becker taking detailed notes about the nilometer's measurements, her pencil moving across grid paper rather than the standard archaeological field notebook. Why would a German academic specializing in authentication find ancient Egyptian water gauges so fascinating? Another data point suggesting she wasn't what she claimed to be.

She caught me watching and adjusted her pince-nez with calculated indifference, her gaze assessing me with the clinical detachment of an entomologist pinning a specimen.

As the tour continued, I found myself instinctively looking for Quinn whenever I discovered something suspicious—only to remember we weren't speaking. My brain kept categorizing observations as *things to tell Quinn* before my hurt feelings could intercept them.

In the sanctuary, we gathered where the statue of Horus had once stood. The stone shrine had survived millennia of history, outlasting empires and religions.

Something else caught my attention—an exchange between Montague and Fraulein Becker. They stood near a side chamber, apparently discussing a hieroglyphic sequence, but their postures suggested more intimate acquaintance than academic colleagues. I edged closer, pretending to examine a carved falcon.

"—amplify certain frequencies to extraordinary effect under the right conditions," Montague was saying. "We are ready."

Fraulein Becker nodded, her severe face showing rare animation. "The measurements confirm it. All components are accounted for."

My stomach tightened into a cold, hard knot. Components. Mullen's last words in his portfolio echoed in my mind: "They're not collecting artifacts—they're assembling components."

I moved to better overhear their discussion when a hand touched my elbow. Quinn.

"Careful," he murmured. "They're watching you."

Despite everything, we fell into our natural pattern—his body angled to block others' view, my notebook at the ready, to capture what we needed.

"Colonel Hartwell has again been intercepting Mrs. Pemberton all morning," I said quietly, not looking at him.

"And Fraulein Becker hasn't let Lady Penelope out of her sight," he replied.

"Organized, coordinated, and deeply connected," I summarized. "But to what purpose?"

Quinn didn't answer immediately. When he did, his voice was low enough that only the chamber's perfect acoustics allowed me to hear him. "I would choose you over the mission. That's what I told my handler."

The statement struck me with the force of a falling limestone block. I nearly dropped my notebook, fumbling it against ancient stone while my mind raced.

"You don't need to say that," I managed, focusing intently on the hieroglyphs before me. "Our cover doesn't require—"

"It's not about the cover, Clarissa." His voice remained low, but carried that intensity I'd categorized as *genuine Quinn* rather than *performance Quinn*. "When my handler asked if I could complete mission objectives even if it required sacrifice, I said I would choose you over the mission. Every time."

I kept my eyes fixed on the carved falcon, afraid of what my expression might reveal. My cataloging system for emotional responses was proving woefully inadequate—there was no appropriate filing method for the sensation spreading through my chest.

"That's why I'm considering resignation," he continued, shifting slightly to block Fraulein Becker's view. "I can't be an effective operative when I'm... compromised."

I finally looked at him. "Is that what I am? A compromise?"

The corner of his mouth lifted slightly. "The most beautifully catastrophic compromise I've ever made."

I couldn't deal with that information properly, not here or now, so I left Quinn to approach Montague. It was time to plant more seeds.

I found the professor near one of the temple's side chambers, studying a column as if it might confess its secrets under sufficient scrutiny.

"You're not collecting antiquities," I said lightly. "You're assembling something."

He did not turn immediately. "Aren't all collections assemblages?"

"Not of this precision." I stood shoulder-to-shoulder with him, studying the carved reliefs. "You've selected pieces with specific mathematical relationships. Ratios that align."

Now he looked at me fully.

"If the system is real," I continued, "it would represent the most sophisticated architectural acoustics in the ancient world."

"And you doubt it?" he asked softly.

"I doubt everything," I replied. "But I would very much like to see the calculations."

For the briefest moment, admiration eclipsed suspicion in his expression.

Before I could press further, Hassan approached, his expression grim beneath the formal courtesy. "Dr. Bell, Mr. Quinn, we must return to the ship. Immediately."

"Has something happened?" Quinn asked, seamlessly switching to concerned fiancé.

"Egyptian police have been conducting searches as part of the murder investigation." Hassan's eyes fixed on mine with uncomfortable intensity. "They found something in your cabin, Dr. Bell. Something that requires explanation."

My stomach dropped. Mullen's portfolio—the evidence I'd hidden after finding his body.

"What sort of something?" I kept my voice steady through years of practice presenting controversial findings to skeptical academics.

"Documentation connecting you to the victim." Hassan's tone was carefully neutral, but his posture had shifted from colleague to interrogator. "Including notes suggesting you knew more than you've shared with authorities."

My fingertips tingled with adrenaline, a wave of numbness

spreading upward. I opened my mouth to explain when Quinn appeared at my side.

Montague cleared his throat. "Most concerning, especially given recent events." He glanced between Quinn and me.

Lord Ashford appeared at my other side, his customary flirtation replaced by careful calculation. "I'm sure there's a perfectly reasonable explanation. Dr. Bell has always struck me as the soul of integrity."

The sanctuary suddenly felt claustrophobic, ancient walls pressing in as the Brotherhood members encircled us with polite concern masking predatory interest. I glanced at Mrs. Pemberton, who watched with terrified eyes, and Lady Penelope, whose narrowed eyes suggested she was cataloging every reaction.

"I'd be happy to explain everything," I said with far more confidence than I felt. "Though perhaps not in a three-thousand-year-old sacred space."

Quinn's hand found mine, his grip communicating both support and warning. Whatever confrontation awaited on the ship, we were facing it together—both the performance and what lay beneath it.

As our group filed out through the hypostyle hall toward blinding sunlight, I noticed Dr. Waverly and Colonel Hartwell exchanging satisfied glances. If there was evidence in my cabin, beyond Mullen's portfolio, it was no accident. Someone had deliberately compromised me.

Annie fell into step beside me, her practical presence a reminder of the normal world beyond this nightmare. "Don't worry," she whispered. "Freddie's watching your cabin. Nobody could have planted anything without him seeing."

I squeezed her hand gratefully. "Thank you."

The donkey ride back to the ship passed in tense silence, the chaotic vitality of Edfu town a jarring counterpoint to the deadly serious game unfolding among our party.

Quinn leaned close as we dismounted, his lips brushing my ear. "Together?"

I nodded once. "Together."

Quinn's presence beside me was more reassuring than it had any logical right to be.

The emotions remained uncategorized, the partnership undefined, but for the first time since this journey began, I was certain of one thing: in telling me he would choose me over his mission, Benedict Quinn had given me the most honest words of our fake engagement.

# CHAPTER TWENTY-FOUR

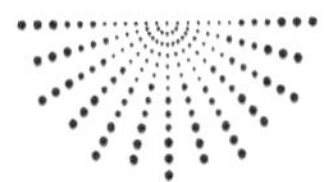

The police captain who boarded at Edfu had a mustache so elaborately waxed it appeared capable of independent movement, rather like an Egyptian version of my dig director, Dr. Bradford. The mustache twitched with suspicion as he examined Mullen's portfolio spread across the salon table.

"And you say you found these documents... how?" He directed the question at Hassan, but his eyes remained fixed on me.

Hassan's face was a masterpiece of professional neutrality. "Dr. Bell discovered Mr. Mullen's body and immediately alerted ship authorities."

*Thank you, Hassan.*

The portfolio's contents lay exposed between us: authentication records, observation notes on passengers, and detailed entries about the Brotherhood of the Blue Flame. My fingerprints were undoubtedly all over them, along with whatever remained of Mullen's.

"Yet these papers were not reported in the initial evidence catalog." The captain's mustache performed an impressive leap of skepticism.

I smoothed my skirt against the blood-red velvet of the salon chair, buying precious seconds to compose my response.

"I have an unnatural curiosity," I admitted, pressing my thumbnail into my forefinger to maintain composure. "It's something of an occupational hazard for archaeologists. We're essentially glorified busybodies with academic credentials and better tools for digging through other people's belongings."

Quinn, positioned behind me like a well-dressed sentinel, added helpfully, "It's true, Captain. My fiancée once spent three days analyzing a single pottery shard that everyone else had dismissed as debris."

His hand squeezed my shoulder briefly, a gesture of solidarity despite last night's argument. The casual touch sent a wave of comfort through my frayed nerves.

"This 'Brotherhood' you mention," the captain continued, examining Mullen's notes with obvious skepticism. "You believe it is connected to these murders?"

"The evidence suggests—" I began.

"A philosophical society," Hassan interrupted smoothly. "Wealthy Europeans and Americans with wildly romantic notions about ancient Egypt. Nothing more sinister than that."

Around us, the Brotherhood members had positioned themselves in an almost perfect circle, like specimens arranged in a museum case.

Dr. Waverly thumbed through a book with elaborate nonchalance, Colonel Hartwell stood at parade rest near the windows, and Lord Ashford lounged against a pillar in his pristine white dinner jacket from the previous evening. Lady Penelope fidgeted with her lapis lazuli necklace, the beads clicking softly together in a rhythm that betrayed her nervousness.

From the mezzanine above, Fraulein Becker watched silently, her face betraying nothing. She remained the one passenger whose room I hadn't searched—and consequently, the one whose allegiance remained most uncertain.

"I merely found Mr. Mullen's theories... intriguing," I said carefully. "Many scholars develop unusual hypotheses that seem incomprehensible to outsiders."

"And you took these papers because...?"

"Professional interest," I replied with more confidence than I felt. "The Brotherhood's theories about harmonic resonance in temple architecture align with some of my own research."

This wasn't entirely untrue.

The captain's colleague whispered something in Arabic. Hassan responded tersely, and I caught enough to understand they were discussing jurisdiction issues.

"Dr. Bell has been assisting my investigation," Hassan said finally, the admission clearly painful. He gathered Mullen's papers, aligning their edges. "I will take full responsibility for her... enthusiasm."

The captain's mustache performed another twitch. "See that you do, Inspector. We will need to question all passengers again when we reach Aswan."

"Of course," Hassan said.

"Nicely done," Quinn murmured once the police had exited. "Though perhaps next time, inform me before you steal critical evidence from a murder victim."

"I forget that I don't always work better independently." The words sounded hollow even to me.

His eyes met mine, and I saw the unspoken question there: *Would you have told me if you trusted me completely?*

Hassan interrupted our silent standoff. "I cannot continue protecting you if you interfere with evidence, Dr. Bell. The portfolio remains with me now."

"Of course," I nodded, grateful I'd already memorized the most critical sections. "Thank you for your support, Inspector."

"It was not support," Hassan corrected. "It was pragmatism. I need your expertise, but I will not tolerate further complications."

As he departed, Mrs. Pemberton approached, her expression artificially bright.

"Such excitement," she chirped. "Though I'm sure it's all a misunderstanding. Mr. Mullen was so... intense about his work."

Colonel Hartwell materialized at her elbow. "Indeed."

They retreated together, his hand firmly guiding her away. I turned to Quinn, who was watching the exchange with narrowed eyes.

"The coaching continues," he said quietly.

"Indeed. Though her acting skills need refinement."

"Unlike yours." His tone was impossible to categorize—somewhere between admiration and accusation.

Before I could respond, Annie appeared with a fresh cup of tea.

"You look like you need this," she said, pressing the cup into my hands. "And perhaps a reminder that dinner is in one hour."

The tea was bitter and over-steeped, but I drank it gratefully. I had been on high alert since waking at since dawn, and my mind felt stretched thin across too many competing theories.

"Thank you, Annie." I sighed, watching the Brotherhood members disperse to their cabins. "I believe tonight we abandon subtlety."

Quinn raised an eyebrow. "That sounds ominous."

"It's time to ask direct questions," I said. "We've established they're all connected. Now we need to understand why."

"And you think they'll simply tell you?"

"No," I admitted. "But their evasions will be informative."

~

The dining salon vibrated with tension beneath the veneer of civilized conversation.

Heavy velvet drapes were partially drawn against the darkening Nile, and the distant thrum of engines provided a constant reminder of our isolation—and our inexorable progress toward Aswan.

From a gramophone in the corner, the latest American jazz hit "Tea for Two" played with incongruous cheerfulness. I had dressed carefully in a pale peach with a fashionable dropped waist—professional enough for a confrontation, elegant enough for the formal dinner setting. Around me, the gentlemen's white dinner jackets and black bow ties stood in stark contrast to the ladies' colorful evening gowns, creating a festive tableau that belied our dangerous circumstances.

Quinn wore his customary evening attire with perfection. Despite everything, my gaze kept returning to the strong line of his jaw, now set in determination as we entered this next phase of our investigation.

I waited until the main course had been served before launching my offensive.

"I've been studying your Brotherhood of the Blue Flame," I announced to the table at large. "Which it seems may include all of you. Perhaps someone could explain its actual purpose?"

The clatter of silverware faltered momentarily before resuming with studied casualness.

"It's merely a scholarly association," Dr. Waverly offered, her silver hair catching the light as she leaned forward. "Studying various ideas."

"Particularly acoustic properties," Colonel Hartwell added, cutting his meat with force.

"The emerging field of archaeoacoustics," I noted, "has documented such phenomena, though without attributing supernatural properties to them."

Dr. Waverly's jaw muscles worked silently as she forced herself not to respond to my provocation. "Science often dismisses what it cannot immediately explain, Dr. Bell. The Brotherhood simply maintains an open mind."

"Yes, so you've mentioned." That line was beginning to sound extremely rehearsed.

Lord Ashford smiled disarmingly. "Really, Dr. Bell, it's all rather dry and academic. I mainly joined for the excellent brandy at meetings."

"And what precisely will you be demonstrating at Aswan?" I asked, watching their reactions carefully.

Another pause in the rhythm of dinner. Dr. Waverly and Colonel Hartwell exchanged a glance so brief I might have missed it had I not been looking for exactly such coordination.

"I wasn't aware we had scheduled any demonstrations," Lady Penelope said with practiced lightness, though her fingers nervously twisted her napkin.

"Scientific theories require testing," I pressed. "Surely you intend to validate your harmonic principles at some point?"

"Validation comes in many forms," Montague interjected smoothly from the far end of the table. "Not all require public demonstration."

Quinn's knee pressed against mine beneath the table—a warning I ignored.

"Two men have been murdered," I said bluntly. "Both were investigating anomalies in artifact authentication records."

"How shocking to bring up such unpleasantness at dinner," Mrs. Pemberton murmured, though her eyes darted anxiously toward Colonel Hartwell.

"Perhaps Dr. Bell's archaeological enthusiasm has extended into amateur detection, as it so often does," Montague suggested with a patronizing smile. "Though solving murders requires different expertise than cataloging pottery."

Fraulein Becker watched this exchange with unnerving intensity, her spectacles reflecting the chandelier light in a way that obscured her eyes completely.

"The police seem quite convinced these deaths resulted from professional disputes," Captain Mason said firmly. "Nothing to do with philosophical societies or archaeological theories."

The contrast was striking—the dense, detailed evidence in Mullen's portfolio versus the airy, vague explanations offered by passengers. Yet they maintained perfect coordination, each member filling gaps the others left.

Perhaps it was time for a different tack.

"You speak of harmony as though it were poetry," I said, letting my gaze pass deliberately from Ashford to Hartwell to Waverly. "But harmony is mathematics. If your theory holds, it would redefine every sacred structure along this river."

Dr. Waverly's eyes gleamed. "Exactly."

The silence that followed felt less hostile than before.

Perhaps thoughtful.

I caught Quinn watching this verbal choreography with professional assessment, undoubtedly cataloging patterns for later analysis. The conversation fragmented after that, Brotherhood members smoothly redirecting to innocuous topics despite my continued probing. By dessert, I had gleaned nothing concrete beyond confirmation that they were indeed working in concert.

As the meal concluded, I found myself uncharacteristically discouraged. Quinn eyed me with an expression I couldn't quite read—concern mixed with something like admiration.

"You were rather direct," he murmured as we rose from the table.

"Subtlety has gotten us nowhere," I replied. "And we're running out of time before Aswan."

Before he could respond, Montague appeared at my elbow.

"Dr. Bell, might I have a word?" His academic demeanor was firmly in place, but something harder lurked beneath it.

I smiled and waited.

"I sense you are beginning to understand our... enthusiasm... for our work."

"Such claims cannot be based on enthusiasm alone. There would need to be projections. Diagrams. Experiments."

His lips curved slowly. "You surprise me, Clarissa."

"I dislike incomplete arguments," I replied. "Particularly ones that threaten to rewrite history."

He was slow to respond. "Then perhaps," he said at last, "you should hear the complete argument." His smile warmed slightly. "I'm giving a small lecture this evening on 'The Harmony of Heaven and Earth' focusing on how Egyptian astronomical knowledge aligned with architectural acoustics. I'd be honored if you would attend."

My pulse jumped at the phrase, and a chill ran down my spine despite the salon's warmth. The Egyptians had indeed possessed remarkable astronomical knowledge, correctly calculating solar years and planetary movements with stunning accuracy. But Mullen's notes suggested the Brotherhood had twisted this genuine science into something far more sinister. I kept my expression neutral with effort.

"What time?"

"Nine o'clock. A private salon on the lower level." He glanced at Quinn, then back to me. "A scholarly gathering only, I'm afraid. Your fiancé would find it terribly dull."

"I assure you, I find scholarship fascinating," Quinn said, his tone pleasant but his eyes hard.

"Perhaps another time," Montague smiled thinly. "Tonight's private discussion involves specialized archaeological knowledge beyond most laymen's understanding."

The implication that Quinn was merely a wealthy collector without scholarly credentials was deliberate—and effective.

"I'd be delighted to attend," I said, matching his academic civility.

As Montague departed, Quinn turned to me with alarm barely concealed beneath his performance.

"You can't seriously be considering going alone."

"Of course I am." I watched Montague retreat across the salon. "This is our first opportunity to learn what they're actually planning."

"It's also the perfect opportunity for them to—" He stopped, jaw tightening.

"To what? Murder me in the middle of the ship with witnesses everywhere?"

"They've managed two murders already," he reminded me, voice low. "Aboard this very ship."

Annie appeared at my side, her practical presence a welcome interruption.

"Your evening shawl, Dr. Bell," she said, draping silk across my shoulders. "It gets rather cool on the river at night."

The weight of the fabric steadied me. "Thank you, Annie."

"You're welcome." She glanced between Quinn and me, reading the tension with uncanny accuracy. "I suppose you'll be gathering information tonight? Far better than speculating, I always say."

Quinn's expression darkened. "It's not information gathering I object to. It's the method."

"This is the first concrete lead connecting Mullen's notes to the Brotherhood's activities. We're less than two days from Aswan—we don't have the luxury of caution. And I don't recall asking permission," I added quietly.

Something flashed in his eyes—hurt, perhaps, or frustration. "No, you certainly didn't." The formal perfection of his evening wear only emphasized the rigid tension in his shoulders as he stepped back. "Just remember that your academic curiosity has already gotten one scholar killed."

He turned and walked away, leaving me with a hollow sensation in my chest that defied categorization.

"Men," Annie sighed. "Always thinking protection means control. As if you haven't been solving your own problems for years."

"Yes, well, before Quinn, my problems typically involved missing artifact catalog numbers or academic rivals stealing my research—not people actively trying to murder me," I admitted. "Though Professor Smythe at Oxford did once threaten me with bodily harm when I corrected his translation of a particularly vulgar hieroglyph."

Annie smiled, but didn't respond.

"Besides, this isn't about control," I said finally. "It's about trust."

"Then perhaps you should both try it sometime," Annie suggested mildly, before drifting away to seek out Freddie, who was clearing plates from tables.

As nine o'clock approached, I gathered my notebook and pencil.

Quinn was right about the danger, but I'd spent my entire career examining artifacts others dismissed as insignificant.

The Brotherhood's theories might blend legitimate archaeology with pseudoscientific nonsense, but their murders were quite real—and I intended to uncover both their methods and their motives before we reached Aswan.

# CHAPTER TWENTY-FIVE

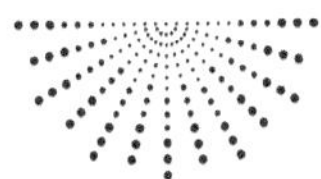

*I* followed Montague down corridors I'd never realized existed, descending toward the lower deck where passengers rarely ventured. Each step took me further from Quinn's protection and Annie's support, leaving me with only my wits as defense.

"We have a private salon here," Montague explained, his tone unchanged despite our surreptitious journey. "The captain reserves it for gatherings of a scholarly nature."

The narrow passageway opened into a chamber that defied the ship's predictable layout. Chairs arranged in the start of a strange semicircle—I recognized as an attempt at the golden "phi ratio"—faced a demonstration table laden with artifacts. Oil lamps cast dramatic shadows across walls hung with temple diagrams and mathematical notations. The windows were covered with heavy drapes despite the evening heat, ensuring whatever happened here remained unseen from the river.

Several sets of eyebrows rose at my entrance. All wore identical lapis lazuli amulets with the now-familiar blue flame symbol—even Mrs. Pemberton, who perched at the edge of her seat like a sparrow contemplating flight, and Fraulein Becker, whose involvement had been uncertain until tonight.

Dr. Waverly arranged small brass objects on a side table—a

miniature solar system with additional spheres corresponding to no planets I recognized. "The Seven Globes of the Root Race Evolution," she explained. "Each representing one phase of human spiritual-physical development."

I nodded politely, recognizing Madame Blavatsky's Theosophical theories about humanity evolving through seven spiritual phases, with Atlanteans as the supposedly advanced Fourth Root Race.

Colonel Hartwell closed the door behind us, and I heard the unmistakable sound of a key turning in the lock.

"Dr. Bell has graciously accepted our invitation to learn more about our philosophical approach to ancient wisdom," Montague announced.

The others straightened visibly—oddly deferential, beyond what one might show a respected academic colleague.

"The High Priest of the Lapis Sun honors us with this teaching," murmured Colonel Hartwell.

I maintained my neutral expression, though my pulse quickened. This was no mere academic society with eccentric theories—these people viewed Montague as a spiritual authority. The realization sent an involuntary chill across my skin.

I took the remaining seat, cataloging the artifacts displayed on velvet-covered tables: tuning forks, crystal bowls filled with water, bronze instruments resembling surveying tools, and architectural models of temple chambers.

"I appreciate scholarly discourse of all kinds," I said, extracting my notebook. "And am very interested in acoustic properties of ancient structures."

Montague's smile didn't reach his eyes. "Then you'll find tonight's discussion fascinating."

He began with legitimate archaeological information—the measurable acoustic properties of hypostyle halls, the echo patterns in burial chambers, the way certain temple corridors carried whispers with remarkable clarity.

Then came the subtle shift. Montague placed his hands palm-down on the demonstration table and spoke a brief invocation in a language I didn't recognize. The other members mirrored the gesture with practiced synchronicity.

"We acknowledge the Akashic Field before drawing knowledge from it," Dr. Waverly whispered. "The vibrations must align properly."

"Orthodox archaeology would have us believe these acoustic properties were architectural accidents," Montague continued. "But the evidence suggests otherwise. The Fifth Root Race—our current era of mental evolution—must recover what the Fourth Race mastered before their fall."

"The Fifth Root Race," I repeated. "You mean what Madame Blavatsky termed the 'Aryans' in her Theosophical writings."

"Precisely. Though we speak of spiritual-evolutionary categories, not the biological distortions currently fashionable in certain European circles."

Blavatsky's framework divided human evolution into "root races," with Atlanteans supposedly having mastered sciences lost to modern humanity. Montague had wrapped legitimate archaeological acoustics in mystical language, explaining the Brotherhood's peculiar blend of scientific terminology and religious reverence.

"Dr. Bell," Montague addressed me directly, "your expertise in pigmentation has proven valuable in distinguishing Egyptian blue from true lapis lazuli. But have you considered why certain knowledge was encoded specifically in lapis rather than common pigments?"

"Lapis lazuli was imported from Afghanistan at considerable expense," I replied neutrally. "Its rarity made it appropriate for high-status documentation."

"Its rarity, yes," Montague agreed. "But also, its physical properties."

Colonel Hartwell leaned forward. "Certain minerals respond to specific frequencies. The ancients understood this principle and applied it systematically."

"These pieces—all from the workshop of the scribe Amenemhat—form components of a unified system designed to amplify and direct specific frequencies."

*So, this is what it's all been about?*

The black-market dealings, even the murders? The archaeologist in me recognized the collection's legitimate historical significance—artifacts from a single New Kingdom scribal workshop represented a scholarly treasure regardless of the Brotherhood's interpretations.

Dr. Waverly approached the demonstration table and selected two crystal goblets. "Allow me to demonstrate harmonic resonance."

She filled them with varying levels of water and ran her dampened finger around their rims. The glasses emitted clear tones that seemed to vibrate through bone rather than air.

"These frequencies exist in specific mathematical relationships," she explained. As she adjusted the water levels, the second goblet began vibrating without being touched. The crystal suddenly shattered with a musical ping.

"Forgive me," Dr. Waverly said, flustered. "The frequency was too pure."

Impressive party trick, I thought, though entirely explicable through standard physics. If parlor tricks with wine glasses were proof of ancient Egyptian supernatural knowledge, then my Aunt Gertrude's bridge club had been channeling pharaonic wisdom every Thursday since 1912.

"Now imagine this principle applied at architectural scale," Montague continued, "with chambers designed to amplify specific frequencies during celestial alignments."

The Brotherhood's "scientific" explanations grew increasingly mystical, each member contributing specific details.

At some unspoken signal, Fraulein Becker approached a cloth-covered object. She removed the black velvet covering, revealing Jasper Thorne's "Astral Sphere"—the disc stolen during the Blackwood House affair. Its deep blue surface was etched with astronomical markings that seemed to shift under the lamplight.

"The Resonant Key," Montague announced reverently.

"After centuries apart, these items are reunited in preparation for the Convergence."

The Brotherhood members repeated their strange gesture, palms down, eyes briefly closed.

"These artifacts seem to form a coherent collection," I said. "What's their purpose when assembled correctly?"

"When properly arranged during the correct celestial alignment, they create what we call 'harmonic convergence'—a state where vibrational frequencies align to produce extraordinary effects."

"What kind of effects?" I pressed.

"Elevated perception," Dr. Waverly offered. "Access to knowledge beyond normal consciousness."

"Strategic advantages," Colonel Hartwell added.

My stomach tightened into a knot. These weren't merely academic eccentrics—they genuinely believed they could unlock supernatural powers through sound.

"The ancients understood that reality itself has a fundamental frequency," Montague explained. "By aligning with that frequency through precisely calculated sound vibrations, one can access levels of awareness typically dormant in human experience."

I nodded thoughtfully, as if considering this absurdity rather than filing it under *Dangerous Delusions: Archaeological Variety.*

Thanks to my Episcopal upbringing, I recognized the difference between genuine spiritual reverence for ancient beliefs and the Brotherhood's exploitative mysticism masquerading as scholarship.

"And you believe this... convergence... can be achieved at a specific location?" I asked.

"The ancients constructed temples as vibrational instruments," Montague confirmed. "Their dimensions and proportions are mathematically precise. But certain sites are particularly effective due to geological and astronomical factors."

"Such as?"

"We've been conducting acoustic measurements at each temple site during our cruise," Dr. Waverly interjected eagerly. "Testing resonance patterns, measuring harmonic frequencies, calculating optimal positioning for the artifacts."

Colonel Hartwell nodded. "Abydos showed promise, but the chamber dimensions weren't quite suitable. Dendera had excellent acoustic properties, though the celestial alignment was imprecise."

"So, you're still determining the exact location?" I pressed, though the answer seemed obvious given our itinerary.

Montague's smile was enigmatic. "Let us say that each temple visit has been... instructive. The optimal site will reveal itself through scientific measurement, not speculation."

I glanced around the room, noting the subtle anticipation in their expressions. With only one major stop remaining on our itinerary, their destination was hardly mysterious.

Lady Penelope spoke for the first time, her voice deliberately light. "Philae is particularly suited, according to my late husband's research."

Philae. The temple complex near Aswan. Our final destination.

"And these artifacts—how precisely do they function together?" I asked, touching a small architectural model that resembled a temple chamber.

Colonel Hartwell stepped in. "Each component serves a specific purpose. The Resonance Bowl establishes the fundamental tone. The Architect's Measuring Rod determines proportional ratios. The Calculation Tablet provides the sequence of activation. The Astronomer's Alignment Tool ensures correct orientation."

"Fascinating," I said. "But surely some components are missing? Mullen's notes mentioned—"

"Mr. Mullen was somewhat confused about the catalog," Montague interrupted. "The complete collection includes several pieces already in trusted hands."

"The scientific community would require evidence for

such claims. Have you documented these effects under controlled conditions?"

"Modern interference makes complete demonstration difficult," Dr. Waverly admitted. "Electronic frequencies, industrial vibrations create disruptive patterns."

"Which is why we must conduct our convergence at a location removed from such interference," Montague added. "Philae, with its partially submerged halls, will increase the frequencies."

I made detailed notes, mentally translating their mystical terminology into concrete plans. They intended to assemble all the artifacts at Philae, believing this would create some kind of harmonic resonance effect. Was this merely ridiculous pseudo-science, or something genuinely dangerous?

After an hour of increasingly esoteric discussion, Montague concluded the formal presentation. I approached the small architectural model, noting its precise interior dimensions.

"Your thoughts, Dr. Bell?" Montague appeared beside me, studying my reaction more than the artifact.

"The historical significance of a complete workshop collection is undeniable," I said carefully. "Though I confess some skepticism about the more... metaphysical interpretations."

"Skepticism is the beginning of wisdom," he replied. "Few members understood immediately. True comprehension comes through demonstration."

"Speaking of demonstrations—I understand the auction is merely ceremonial? These artifacts already belong to Brotherhood members."

Surprise flickered briefly across his face. "You've been investigating thoroughly."

"I'm an archaeologist. Observation is my profession."

"The auction serves a symbolic purpose, formalizing the unification of artifacts that have been scattered for centuries."

"So, the cruise wasn't just about gathering people—it was about gathering their artifacts," I observed.

"Who could resist participating in humanity's greatest archaeological discovery?"

"And do you have other pieces not displayed tonight?" I asked directly.

Montague's fingers tightened almost imperceptibly. "You have excellent sources, Dr. Bell. Or perhaps excellent deductive skills."

"Both, actually."

"Then you understand why we must proceed carefully. Knowledge of this significance cannot be casually shared."

"Of course not," I agreed, allowing scholarly enthusiasm to color my voice.

"Most academics would dismiss these principles without investigation," he continued. "But you've demonstrated remarkable openness to evidence that challenges orthodox interpretation."

"I find that truth often emerges at disciplinary boundaries," I said. "Such as between archaeology and acoustics, mathematics and architecture."

Montague nodded approvingly. "The Brotherhood has always sought members who recognize these intersections. Your expertise in pigment authentication makes you particularly valuable." He lowered his voice. "Would you consider joining us at Philae for the demonstration? Your expertise would be invaluable in authenticating certain... convergence conditions."

The trap was baited perfectly—scientific curiosity and professional recognition.

"I'd be fascinated to observe," I said, watching his reaction. "Though I'd need to understand more about what this demonstration entails."

"Some aspects cannot be explained, only experienced," he replied. "What we will witness at Philae hasn't been seen for three millennia. A convergence of knowledge, celestial alignment, and human consciousness that transcends ordinary perception."

The religious fervor in his eyes was more alarming than any

detailed explanation. This wasn't merely academic fraud—Montague genuinely believed in whatever transcendent experience he was orchestrating.

"You've given me much to consider."

His gaze intensified. "I should warn you, Dr. Bell—once certain knowledge is gained, one's perspective changes permanently. The veil, once lifted, cannot be lowered again."

I nodded solemnly, as if contemplating cosmic revelations rather than calculating how quickly I could warn Quinn and Hassan.

"I look forward to continuing our discussion," I said, gathering my notebook.

"Indeed. And after Philae, the academic world will be forced to acknowledge what we've known all along. The Fifth Root Race will take its first step toward the Sixth."

As he spoke, the Brotherhood members rose in perfect unison and formed a circle around me. For one terrifying moment, I thought they meant to prevent my departure, but they were simply performing some kind of closing ritual—hands extended toward the center of their circle, palms down, creating an invisible canopy over the artifacts.

"The Blue Flame illuminates the path," Montague intoned.

"From matter to vibration, from vibration to spirit," they responded in unison.

Colonel Hartwell unlocked the door, and I was finally permitted to leave, notebook clutched to my chest like a shield.

As I climbed the stairs back to familiar territory, the weight of new information settled like stone dust in my lungs, along with something else—a visceral dread that went beyond academic disapproval. I had witnessed not just scholarly delusion, but religious fanaticism clothed in scientific language. These people weren't merely searching for archaeological treasures; they believed they were unlocking cosmic powers.

Montague thought he was recruiting a convert to his mystical Fifth Root Race philosophy.

But what would his response be, when he discovered my supposed conversion was all an act?

# CHAPTER TWENTY-SIX

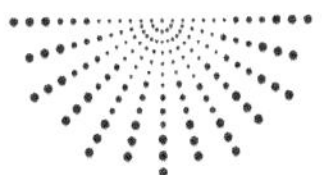

We had one more stop before Aswan, and whatever the Brotherhood planned for the Temple of Philae.

This afternoon, the double temple at Kom Ombo rose before us, built with perfect symmetry to honor both Sobek, the crocodile god, and Horus the Elder simultaneously. Each side mirrored the other in layout but contained entirely different ritual spaces.

We'd passed the temple's nilometer earlier—the ancient device that once measured the life-giving Nile floods, a reminder that water levels had always been matters of life and death in Egypt.

We moved through the columned court with its duplicate entrances. Duplicate sanctuaries. Duplicate lives. The metaphor wasn't lost on me as I glanced at Quinn, who walked slightly ahead, pointing out architectural features to Annie with an expertise that still surprised me. For more than a week now, I'd been living a duplicate existence—Dr. Clarissa Bell, archaeologist, and Clarissa Bell, fiancée. The boundaries between these identities had begun to blur in ways both exhilarating and terrifying. But even before that... my alter ego as a would-be detective had begun to overshadow my chosen career.

And what of Benedict Quinn, and all his duplicity?

"The crocodile mummification chambers would have been located near the river," Quinn was explaining to Annie. "They've found hundreds of mummified crocodiles in the area."

"How perfectly ghastly," Annie replied with a delighted shiver.

Our excursion group moved toward the exit and the bustling marketplace that had grown up alongside the temple complex. The revelations of the Brotherhood's lecture still churned in my mind as we entered the bazaar, a chaotic counterpoint to the temple's calm order.

"I'm going to look at those papyrus scrolls," Quinn said, nodding toward a merchant's stall. "Would you like anything?"

"I'll just browse," I replied, grateful for a moment alone, as the others of our group also fanned out to explore and shop.

The market sprawled in concentric circles radiating outward from the temple entrance—spice merchants with pyramids of ochre, crimson, and golden powders; fabric sellers displaying lengths of cotton in every color; artisans selling reproduction statuary of varying quality and dubious authenticity. The air hung heavy with the scent of cardamom, cinnamon, and the distinctive dusty perfume of sun-baked stone.

I was examining a rather poorly executed Bastet figurine when I felt a hand close around my wrist. I turned, expecting Quinn, but found Mrs. Pemberton instead. Her face was flushed, eyes darting nervously over my shoulder.

"Please," she whispered, her accent thickening with anxiety. "I need a word. Now."

Without waiting for my response, she pulled me between two fabric stalls and into a narrow alcove created by the junction of ancient temple wall and more recent market construction. The rough stone wall of the alcove scraped against my back as I pressed deeper for privacy, ancient limestone catching at the cotton of my blouse.

"Mrs. Pemberton, what—"

"No time." She fumbled with the clasp of her handbag. "I've been watched every minute since... since Mullen..." Her voice cracked. "Colonel Hartwell barely lets me visit the powder room alone."

Her hands trembled so violently that she dropped her bag, spilling its contents.

My shoulders tensed progressively higher with each whispered revelation.

We both crouched to retrieve the scattered items—a handkerchief, compact mirror, small pill case, and several folded papers. As I helped gather them, my fingers brushed against a diagram inked on thick paper.

"That's it." She snatched it and unfolded it with trembling fingers. "My husband's last work. The reason they killed him."

*Killed him?*

The diagram showed temple chambers—not the familiar floor plans I'd studied, but underwater structures. Specifically, submerged chambers beneath Philae temple near Aswan. The drawing was meticulous, with measurements noting water levels and precise mathematical ratios.

"Your husband documented these chambers?" I traced the carefully inked water level markings with my fingertip, immediately recognizing the significance of undocumented substructures.

"Albert discovered them during the flooding season two years ago. He was a hydraulic engineer, you see, consulting on water table changes near the monuments." Her voice steadied slightly when discussing her husband's expertise. "He found that these particular chambers create extraordinary acoustic effects when partially flooded—amplification beyond anything that would be expected."

I studied the diagram more carefully, trying to understand why she would think them worth killing for.

"Albert was ever so excited." Mrs. Pemberton's fingers unconsciously straightened the edges of the paper. "He thought he'd made an important archaeological discovery. He shared his findings with Lord Ashford, who seemed very interested." Her voice dropped. "Three days later, Albert died in his sleep. Heart attack, they said."

The hair on my arms rose despite the market's heat. "You believe he was murdered."

It wasn't a question.

"I know he was." Her pale eyes met mine directly for perhaps the first time since we'd met. "The night before, he'd told me he found something troubling in Lord Ashford's reaction. Something about collecting artifacts with specific properties. Albert was worried someone would create some sort of... amplification system. He was going to speak with museum authorities in the morning."

"And that's why you've been so afraid."

She nodded. "After the funeral, Lord Ashford and Colonel Hartwell visited me. Such concern they showed." Her bitter tone made clear the nature of their visit. "They suggested I join their little club to honor Albert's memory. Made it quite clear refusal wasn't an option if I wanted to keep my lovely house and reputation."

A tear tracked down her cheek, leaving a pale line through her carefully applied powder.

"I told Mr. Mullen," she confessed, voice barely audible above the market's bustle. "He seemed so concerned about the auction catalog. I thought he would be the one—that he could find someone who could help. And now he's dead too, and it's my fault."

"It's not your fault." I straightened the crumpled edge of the diagram, fighting the urge to look over my shoulder. "You couldn't have known."

"But I did know," she insisted. "I knew exactly what they're capable of. I've seen what happens to people who threaten their plans."

"What exactly are they planning at Philae?" I asked, attempting to keep her focused.

Mrs. Pemberton's eyes darted nervously past my shoulder. "The artifacts—they form components of a system. The Brotherhood believes when assembled correctly during the right celestial alignment, they'll create a harmonic convergence that reveals ancient wisdom. Utter nonsense, of course."

"Then why kill for it?"

"Because they've modified the underwater chambers," she said, tapping the diagram. "Albert's measurements showed the chambers are already unstable. The modifications they've made—adding modern equipment to enhance the acoustic properties—could cause catastrophic collapse if subjected to the resonant frequencies they're planning."

I stared at her, the implications sinking in. "They would destroy ancient chambers for an experiment based on pseudoscience?"

"Professor Montague believes with absolute conviction. The others follow for their own reasons—prestige, fear, greed." Her hands shook as she folded the diagram. "They don't care what gets destroyed in the process."

A horrifying thought occurred to me. "Mrs. Pemberton, have you shown this diagram to anyone else aboard the *Nefertiti*?"

She shook her head. "Only Mr. Mullen. I've kept it hidden in my—" Her eyes suddenly widened, focused on something behind me. "Oh, oh my goodness."

I turned to see Colonel Hartwell's imposing figure moving through the crowd, his walking stick tapping rhythmically against the stone pavement. He hadn't spotted us yet, but his methodical progress through the market suggested he was searching for something—or someone.

"He's looking for me." Mrs. Pemberton shoved the diagram into my hands. "Take it. Please." The marketplace narrowed toward the river, its funnel shape suddenly striking me as a trap rather than a pathway.

"Come with me," I urged. "Hassan can protect you."

She gave a brittle laugh. "No one can protect me now. Just stop them." She squeezed my hand once, then stepped back. "Your engagement—is it real?"

The question caught me off-guard. "I—"

*Yes, we're genuinely pretending to be engaged while investigating murders while possibly falling in love. Perfectly straightforward.*

"Never mind. It doesn't matter what you call it. I've seen the way he looks at you." A sad smile touched her lips. "Just don't waste time, dear. Life's too short for that."

Before I could respond, she slipped away, moving perpendicular to Hartwell's path through a row of fabric merchants. I quickly folded the diagram and tucked it into my satchel alongside Mullen's notes, then moved in the opposite direction, weaving through spice stalls and pottery displays toward where I'd last seen Quinn.

My mind raced to fit together the pieces of this deadly puzzle. The Brotherhood wasn't just collecting artifacts—they were assembling components of an acoustic system designed to exploit the architectural properties of specific temple chambers. Whether or not their "harmonic convergence" would reveal ancient wisdom was irrelevant. The real danger was structural damage to irreplaceable archaeological treasures. Not to mention anyone who might be in the path of the destruction.

I needed to find Quinn. We had to reach Aswan before—

A flash of pale yellow caught my eye. I paused behind a display of brass lanterns, peering through their intricate patterns at Lady Penelope Fairfax. She stood in a secluded corner of the market, partially concealed by hanging carpets. What caught my attention wasn't her presence but her actions. She was passing what appeared to be documents to a local man in a simple *gallabiyah*. As I watched, he nodded once, tucked the papers into his robe, and departed.

Lady Penelope remained motionless for a moment, her usually animated face uncharacteristically solemn. Then she smoothed her skirts, adjusted her fashionable hat, and transformed back into the frivolous socialite I'd come to know, complete with fluttering hands and vapid smile as she rejoined the main market.

Was she working with the Brotherhood or against them?

The question nagged at me as I continued searching for Quinn, the weight of Mrs. Pemberton's diagram burning through my satchel with its urgent warning.

I found him examining a display of papyrus scrolls, his tall figure easily visible above the crowd.

"There you are," he said, turning as I approached. "I was about to—" He stopped, studying my face. "Let me guess—you've either discovered ancient treasure, mortal danger, or they've run out of those almond pastries you like. Judging by your expression, I'm guessing it's not the pastries."

"Not here," I murmured, taking his arm in what would appear to casual observers as a gesture of affection. "We need to return to the ship immediately."

To his credit, Quinn asked no further questions. He simply covered my hand with his, leaned close as if sharing an intimate comment, and whispered, "Lead the way, darling."

The endearment, which would have irritated me just days ago, now felt like warmth flowing down my spine. This too was part of the duplicate life I was living—the simultaneous irritation and attraction, suspicion and trust. The old Clarissa would have found these contradictions methodologically unsound, requiring categorization and resolution.

But as we navigated back through the market, Quinn's steady presence beside me, I realized I was becoming someone new—someone who could hold these contradictions comfortably. Someone who could be both archaeologist and investigator, independent and partnered, suspicious and trusting.

Mrs. Pemberton was right. Life was too short for rigid categories.

# CHAPTER TWENTY-SEVEN

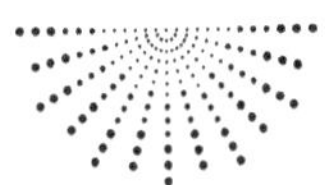

eturning to the ship felt like retreating to a battlefield rather than a sanctuary.

The golden evening light across the Nile did little to soften my unease as Quinn and I made our way aboard, Mrs. Pemberton's diagram weighing in my satchel like a time bomb.

"We need to find Montague immediately," I said, keeping my voice low despite the relative privacy of the upper deck.

Quinn nodded, his expression grim. "The sooner we confront him about these modified chambers, the better."

We made our way to the main salon, but found it occupied only by Lady Penelope and Marcus Waverly engaged in what appeared to be an intensely polite conversation about Egyptian textile exports. I asked whether Professor Montague had returned, but neither had seen him. Their eyes followed us with unsettling attention as we moved toward Captain Mason's small office near the navigation deck.

The Captain looked up from his logbook as we entered, his weathered face registering mild irritation at the interruption. "Dr. Bell, Mr. Quinn. I trust you enjoyed the temple excursion?"

"Where's Professor Montague?" I asked, bypassing pleasantries.

Mason's expression shifted to practiced neutrality. "Dr. Montague departed by train to Aswan approximately three hours ago. Urgent business, he said. He'll rejoin us tomorrow when we dock."

Quinn and I exchanged glances. "Did he mention the nature of this urgent business?" Quinn asked.

"I don't make a habit of interrogating my passengers, Mr. Quinn." Captain Mason adjusted his uniform cuffs. "He mentioned only that he had preparations to oversee and would meet us at the temple site."

Preparations. The word sent a chill through me despite the evening heat.

"If there's nothing else?" Mason prompted, clearly eager to return to his documentation.

We thanked him and retreated to the corridor, where Quinn immediately guided me toward a quiet alcove beneath the stairs.

"This changes everything," he whispered. "If Montague's already at Aswan—"

A steward approached with a silver tray bearing a sealed telegram and an envelope. "Messages for you, sir. And for you, madam. Just arrived with a boy from the shore."

My stomach dropped. No one ever telegraphed unless circumstances were dire.

I broke the seal, the familiar yellow paper of the Western Union telegram form feeling brittle between my fingers. The typed message conveyed with the impersonal efficiency that had become the hallmark of modern communication:

CLARISSA STOP FATHER GRAVELY ILL STOP RETURN NEW YORK IMMEDIATELY STOP PASSAGE ARRANGED FROM ALEXANDRIA STOP FAMILY LAWYER WILL MEET YOU STOP RICHARDS

My breath caught. Father ill? But my father's lawyer was named Peterson, not Richards. And why would a lawyer arrange passage from Alexandria when I was nowhere near there?

"Someone wants me off this ship," I muttered, showing Quinn the telegram.

He nodded grimly. "And I think I know why." He handed me his own message.

I scanned Quinn's handwritten note, my eyes widening as I processed the contents:

*Quinn-*

*Critical: INDIGO compromised. Original mission was academic suppression of advanced Egyptian knowledge to maintain British superiority. Head became convinced of weaponization potential and has diverted into occult applications. Extremely dangerous.*

*Terminate operation immediately. Abandon ship at next port and await retrieval.*

*Trust no one.*

*-K*

I looked up at Quinn, my mind racing. "Your handler finally learned what's actually happening."

"And conveniently timed to arrive just as Montague heads to Aswan alone." Quinn's voice was tight with barely contained fury. "All this time, they've had me investigating Operation Indigo while withholding its true purpose."

"Montague." The name fell from my lips with absolute certainty. "It must be. That's why he was so interested in my pigment authentication work—not just to identify genuine artifacts, but to assemble the complete system. But I never would have pegged him as working for the government, let along going rogue."

"Well, if it's true, he's already at Aswan preparing... whatever this is." Quinn folded the note carefully, his expression darkening. "The harmonic convergence isn't just pseudoscience to him. He genuinely believes... what? That he can weaponize these acoustic properties? Or does he believe the nonsense he's been spouting about lifting humanity to a new plane?"

I pulled Mrs. Pemberton's diagram from my satchel, smoothing it on the polished wooden railing. "Look at these modifications to the underwater chambers. Albert Pemberton discovered them a year ago—structural changes that amplify acoustic properties. She thinks he was killed because of it. If it's true, Montague has been planning this for years."

"And killing anyone who threatens to expose him." Quinn's voice was grim. "Pulling the strings behind Elias Hawke?"

My memory flashed to Hawke, and the bullet that had narrowly missed me when it killed him at the symposium.

I shuddered. "And what about Harrison Foster? Could Montague have been the one who was paying Foster to steal the Astral Sphere?"

Quinn's hands tightened around the rail. "Possibly Mrs. Pemberton's husband. And then we must assume Faraj and Mullen here on the ship."

"But how? Montague wasn't even here when Faraj was killed."

"He must be working with someone else."

"Or *everyone* else."

Our eyes met in shared understanding, and he covered my hand on the rail. Whatever Montague was preparing at Philae, he was determined that we wouldn't interfere.

"We need to speak to Hassan," I said, gathering the diagram and telegrams. "And we need to get Mrs. Pemberton somewhere safe, before they realize she's spoken to us."

Quinn nodded, his hand still covering mine. "And we absolutely cannot let anyone know we've figured all of this out." He pointed to my telegram. "Including that."

"Indeed," I replied, allowing myself a moment of dark humor. "After all, my poor father requires my immediate attention."

"Hassan is going to want to see some proof."

I frowned. "So, we need to see what Montague left behind. Maybe there's something there."

"Do you think Annie's young man might be persuaded to help again?"

I nodded, already calculating the safest approach. "After midnight, when the other passengers are asleep."

We parted to our separate cabins, agreeing to meet at Quinn's door at half past midnight. I spent the intervening hours reviewing Mullen's notes and Mrs. Pemberton's diagrams, searching for clues about Montague's modifications to the Philae chambers.

The evidence was terrifying. Montague had installed modern acoustic amplification equipment in ancient chambers already known for unusual sound properties. According to Mrs. Pemberton's husband's calculations, the resonant frequencies Montague planned to generate could cause catastrophic structural collapse if the experiment was followed precisely.

This wasn't mere pseudoscience. It was insanity.

When I slipped from my cabin at the appointed time, Quinn was waiting. Without a word, we made our way to the service corridors where Annie had arranged for Freddie to meet us.

The young steward looked both thrilled and terrified by his role in our investigation. "'Annie says you're tryin' to stop someone dangerous," he whispered, pressing the brass master key into my palm once more.

"That's right," I assured him. "And the fewer details you know, the safer you'll be."

Freddie nodded earnestly. "I've checked the passenger cabins on me rounds. Everyone seems to be in for the night except—" He hesitated.

"Except?" Quinn prompted.

"Waverly—Marcus, not 'is mother. 'E's in one of the storage compartments near the galley. Mixin' something wiv chemicals from 'is valise." Freddie's expression grew troubled. "Didn't look like medicine to me, I'll tell ya that much."

Another piece of the puzzle. Marcus had pharmaceutical knowledge—potentially enough to have prepared the poison that killed Faraj.

We thanked Freddie and made our way through the

labyrinthine service passages toward Montague's cabin, pausing only once when a cabin steward crossed our path. The ship hummed with muted nighttime activity—distant clanks from the engine room, the occasional creak of wooden panels adjusting to the Nile's gentle current.

Montague's cabin was located on the upper deck, a spacious suite befitting his status. I inserted the master key with trembling fingers, feeling ridiculously like a character in one of Annie's secret dime novels.

The lock yielded with a soft click, and we slipped inside, closing the door silently behind us. Quinn produced a small electric torch, its beam revealing a cabin of fanatical orderliness.

Montague's possessions weren't merely organized—they were arranged with the same precision I'd use for categorizing tomb goods—methodical to the point of revealing psychological significance. The effect wasn't merely tidy—it was unsettling, suggesting a mind where obsessive patterns dominated every aspect of life.

"We need to work quickly," Quinn whispered, already moving toward a leather portfolio on the writing desk.

I nodded, heading for the steamer trunk against the far wall. We moved in practiced synchronization, as if we'd conducted countless investigations together rather than just two. While I carefully examined Montague's packed belongings, Quinn sifted through the papers on his desk.

"Look at this," he breathed after several minutes, his hand moving unconsciously to his waistcoat pocket where I knew he kept his service revolver, a gesture so subtle he likely didn't realize he'd made it.

I joined him, examining the detailed architectural drawings he'd discovered. The plans showed the hypostyle axis at Philae marked with careful measurements, notes in the margins where columns, water, and stone aligned. In the sketches he had added his own apparatus—horn loudspeakers on tripods, a carbon microphone wired to battery boxes, tuning forks spaced at deliberate intervals, and a metal plate dusted with sand to record the vibration.

"He's built a primitive amplification rig," I murmured, recognizing the ratios that matched Mullen's notes. I leaned forward, shoulders hunching as if physically trying to contain the terrible implications of what we were seeing. "These carbon microphone assemblies connected to amplification circuits— it's the same technology now revolutionizing radio broadcasts across Europe, repurposed for his archaeological madness."

"And why?" Quinn asked, his finger tracing the careful measurements. The perfect circles of Montague's modified chamber designs, obsessively drawn and redrawn with a compass, created concentric patterns like ripples in a dangerous pond. "What does he actually believe will happen?"

"According to the Brotherhood lecture, he thinks reuniting these artifacts during a specific celestial alignment will create a harmonic convergence that reveals ancient wisdom." I shook my head at the absurdity. "But the real danger is structural. These modifications have compromised the chambers' stability. If he generates these frequencies—"

"The entire structure could collapse." Quinn's expression darkened. "Killing everyone inside and destroying priceless archaeological treasures."

"Along with anyone who might expose his madness," I added, thinking of Mullen and Faraj.

We continued our search, finding additional evidence of Montague's obsession—journals filled with harmonic calculations, correspondence with Brotherhood members spanning years, and most damning of all, official documents bearing the Operation Indigo letterhead.

"This confirms it," Quinn said, indicating a personnel file. "Montague wasn't just involved with Operation Indigo—he created it. Used government resources to track down these artifacts while pretending to protect British interests."

I was examining a drawer of personal items when something caught my eye—a flash of familiar burgundy silk partially hidden beneath Montague's monogrammed handkerchiefs. I carefully extracted the fabric, recognizing the distinctive zigzag pattern.

"This belongs to Lady Penelope," I said, holding up the scarf. The feminine rose perfume from the burgundy silk hung in the air, startlingly out of place amid Montague's sterile, masculine domain. "I've seen her wear it several times."

Quinn took it carefully. "What was she doing in Montague's cabin?"

"Either they're working together, or—" I paused, reassessing everything I knew about the young widow. "Or she's conducting her own investigation while wearing considerably better accessories than either of us."

"We need to go," Quinn said suddenly, returning the scarf exactly as we'd found it. "If she comes back for it—"

We carefully restored everything to its precise original position, leaving no trace of our intrusion.

Moving silently through the ship's corridors, we encountered an unexpected number of passengers still awake despite the late hour—Colonel Hartwell apparently taking air on the port deck, Dr. Waverly consulting star charts near the observation lounge, Lord Ashford engaged in what appeared to be a casual midnight snack in the small dining salon.

"Is it just me," I whispered, "or is everyone positioned to observe movement throughout the ship?"

Quinn nodded grimly. "Like sentries at a military installation."

We needed somewhere private to compare notes and plan our next steps. The deck was too exposed, our cabins potentially monitored. Quinn led us downward, through increasingly utilitarian corridors until we reached the machinery room on the lower deck.

The space hummed with the rhythmic thudding of steam engines and the heat of coal furnaces. Pipes snaked across the ceiling like mechanical vines, their metallic surfaces gleaming dully in the dim electric light.

"No one will overhear us here," Quinn said, pulling me behind a massive boiler that blocked us from view of the doorway.

I laid out the various threads of evidence, my mind categorizing and connecting facts.

"Montague theorized that these harmonic artifacts were components of an actual ancient acoustic system," I summarized. "But instead of documenting this legitimately, he became obsessed with the idea that they could access some kind of transcendent knowledge."

"Or power," Quinn added. "My handler indicated he initially believed they had weapon potential."

"He must be waiting for all the participants to arrive with their artifacts." I checked my watch—nearly 2 AM. "But by taking the train, he's gained almost a full day to complete his preparations."

"And the Brotherhood members are keeping us under surveillance to prevent interference."

"But why allow us to reach Aswan at all?" I wondered. "Why not simply eliminate us like Mullen?"

"Because Montague still hopes to recruit you," Quinn said grimly. "Maybe he needs your expertise to verify the final harmonic sequence?"

The full picture was beginning to come into focus.

But just then, a metallic click echoed through the machinery room.

Quinn was at the door in an instant, his face confirming my suspicion.

"Locked," he said quietly. "Someone doesn't want us leaving this ship tonight."

I reached for the nearest pipe, testing its solidity. "Then we'd better start making noise."

Quinn's half-smile in the dim light sent a shiver down my spine. "Dr. Bell, you never cease to surprise me."

"Consider it a comprehensive course in archaeological improvisation," I replied, scanning the room for potential tools. "Though I suspect there's still much we could teach each other."

The suggestive undertone in my voice surprised even me. Perhaps being locked in a steam-filled engine room while a megalomaniacal professor prepared to collapse an ancient temple created unusual courage.

Or perhaps I was finally accepting what Annie had been telling me all along—that Clarissa the archaeologist and Clarissa the woman were not separate categories.

Quinn's eyes darkened as he moved closer, his hand brushing mine as we both reached for an iron tool hanging on the wall.

"When we get out of here," he said, his voice low against the mechanical symphony surrounding us, "we should discuss renegotiating the terms of our engagement."

"To something more... ?" I waited for him to fill in the adjective.

His smile illuminated the dimness. "Precisely."

I hefted the iron bar. "But first, let's go stop a madman from destroying several thousand years of Egyptian cultural heritage."

"As you wish, darling," Quinn replied, with an emphasis on the endearment that was entirely unprofessional, completely inappropriate, and absolutely perfect.

# CHAPTER TWENTY-EIGHT

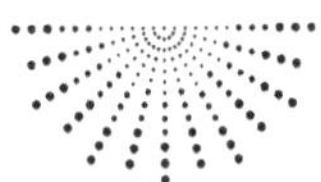

Freddie's arrival at the machinery room door sent waves of relief through me. His worried face appeared in the small window moments after our makeshift percussion symphony had reached what I considered a rather impressive crescendo.

"Bloody 'ell," he whispered as the lock yielded. "What're you doing down 'ere?"

"Impromptu engineering study," I said, squeezing through the doorway. "The acoustics are marvelous, but the accommodations leave something to be desired."

Quinn followed me into the narrow service corridor. "Someone locked us in deliberately. We need to get off this ship immediately."

Freddie's eyes widened. "Off the ship? But we're anchored midstream. And there's fog rolling in something terrible."

"Fog?" I asked.

"Started about an hour ago. Captain says we'll 'ave to delay departure in the morning. Can't see more than a few feet past the rail."

Quinn and I exchanged glances. Dangerous navigation conditions would delay the Brotherhood's departure as well, giving us precious hours to reach Philae ahead of them.

"Freddie," I said, "we need a boat. Something small and quiet that won't attract attention."

The young steward shifted uncomfortably. "Annie said you're trying to stop something bad, but this is—"

"People could die if we don't reach Philae before dawn," Quinn said, his voice low and urgent.

Freddie hesitated, then nodded. "There's a service launch tied up port side. Used for shore errands. I could say I'm fetching fresh milk for morning tea."

"Perfect. We'll meet you there in five minutes," Quinn said. "I need to retrieve something from my cabin first."

Freddie disappeared down the corridor, leaving us alone in the dim passage that smelled of engine oil and river water.

"My revolver," Quinn explained. "And warmer clothing for both of us if we're going to be on the river in this weather."

I nodded and pressed my cabin key into his hand. "I'll head to the port launch and make sure Freddie doesn't lose his nerve."

Quinn caught my arm. "Be careful. Someone just tried to lock us below deck indefinitely." His eyes held mine. "I meant what I said earlier. I'd choose you over the mission. Every time."

The sincerity in his voice stole my capacity for clever retort. "Five minutes," I managed. "Don't be late."

We parted at the service stairs, Quinn heading toward our cabins while I made my way up to the main deck. Emerging from below, I found myself stepping into another world entirely.

The fog had transformed the familiar ship into a ghostly apparition. Here along the Nile near Aswan, where granite boulders and rocky islands retain the desert's overnight chill while the river maintains its warmth, moisture settles low across the river's surface like nature's own chemistry experiment.

Tonight, that moisture hung in a dense white shroud that muffled sound and obliterated distance. The deck lamps created perfect circles of light, eerie haloes that barely penetrated a few feet before dissolving into swirling whiteness. I couldn't see the river, the shore, or even the bow of our own vessel.

I moved carefully along the port side, one hand trailing the rail. The fog seemed to press against my skin, cool and slightly oily, carrying the smell of river mud and wet stone.

Sound behaved strangely—distant voices floated disembodied through the whiteness, while the lap of water against the hull echoed with unnatural clarity. The midnight blue of the river, nearly black beneath the foggy sky, rippled beneath a ghostly white veil.

The service launch should be just ahead, down the short ladder where supplies were loaded. I strained to see through the misty darkness, wiping condensation from my eyelashes.

Footsteps sounded behind me, muffled but approaching steadily. Relief coursed through me—Quinn had returned more quickly than expected.

"That was fast," I said, turning. "Did you manage to—"

The fog revealed no one.

The footsteps had stopped.

"Quinn?" I called softly.

Only silence answered, thick and oppressive.

Then the footsteps resumed, closer now, still obscured by the impenetrable whiteness. Something about their rhythm felt wrong—too light for Quinn's confident stride, too purposeful for a casual nighttime wanderer.

I backed toward where I thought the service ladder must be, my hand gripping the damp railing. The fog parted momentarily, revealing a shadowy figure approaching—smaller than Quinn, moving with deliberate intent.

Before I could call out or move, hands emerged from the whiteness and shoved hard against my chest.

The sudden force sent me stumbling backward. My ankle caught on something—the top rung of the ladder—and as I fell, my temple glanced against the metal railing. Pain exploded behind my eyes.

Then gravity claimed me completely.

The impact with the water stole my breath. Coldness closed over my head, shocking my system with its icy bite. My mind—my methodical, analytical mind—immediately calculated the danger: water temperature, constrictive clothing, night conditions, moderate current, fog disorientation.

*Combined survival probability: concerning.*

I kicked upward, fighting the weight of my waterlogged clothing. My cotton skirt had become heavy as chainmail, threatening to drag me under. Breaking the surface, I gasped for air and tried to orient myself in the swirling whiteness. The ship's lights were barely visible, distorted glows in the fog. I treaded water, reaching for the practiced calm that had served me through other adventures. My heartbeat thundered in my ears, loud enough to drown out the river itself.

The current pulled at me, stronger than expected, dragging me away from the dim lights of the ship.

I attempted to swim toward what I hoped was the shore, but my water-heavy skirt tangled around my legs. Each stroke became more labored, my muscles protesting the cold.

Above me, I heard a shout, then what sounded like a brief struggle. A splash followed—large and deliberate.

"Clarissa!" Quinn's voice carried across the water, urgent and strained.

"Here!" I called, my voice weaker than I'd have liked.

Swimming in the dark was disorienting enough, but the fog transformed it into a nightmare of confusion. Water filled my mouth as I tried to call again. I could no longer see the ship's lights—only uniform whiteness in every direction.

"Keep calling out!" Quinn's voice came from somewhere to my left.

I did as instructed, though my teeth had begun to chatter. How could it be so cold, here in such a warm country? The chill seeped into my bones with remarkable efficiency.

*Hypothermia will begin affecting your coordination in approximately ten minutes.*

"Your timing is impeccable, Dr. Bell," I muttered to myself.

"Drowning just before solving the case would be rather anti-climactic."

Something brushed against my arm in the water—a branch or debris carried by the current. I tried to kick away, but my sodden skirt wrapped around my legs like a burial shroud.

Ironic, for an Egyptologist to be claimed by the very river that had nurtured the civilization she studied.

Then strong hands gripped me, pulling me against a solid form.

"I've got you," Quinn said, his breath warm against my cold cheek.

He supported me with one arm while swimming with the other, moving us through the water with surprising strength. I couldn't see where we were headed in the fog, but Quinn seemed to have a destination in mind.

"Someone pushed me," I managed between chattering teeth.

"I know. I saw them." His arm tightened around me, a futile attempt to generate warmth.

"Who?"

He hesitated. "Couldn't see clearly. Feminine build. Dark hair."

Lady Penelope. The revelation shouldn't have surprised me, yet it did. I'd suspected her of investigating the Brotherhood, not participating in its violence.

"Did you see where she went?" I twisted in his grasp, scanning the impenetrable whiteness as water sputtered from my lungs.

"I was somewhat preoccupied with preventing your untimely demise." Quinn adjusted his grip around my waist, his fingers testing my ribcage as if cataloging possible injuries.

Despite the cold, despite the danger, I felt a ridiculous smile forming. "You're prioritizing me over capturing a suspect? Your superiors would be appalled."

"My superiors can go to hell," Quinn muttered, adjusting his grip around my waist.

Our sodden clothing dragged us both down, making our

progress painfully slow. The fog concealed everything, creating the unsettling sensation of swimming through an endless void.

But Quinn maintained our direction with unwavering confidence. How he navigated in these conditions remained a mystery.

Finally, my feet brushed against something solid—a submerged rock, then sandy riverbed. We had reached the shore.

Quinn half-carried me onto the bank, where we collapsed together on the muddy ground. For several minutes, we simply lay there, catching our breath, my head resting against his chest where I could hear his heart pounding.

"That's twice you've saved my life this week," I said when I could speak normally again. "People will talk."

"People are already talking." He pushed himself up to look at me, his expression unusually vulnerable in the diffused moonlight that filtered through the fog. "Are you hurt?"

I took inventory. "Cold. Wet. Dignity somewhat compromised. But otherwise intact."

His hand touched my cheek, brushing away rivulets of water. The gesture held none of the calculated affection of our public performances. This was something else entirely—raw and unguarded.

"I thought I'd lost you," he said quietly.

"It would take more than an impromptu swim to rid yourself of me, Mr. Quinn."

He smiled, the tension in his face easing slightly. "Thank God for that."

We sat up, surveying our surroundings. The fog had transformed the familiar riverbank into an alien landscape. Palm trees loomed as ghostly silhouettes, while nearby granite boulders seemed to shift and change shape with each swirl of mist.

"We need to find Freddie and that boat," Quinn said, helping me to my feet. "And dry clothing, if possible."

We made our way along the shore, guided by the distant glow of the ship's lights. Our sodden clothes clung uncomfortably, and my teeth had resumed their chattering.

Quinn put his arm around my shoulders, sharing what warmth he could.

"About what I said in the engine room," he began.

"You mean about renegotiating our engagement terms?" I asked, keeping my tone light despite the tumultuous emotions beneath.

"Yes." He stopped walking, turning to face me. "I meant it. This charade has become... something else entirely."

I looked up at him, water dripping from both our faces, standing bedraggled and shivering on a foggy riverbank in Egypt. It was hardly the romantic scene one dreams of, yet it felt more authentic than any carefully orchestrated moment could have been.

"I find myself—" I hesitated, searching for the proper archaeological metaphor and finding none. "I find myself rather glad of that."

The smile that spread across his face was worth every ounce of cold and discomfort. He leaned closer, and I waited for him to kiss me. Instead, he gently tucked a strand of wet hair behind my ear.

"We should continue this conversation somewhere warmer. And drier."

"And after we've prevented the Brotherhood from destroying an ancient temple," I added.

"There's always something, isn't there?"

We continued along the shore until we spotted Freddie's anxious face peering through the fog from a small wooden boat. The Egyptian boatman sat at the rudder, adjusting his damp *gallabiyah* as he evaluated our bedraggled Western attire. The young steward's eyes widened at our soaked appearance.

"What the—? What 'appened to you two?"

"Swimming is quite refreshing this time of year," I said. "I highly recommend it. If one enjoys near-death experiences."

Freddie helped us aboard, the boatman's face still impassive.

"Philae," I said, my voice hoarse from river water. "We need to reach the temple before dawn."

The boatman shook his head. "Impossible, *sitt*. No one goes to Philae in this fog."

Quinn placed several gold coins in the man's palm. "Someone already has. We need to follow."

The boatman hesitated, then pocketed the coins. "There is a path through the boulders. But in this fog..." He gestured at the impenetrable whiteness surrounding us.

He jutted his chin toward a pile of ragged blankets in the prow. Apparently as close as we would get to warmer and drier.

As we pushed off from shore, the mist parted momentarily, revealing a fleeting glimpse of the dark river ahead. In the distance, barely visible through swirling fog, pinpricks of light moved across the water toward Philae.

"I fear we're not alone," I whispered, gripping Quinn's arm. "The Brotherhood is already on their way."

# CHAPTER TWENTY-NINE

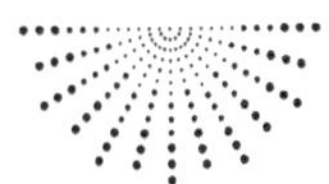

The fog swallowed sound as efficiently as it devoured sight, transforming our small boat into an island suspended in gray . Sound traveled strangely—some noises muffled to nothing while others amplified, as if the mist itself were deciding what we should and shouldn't hear.

I huddled at the bow, clutching Mrs. Pemberton's now-soggy diagrams while our Egyptian boatman guided us through the First Cataract—though "cataract" failed to convey the labyrinthine maze of deadly granite boulders that had terrorized river navigators since pharaonic times.

"You're certain this is the best approach?" I asked Quinn, who crouched beside me, his attention divided between the darkness ahead and the darkness behind.

"I'm certain it's the only approach." He adjusted his grip on the small revolver he'd somehow managed to keep dry during our impromptu swim.

Our boatman muttered something in Arabic that made Quinn's eyes widen.

"What did he say?" I asked.

"That we're navigating the Path of Seventy Questions." Quinn's voice was tight. "A route even experienced boatmen avoid in daylight."

"Lovely." I returned my attention to Mrs. Pemberton's diagrams, tracing my finger over the detailed schematics of Philae's underground chambers. Her late husband had meticulously documented the temple's acoustic properties, mapping precisely where Montague would install modern amplification equipment. The most alarming detail was the resonance diagram—concentric circles marking potential structural fracture points where sound waves would converge with maximum intensity.

"Old man used to say," our boatman offered in careful English, "sound and stone become brothers at Philae. Temple sings in morning light."

Quinn and I exchanged glances.

"Sings how, exactly?" Quinn asked.

The boatman shrugged. "Like humming. Only on special days." He nodded toward the darkness ahead. "Temple sleeps underwater half the year now. British engineers talk of moving stones, but old gods might object." He made another warding gesture. "Isis does not like to be disturbed when she bathes."

The small engine sputtered, its rhythm faltering momentarily before resuming. The sound sent my heart into a similar stutter.

Through the fog, distant pinpricks of light appeared—other boats converging on Philae from multiple directions. The Brotherhood members from our ship, certainly, but possibly others as well. Mrs. Pemberton had mentioned "associates from abroad" gathering for the convergence.

Our boatman throttled the engine lower, reducing its sound to a muted burble. The current caught us, pulling us into a channel between towering granite formations. The boat rocked as water churned against submerged obstacles.

"Should the water be moving quite so enthusiastically?" I whispered.

"We approach the narrows," the boatman answered. "Current strong here."

The engine sputtered again, longer this time, before catching. The boatman frowned, tapping the fuel gauge.

"Tell me we have sufficient fuel," I said.

"Enough. Maybe." The boatman shrugged with the fatalism I'd come to recognize in Egyptians who'd spent lifetimes battling the Nile's caprices.

A sudden surge of current sent us veering toward a granite outcrop. The boatman yanked the tiller, but the engine chose that precise moment to die completely.

"Allah protect us," he muttered, grabbing for the long pole stowed along the gunwale.

Quinn was already moving, seizing a second pole and jamming it against the approaching stone. The impact shuddered through the boat's frame, wood groaning as currents pushed us sideways. The granite scraped against our hull with a sound like fingernails on a tomb wall.

They both lunged with poles as the current accelerated, barely deflecting the boat from a head-on collision. The vessel spun, momentarily out of control, before the boatman's expert maneuvering stabilized our course.

Quinn knelt beside the engine, attempting to diagnose its failure. He checked his luminous-dial wristwatch—one of those military models that had become fashionable after the Great War—before returning to the engine. "Fuel line blockage, perhaps. Or water in the carburetor."

"We're still not close enough to see the temple," I said, examining the most detailed of Mrs. Pemberton's schematics. "According to these measurements, the underwater chambers are on the eastern side, beneath the colonnade. Montague has installed amplifiers at these five points." I traced the markings on the diagram. "If any one of them is disabled, the entire system should fail."

The boatman looked up sharply. "Underwater chambers? Those are forbidden."

"Forbidden by whom?" I asked.

"Old stories. Bad places underwater." He made a warding gesture. "Not for people."

Quinn was still trying to restart the engine, his expression growing more concerned with each failed attempt. The current continued pulling us downstream, our trajectory now entirely at the Nile's whim.

"We need to use the poles," he instructed. "We must reach shore before we're swept into the main channel."

I grabbed another, and we maneuvered desperately, pushing off granite boulders that materialized from the fog with terrifying suddenness. I found my breath unconsciously matching Quinn's rhythm. My arms strained against the current's relentless force, muscles protesting.

"I believe I'm developing new categories of unpleasantness." I braced my shoulder against the pole, feet sliding on the damp deck as I pushed against an unyielding boulder. "Tonight shall be filed under *Nautical Misadventures, Life-Threatening*."

"Quite a specific category." Quinn shifted his grip on the pole, muscles straining visibly through his damp shirt as he fought to prevent our stern from smashing into stone.

"I maintain a detailed taxonomic system for classifying near-death experiences."

"Extensive collection, is it?"

"Distressingly so, since meeting you."

The boat lurched again as the current strengthened. A grinding sound from below suggested our keel had found something unpleasantly solid.

"We're running aground," the boatman warned, thrusting his pole into the murky water to gauge depth.

"Better than the alternative," Quinn observed, gesturing toward the increasingly turbulent water visible beyond our port side.

A strange sound drifted through the fog—not a boat engine, but a low, resonant humming. It seemed to emanate from everywhere and nowhere, vibrating through the air with unsettling persistence.

"The temple is singing," the boatman whispered, his eyes wide.

The humming intensified, taking on a quality that made the water's surface tremble slightly.

I peered through the gray void.
"They've started."

# CHAPTER THIRTY

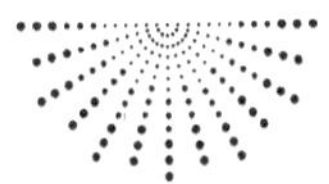

Quinn abandoned the engine and moved to my side, examining the diagrams. "Can you tell what frequency they're generating?"

I shook my head. "But according to these calculations, the initial calibration tone is just the beginning. Mrs. Pemberton's husband documented an entire harmonic sequence—each tone building upon the last, creating increasingly powerful resonance patterns."

"How long before it reaches dangerous levels?"

I studied the logarithmic progression charted on the diagram's edge. "Looks like Pemberton wasn't certain. Hours, perhaps, once they've established the base frequency. The underground chambers will amplify and concentrate the effect until the stone itself begins to fracture."

"We've reached the eastern shore," the boatman whispered, relief evident in his voice as he secured our vessel to a jagged outcropping.

As we disembarked, I clutched the diagrams to my chest.

The massive silhouette of Philae Temple emerged from the dissipating mist, but something was fundamentally wrong with its outline. Dark cables snaked across ancient stone like parasitic vines. Metal equipment gleamed dully in the pale light, their harsh aluminum angles jarring against the temple's graceful lotus-topped columns.

"Montague's been quite busy," I murmured. "And where on earth did he even get amplifiers?"

Quinn's jaw tightened. "Likely British Army experimental models. Not exactly available to your average archaeological expedition."

"Your intelligence friends seem rather generous with their equipment."

"Not my people. But Operation Indigo reaches higher than I imagined. How do we shut it down?" Quinn asked, scanning the temple complex with narrowed eyes.

I traced the central diagram with my finger. "His primary control station should be here, in the main hypostyle hall. If we can disable it before the resonance reaches critical threshold, his entire system should fail."

A fine dust sifted down from a nearby column, shaken loose by the intensifying vibrations. I noticed a hairline fracture running up the stone—possibly new damage that gleamed white against the weathered surface.

"The frequency is already causing structural stress," I said. "And there's our visible gauge."

I pointed to a large mechanical device positioned prominently on the temple steps. Its face featured a needle slowly climbing across graduated markings, currently hovering at "42% RESONANCE."

"How much time do we have?" Quinn asked.

"Impossible to calculate precisely, but once that needle reaches the red threshold line..." I let the implication hang in the air between us.

We reached the northeastern corner of the complex, where a small doorway had been partly concealed by restoration scaffolding. The entrance was narrow, barely wide enough for Quinn's shoulders as we slipped inside.

The passage beyond plunged into darkness, the air thick with the scent of ancient stone and river damp.

Quinn produced a small electric torch, its beam revealing a

narrow corridor decorated with faded hieroglyphs, their once-bright pigments now ghostly traces beneath centuries of Nile silt.

"Offerings for the goddess Isis," I translated, my fingertips registering the contrast between sand-worn hieroglyphs, smoothed by millennia of desert winds, and rough-edged drill holes where cables had been forced through sacred carvings. "This was a processional route for temple priests. The Romans added their own inscriptions here, creating a blend of Egyptian and classical worship."

The humming grew louder as we moved deeper into the complex, accompanied by an unsettling sensation of pressure against my eardrums. The stone floor vibrated beneath our feet like the deck of a steamship pushing against current.

We emerged into a small antechamber filled with stacked crates, each of them open and, upon inspection, empty.

I studied Mrs. Pemberton's diagrams more carefully. "Quinn, these calculations..."

He turned the light on me at the horrified tone of my voice.

"They show a fracturing that could propagate through the bedrock. If Philae falls, the resonance could trigger sympathetic collapse in temples for miles downriver."

Quinn grasped my arm, pulling me back from the threshold. He knelt, pointing to a nearly invisible wire stretched across the floor at ankle height.

"Tripwire," he said quietly. "it must lead to a demolition charge."

"Demolition charges in an ancient temple." The archaeological blasphemy momentarily overshadowed the mortal danger. "Montague has abandoned all pretense of preserving heritage."

"They've rigged the system to destroy all evidence if interrupted," Quinn noted grimly. "One wrong move and not only does the temple collapse, but everything linking this to government officials vanishes with it."

He carefully navigated around the trap, then helped me follow his exact path. The passage beyond opened into one of

Philae's inner courts, now transformed into a nightmarish fusion of ancient architecture and modern technology.

Racks of glowing tubes with large horn speakers had been mounted on stone columns. Electrical generators hummed in corners where incense burners once stood. Metal equipment squatted upon sacred stones like chrome beetles, connected by cables that had been carelessly drilled through thousand-year-old carvings. The Brotherhood's modifications transformed the sacred temple into a grotesque musical instrument, with ancient columns serving as monstrous tuning forks and sacred chambers as resonance boxes.

I recognized Lord Ashford's distinctive profile as he carefully adjusted a valve. Nearby, Dr. Waverly calibrated a series of tuning forks while Colonel Hartwell monitored a complex control panel.

A large mechanical gauge dominated the wall behind them, its needle hovering at "51% RESONANCE," the color gradually shifting from yellow to orange.

"Time isn't on our side," Quinn whispered, gesturing toward the doorway ahead. "If we're going to stop this, we need to find the primary amplifier."

A sudden crack echoed through the chamber as a substantial chunk of ceiling broke free, crashing to the floor mere feet from where Brotherhood members worked. My fingers curled into fists at my sides. None of the Brotherhood appeared surprised or concerned—instead, Lord Ashford made a notation in a ledger, as if documenting the precise moment of structural failure.

"They're measuring the damage progression," I whispered in horror. "This isn't an accident—they're intentionally pushing the structure to its breaking point."

Quinn pulled me toward a shadowed alcove as voices approached from an adjoining corridor. We pressed ourselves into darkness as two figures passed—an armed guard of some sort and Marcus Waverly. Marcus looked pale and anxious, clutching a leather case to his chest.

"Mother says the primary amplifier is reaching optimal

modulation," he was saying. "We're still twenty minutes from resonance cascade."

"Professor Montague assures us the structure will hold until then," the guard replied. "The calculations are precise."

They passed without noticing us, disappearing into the main hall. Once they were gone, I turned to Quinn.

Quinn checked his wristwatch against the resonance gauge.

"We need to split up," I said. "Cover more ground looking for it."

Quinn's expression darkened, his shoulders squaring against the argument he knew was coming. "Absolutely not. We stay together."

"The resonance is increasing faster than anticipated," I argued, pointing to the gauge showing "54% RESONANCE." I swallowed hard against the tightness in my throat as the needle trembled closer to the red line. "If we don't locate the primary amplifier soon, it won't matter what else we do."

Another stone fragment crashed nearby, followed by a shower of ancient plaster. The vibration beneath our feet had intensified to a steady tremor.

"And the better his chances of eliminating us individually," Quinn countered. "These people have military-grade equipment, demolition charges, and armed guards."

I took a deep breath, feeling oddly calm despite our circumstances. "According to what we've overheard, we have less than twenty minutes. Once the amplification becomes self-sustaining, it can't be stopped, even if we destroy the equipment."

Quinn stared at me for a long moment, then gently traced my cheek with his fingertips.

"Find the control room," he said finally. "You locate Montague. He's the only one who might know how to shut it down completely. I'll find the charges."

"I'll start with the hypostyle hall," I said. "The primary amplifier should be there, according to Mrs. Pemberton's diagrams."

Quinn caught my hand before I could move away. "Clarissa."

His tone containing no irony or performance stopped me more effectively than his grasp.

"Be careful," he said, voice low and urgent. "If we survive this, I'd very much like to continue our discussion about renegotiating engagement terms."

I felt a ridiculous flutter beneath my ribs despite the danger. "I'll pencil you in for approximately fifteen minutes from now, assuming neither of us is crushed by ancient masonry."

"It's a date," he replied, his smile genuine despite the grimness in his eyes.

I slipped away with a glance at the gauge.

Fifty-seven percent.

# CHAPTER THIRTY-ONE

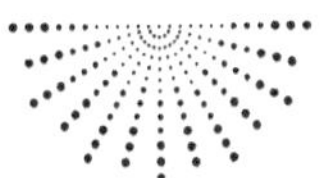

The harmonic hum resonating through Philae's underground chambers vibrated against my ribcage like a tuning fork struck too hard. Cold Nile water seeped into my boots as I navigated the flooded lower level. Given my earlier swim, at least I couldn't get any wetter.

Early dawn light filtered weakly through ancient apertures, casting ghostly fingers across modern equipment that had no business desecrating this sacred space.

Ahead, the warm glow of electric lamps—a jarring anachronism against three-thousand-year-old stone—illuminated what appeared to be Montague's command center.

If the scattered equipment we'd passed earlier suggested desecration, this was outright blasphemy.

The ancient chamber—once a sanctuary only priests could enter—had been transformed into something that would have made Nikola Tesla raise an eyebrow.

In the center stood Montague himself, illuminated by the unholy marriage of harsh electric bulbs and soft dawn glow. The sickly yellow artificial light cast contaminating shadows across hieroglyphs, and he seemed a gaunt, fevered shadow of the man I knew. He was bent over a wooden table where familiar objects were arranged in precise geometric patterns.

Nearby, bound to an ancient stone pillar, was Mrs. Pemberton, her eyes wide with terror. Near her stood a large metal frame supporting what appeared to be a massive tuning fork, nearly as tall as a man.

A low rumble shook the chamber. Ripples formed in the shallow water. Grit and dust trickled from between stones. One loose paving slab began to chatter faintly. A nearby column gave a tiny, sharp cracking tick—no collapse yet, just warning signs, which somehow made it worse.

We needed to get ourselves and Mrs. Pemberton out of here before this whole place collapsed.

But I couldn't tackle him alone. "I need to find Quinn," I whispered to myself.

As I moved toward the exit, another stone cracked behind me with a sound like a gunshot, and water began rushing through a new fissure in the ancient floor.

I escaped into the inner halls, as the hum escalated to a bone-rattling intensity that made my teeth ache.

"Quinn?' I called, my voice swallowed by the strange acoustics.

No answer.

I pressed myself against a wall, maneuvering toward the sound of voices. My fingers traced a crack in the limestone—Montague's equipment was already destroying what it claimed to activate.

The fog that had pursued us from the river had invaded the temple's chambers, turning the space into a ghostly labyrinth.

A figure emerged from the mist. I raised a loose stone I'd acquired as a makeshift weapon.

"Dr. Bell." The voice was feminine, cultured, and entirely too calm for the situation.

Lady Penelope Fairfax stepped forward, looking remarkably composed in a practical khaki outfit that bore no resemblance to her usual society plumage.

"You're going the wrong way," she said. "The primary chamber is east, not north."

I didn't lower my weapon. "Curious that you know the layout so well."

"I should. I've been studying the engineering modifications for months." She regarded me with something like approval. "I rather hoped you'd figure things out sooner."

"Figure what out, exactly? That you pushed me overboard?"

Her eyes widened. "I did no such thing. Though I'm relieved you survived, whoever did it."

Before I could respond, another figure appeared in the corridor behind her.

Marcus Waverly, looking considerably less composed than Lady Penelope—his academic tweeds rumpled, his eyes wide with panic.

"Dr. Bell! Thank God. Have you seen my mother? She's gone completely—"

His words were drowned by a woman's voice echoing through the chambers, reciting what sounded like mathematical equations with the fervor of religious incantations. Even through the disorienting fog and acoustics, I recognized Dr. Waverly's distinctive cadence.

"She believes today is the day of her transcendence," Marcus said, desperation making his voice crack. "She won't listen to reason."

Lady Penelope's expression hardened. "The chambers are already failing."

Another figure materialized from the fog like an apparition.

Colonel Hartwell. "The situation is evolving rapidly," he announced in clipped tones. "Dr. Waverly has commenced the harmonic invocation. Lord Ashford is positioning the artifacts according to Montague's specifications."

"And you're here because...?" I let the question hang.

"Strategic assessment." His eyes darted between Lady Penelope and me. "But I fear the structural integrity cannot withstand the resonant frequencies much longer."

"So, you've abandoned Montague's plan?" Lady Penelope's skepticism was palpable.

"I'm a pragmatist, my dear." The colonel's mouth tightened. "When the evidence suggests imminent failure, one recalculates."

Their multiple agendas swirled around me like the fog, and I struggled to categorize the rapidly shifting alliances.

"We need to evacuate," I said. "The temple can't—"

"Ja, ja, very dramatic." The familiar Germanic accent cut through our conversation. "Always the archaeologist worried about old stones."

Fraulein Becker emerged from a side passage, her severe demeanor somehow more threatening in the eerie lighting. She moved with predatory grace, circling our impromptu gathering.

"Professor Montague anticipated interference," she continued, her accent thickening. "He regrets you did not accept his invitation to participate properly, Dr. Bell."

Marcus stepped forward. "This has gone far enough. My mother is brilliant but deluded, and people are dying for this—this fantasy!"

"And what part did you play, Marcus?" I leaned in. "You were seen mixing something into a syringe—did you kill Mullen and Faraj at your mother's direction?"

"What? No! I—"

"Such devotion," Fraulein Becker mocked. She scowled at Lady Penelope. "And you? Did you share your concerns before or after betraying the Brotherhood to Egyptian authorities?"

Before anyone could respond, a tremendous crash echoed through the chambers, followed by the distinctive sound of stone cracking. The floor beneath us trembled. Water began seeping more rapidly around our ankles.

"The northeastern chamber has failed," Colonel Hartwell reported with clinical detachment. "First stage collapse imminent."

In the moment of distraction, Fraulein Becker lunged toward Lady Penelope's document case.

I swung my stone automatically, catching her across the arm. She staggered sideways, colliding with a modern amplifier.

The resulting feedback screech tore through the chamber like a living thing. Everyone instinctively covered their ears as the harmonics built to a painful intensity.

When I looked up, Fraulein Becker was sprawled against the wall, her thick dark hair distinctly... askew.

The stone floor trembled again. Water surged around our calves.

"The convergence has begun!" Dr. Waverly's voice echoed through the chambers with religious fervor. "The harmonic gateway opens!"

"Mother, stop!" Marcus shouted, his voice breaking. "People are dead. This isn't sacred geometry—it's murder!"

I stared at Fraulein Becker as she slowly regained her footing. Something about her movements had changed—a different fluidity, a familiar arrogance. And her hair—now clearly revealed as a wig—had shifted distinctly to the left.

Understanding crashed over me with the same force as the next surge of water from collapsing chambers.

"You're Violet Hat." I gripped my makeshift weapon tighter. "From Alexandria. You tried to kill us at Pompey's Pillar."

She blinked, momentarily confused by the nickname, then comprehension dawned. Her hand went to her crooked wig, and her lips curved into a smile entirely unlike Fraulein Becker's severe expressions.

"Oh, this ridiculous costume." Her accent vanished completely, replaced by crisp British diction. "I'm surprised you recognized me. Though I suppose I do favor that particular hat rather excessively."

With theatrical flair, she pulled off the blonde wig and false glasses, shaking out her own dark hair.

"Dr. Bell, you really are insufferably persistent." Her voice had transformed along with her appearance. "This charade has become tedious beyond words."

"You've been Montague's operative all along."

"Operative?" She laughed. "So dramatic. I prefer 'specialized assistant.' Professor Montague requires certain practical skills Oxford doesn't teach."

I stared at her, pieces clicking into place. "You killed Faraj. And Mullen too."

"Of course I did." She adjusted her sodden sleeve with fastidious care. "Faraj was becoming troublesome with his questions about the artifacts. Mullen was worse—started making connections, keeping detailed notes."

"And the scaffolding at Abydos?"

Her eyes flashed with genuine hatred. "You should have died in Alexandria. But you're like a cockroach, scuttling away at the last moment."

"But why kill me? I didn't even know who you were."

She sneered. "Yes, well. Montague speaks of you constantly. 'Dr. Bell's authentication techniques,' 'Dr. Bell's brilliance.' As if I haven't been doing his real work for years—removing problems, stealing, manipulating. But he wanted you for this grand moment." She glanced toward the central chamber where the harmonics continued to build. "You have no idea how satisfying it was to see you fall into the Nile."

Another tremor shook the chamber, stronger than before. A chunk of ceiling splashed into the rising water.

I surveyed them all. "Mrs. Pemberton is being held against her will. We need to get her out."

"And my mother!" Marcus cried.

"Your mother is a true believer," Violet Hat/Becker corrected. "You simply lack her vision."

"I lack her delusions," Marcus said, his voice stronger than I'd ever heard it. "Mother may be willing to sacrifice lives for mystical knowledge. I am not."

Colonel Hartwell ran his finger along a crack. "The practical matter remains—this structure is failing. Whatever 'transcendent knowledge' Montague hopes to access will be buried along with anyone who remains."

A new voice joined our increasingly crowded confrontation.

"Which is exactly what he intends."

Quinn materialized from the fog, water dripping from his formal clothes, a bleeding cut across his forehead.

My heart lurched at the sight of him.

"The entire temple is wired with demolition charges," he continued. "Once the convergence activates, Montague plans to eliminate all witnesses."

"Including Brotherhood members," Marcus added bitterly. "We're as disposable as the temple itself."

Lady Penelope crossed her arms. "Egyptian authorities are en route, but the fog has delayed them. I've been sharing intelligence for weeks, but they won't arrive in time."

"My mother..." Marcus's voice broke. "She won't leave. She truly believes she's participating in humanity's spiritual evolution."

Another crash echoed from deeper in the temple. The water rose to our knees. The humming intensified.

"We need to evacuate now," Quinn said, moving to my side with natural protective instinct.

Violet Hat's laugh was cold. "So noble."

"I'm getting Mrs. Pemberton." I moved toward the inner chamber. "Colonel, if you're sincere about abandoning Montague, help me get everyone out."

Marcus stepped in front of me, blocking my path. "We can't just charge in—my mother might interpret it as an attack." His eyes pleaded for understanding.

"Your mother chose this path," I said, more harshly than intended. "Mrs. Pemberton didn't."

He flinched as though I'd struck him, and I immediately regretted my words. "Try to reach her, Marcus. If anyone can, it's you."

Quinn caught my arm. "We go together."

"I need you to disable those charges," I countered.

His fingers tightened. "Clarissa—"

"I know." I met his eyes, all pretense abandoned. "But people will die if we don't split up."

Lady Penelope stepped forward. "I'll go with Dr. Bell. Perhaps I can get through to him."

"And why should we trust you?" Quinn positioned himself between Lady Penelope and me, one hand resting on the ancient column beside us.

"Because my husband discovered what Montague was planning and died for it," she answered simply. "Just like Albert Pemberton."

Violet Hat moved like a striking snake, but this time I was ready. I dodged her lunge, and Quinn intercepted her with practiced efficiency, twisting her arm behind her back.

Another crash, closer this time. The water surged to mid-thigh.

"The chamber is collapsing!" Marcus cried, already splashing toward the sound of his mother's voice. Stone creaked under structural stress, the sound uncomfortably like breaking bones.

Lady Penelope grabbed my arm. "This way—there's a maintenance passage the priests used. It connects directly to the inner sanctum. We need to get above the water before the electricity hits it!"

"Can we trust her?" I asked Quinn.

"We don't have a choice."

He released Violet Hat with a shove toward Colonel Hartwell. "The colonel will escort you to the authorities. I'm sure you'll both have fascinating conversations about your respective career choices."

Her murderous glare promised future retribution.

As Lady Penelope pulled me toward a narrow doorway half-hidden behind modern equipment, Quinn caught my hand one last time.

"Clarissa." Something in his voice made me turn back. His eyes held mine with an intensity that made my breath catch. "Whatever happens, remember what I said on the boat. I chose you. I'll always choose you." He grinned. "But try not to adopt any more homicidal archaeologists before I see you again," he added, his voice lighter than his eyes.

"No promises. They seem to find me irresistible."

Then the next tremor hit, water surged, and we were separated by necessity once more—he toward the demolition charges, and Penelope and I toward the inner chamber where Montague pursued his harmonic convergence with the desperation of a true believer.

# CHAPTER THIRTY-TWO

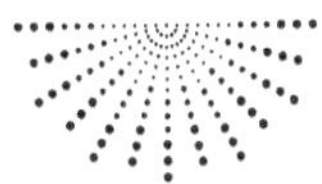

$\mathcal{W}$ater sloshed around my knees as I abandoned the narrow passage Lady Penelope had led me through. Our brief alliance had dissolved minutes earlier when I'd realized her true agenda—she wasn't helping me reach Mrs. Pemberton at all.

"You're not taking me to the inner chamber," I'd said.

Her aristocratic composure had faltered momentarily. "Not directly. We need to secure the artifacts first."

"While Mrs. Pemberton drowns? I think not."

She'd grabbed my arm. "Be reasonable, Dr. Bell. These artifacts represent mathematical principles beyond modern understanding. They cannot be sacrificed."

I'd twisted free, recognizing the familiar gleam of academic obsession in her eyes—not unlike Montague's, though perhaps less homicidal. "Mrs. Pemberton is a living person, not an acceptable sacrifice for your research."

"You don't understand what's at stake—"

"I understand perfectly." I'd started backing away. "You're not Brotherhood, but you're not on our side either. You have your own agenda."

She'd smiled thinly. "Everyone does, Dr. Bell. Even your charming fiancé."

Now I navigated alone through chambers increasingly destabilized by Montague's acoustic madness.

Splashing footsteps echoed from the corridor ahead. I extinguished my light and pressed myself against the wall, feeling hieroglyphs rough against my shoulder blades.

"Dr. Bell?" A crisp British voice called out. Not Quinn's familiar tone, but something adjacent—similar accent, different cadence.

I remained silent, calculating probabilities and escape routes.

"Dr. Bell, I know you're there. I'm Major James Kingsley. Benedict Quinn's handler."

*Osiris's soggy slippers.* The man who'd communicated with Quinn through coded telegrams—the superior officer who had asked whether Quinn was compromised by his "association" with me.

"Prove it," I called, keeping my light off.

A soft chuckle echoed through the chamber. "Pragmatic. Quinn mentioned that about you." A beam of light illuminated a face, and a military-issue identification card. "But perhaps more convincing: Operation Indigo was sanctioned under Foreign Office directive 227, with supplemental Treasury allocation through the Museum Acquisition Fund. Benedict reports directly to my department."

The level of classified detail suggested legitimacy, though in this environment, legitimacy hardly guaranteed trustworthiness.

"Where is Quinn?" I asked, switching my torch back on but keeping it pointed downward to preserve my night vision.

"Currently securing the perimeter with my men." Kingsley stepped into view—a trim, silver-haired man in his fifties wearing surprisingly practical expedition clothing for a British intelligence officer.

I studied him with the same attention I'd give a potentially misclassified artifact. "Perhaps you've been compromised. Operation Indigo has competing factions within British intelligence."

His eyebrows rose fractionally. "You're remarkably well-informed for an American archaeologist."

"I'm remarkably well-informed for anyone." I took a deliberate step toward him. "Your operation began as academic suppression of advanced Egyptian mathematical knowledge to maintain British intellectual superiority, then split into competing agendas. Which faction are you?"

A thin smile formed on his lips. "Direct. Another quality Quinn mentioned." He glanced at his watch. "We're wasting precious time, Dr. Bell. Suffice it to say, my faction believes these artifacts belong in proper British institutions, not destroyed by Montague's acoustic madness or locked away in Egyptian storage facilities."

"Cultural theft as the moderate position?"

"Cultural preservation." He turned toward the passage he'd entered from, his boots making slick sounds against the limestone that had become dangerously smooth underwater. "This way. Quinn is waiting with our extraction team. We have boats positioned to evacuate before Montague's actions destabilize the entire structure. The harmonic frequencies could potentially trigger a chain reaction affecting other nearby temples."

I didn't move. "Mrs. Pemberton is still being held in the inner chamber. And what about Marcus and his mother?"

Water dripped from somewhere above, the *plink-plink-plink* marking seconds we couldn't spare. Kingsley sighed.

"We have men searching for all civilians. But our primary objective must be to secure the artifacts and disable Montague's equipment before the temple collapses entirely." His voice remained measured, reasonable. "Now, shall we proceed? The water is rising rather quickly."

As if to punctuate his statement, a distant rumble shook the chamber. Stone dust sifted down from the ceiling, creating tiny constellations on the water's surface.

I followed, keeping a careful distance. "And what exactly did you instruct Quinn regarding me?"

"To utilize your expertise while maintaining operational security."

"That's diplomatically vague."

"Intelligence work often is."

We splashed through a narrow doorway into a larger chamber where several men in similar practical attire were establishing what appeared to be a radio communications center on the highest portion of the flooded floor. Quinn stood among them, his shoulders tense beneath his soaked clothing. When he turned and saw me, something flashed across his features—relief, concern, and something else I wasn't prepared to categorize.

"Clarissa." He crossed to me in four long strides. "You're alright. Where's Lady Penelope?"

"Gone to pursue her own agenda. She was never taking me to Mrs. Pemberton."

His eyes held mine, then flicked toward Kingsley in a way that communicated volumes.

The major cleared his throat. "Status report, Quinn."

"Hassan reports Egyptian authorities approaching from the south dock. Twenty minutes, perhaps less." Quinn's posture shifted subtly, more formal. "Brotherhood members are positioning the artifacts in the central chamber."

"And the demolition charges?"

"Still in place. Set to detonate."

"After he achieves his convergence and escapes," I added. "With everyone else still inside."

"Precisely why we need to move quickly." Kingsley began issuing orders to his team. "We need to split up. Parker, Wilson —secure the perimeter. Thompson, maintain communications. Quinn, you're with me—we're securing those artifacts."

"And Dr. Bell?" Quinn asked, his tone carefully neutral.

Kingsley glanced at me as if I were an afterthought. "She'll accompany Hassan to document the Brotherhood's activities for evidence. Then evacuate with the Egyptian authorities."

"Absolutely not." Quinn's voice remained measured but took on an edge I recognized from our confrontations with Lord Ashford. "She comes with us."

Kingsley's eyes narrowed. "Is this the compromise your

previous reports mentioned, Quinn? I was concerned when you suggested a personal attachment might be developing."

I touched Quinn's ring for reassurance, the cool stone centering me despite the chaos.

"Dr. Bell's archaeological knowledge is essential," Quinn said evenly. "If your priority is securing them for British museums, you'll want her assessment."

The major studied me for a long moment. "Very well. But understand this, Dr. Bell—these artifacts must be secured for proper study by qualified British institutions."

Before I could deliver a scathing response about colonial entitlement, Hassan appeared at the chamber entrance, water streaming from his formal coat.

"Egyptian authorities are on their way," he announced, his gaze hardening as he took in Kingsley and his team. "These are Egyptian artifacts on Egyptian soil. Your jurisdiction ended at the water's edge, Major. Egypt's newfound independence may be limited, but it explicitly includes archaeological sovereignty."

"This is hardly the time for jurisdictional disputes, Inspector," Kingsley replied smoothly. "We all want to prevent Montague from destroying priceless historical treasures."

"And ensure they remain in Egyptian custody," Hassan added.

A substantial section of ceiling crashed into the water near Thompson's radio equipment. He yanked the transmitter sideways, barely avoiding being crushed.

"We're running out of time," I said, cutting through the diplomatic standoff. "We need to evacuate everyone and disable Montague's equipment immediately."

As Kingsley issued orders to his team, Quinn drew me slightly aside, his voice dropping to a whisper and eyes gleaming with the light that always accompanied his more outrageous plans.

"How do you feel about becoming a Brotherhood convert?"

# CHAPTER THIRTY-THREE

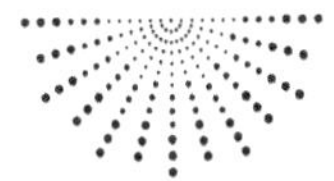

The harmonic resonance had transformed from annoyance to physical pain, vibrating through my skull with unrelenting force.

Water lapped at my thighs as I navigated the flooded inner chamber. The acoustic pressure built until my eardrums felt like papyrus threatening to tear at the seams.

"The primary amplifier should be through here." Hassan followed close behind, his usually immaculate coat torn and waterlogged, his expression grim beneath a layer of stone dust.

We pushed through the flooded hypostyle hall where once-majestic columns now stood half-submerged.

Professor Montague stood at the center of the chamber upon a raised platform surrounded by water. The artifacts we'd identified in the cargo hold were arranged in a precise geometric pattern around him—the measuring rod, the tablets, the sistrum.

And there, at the center—a flat, circular disc gleaming with lapis lazuli inlay. The piece that had gone missing almost six weeks ago, the morning of the Winter Solstice.

Mrs. Pemberton was still strapped to the ancient pillar, her eyes wide with terror above her gag.

I waved Hassan back, out of Montague's line of sight.

"You're early, Clarissa," Montague said without turning. "I'd expected you'd need another ten minutes to work through the eastern passage."

I took a cautious step forward, scanning for the best approach. "Did you leave a trail of breadcrumbs for me, Professor? How thoughtful."

He finally turned, and I barely suppressed a gasp. His eyes burned with an intensity I'd never seen—the focused intelligence that had once made him a brilliant archaeologist now twisted into something feverish and dangerous.

"Not breadcrumbs. I simply calculated your methods. Your persistence. Your inevitable arrival." He gestured toward the artifacts. "You would have been my best student. Who else would I want to witness the culmination of my life's work?"

Despite Quinn's suggestion that I play along with Montague's madness and appear to be convinced, I couldn't give him the satisfaction.

"By *culmination*, I assume you mean *catastrophic architectural failure*?" I nodded toward hairline fractures already creeping up the nearest column. "Your harmonic resonance is destroying the temple."

"Temporary structural adjustment," he dismissed. "The stone will adapt to the frequencies."

"The stone is three thousand years old." My voice was tight with controlled rage. "It will not adapt. It will collapse."

"Such limited thinking. You surprise me." Montague sighed dramatically. "Always worried about preservation without understanding what we're preserving."

Hopefully Hassan was edging around the chamber, closer to the control panel that would shut this nightmare down.

I inched toward Montague, noting the sand patterns vibrating across a metal plate—Chladni patterns, forming perfect geometric shapes. My gaze traveled from artifact to artifact, and suddenly the arrangement clicked into place.

"You've positioned them according to the disc's diagram," I said, gesturing to the central piece.

Montague's eyebrows rose with genuine pleasure. "Very

good, Clarissa. Jasper Thorne was an idiot in many ways—witness his ridiculous moniker of 'Astral Sphere' for what is clearly a disc—but he did recognize the piece's importance."

"It was you who arranged to have Harrison Foster steal it at Lady Blackwood's estate," I added, watching his reaction. "And you killed Elias Hawke."

He shrugged. "Foster was merely another tool. As was Hawke. Although you can't pin that one on me."

"Your *Fraulein* handled that one?"

He only smiled.

More pieces fell into place. "This goes back to the scribe's palette. The one that disappeared from my Giza excavation."

"Precisely." His eyes lit with the fervor of a man who'd waited years to reveal his greatest achievement. "When you identified it as belonging to the New Kingdom scribe Amenemhat, I knew you were special. Sutherland recognized its importance too, though not the full implications. He passed it to Hawke, who brought it to me."

"And you realized all these artifacts came from the same scribe's workshop," I concluded. "All with genuine lapis lazuli pigment, not Egyptian blue."

"Amenemhat wasn't just a scribe." Montague adjusted something on his control panel, his movements precise despite his mounting excitement. "He was a keeper of sacred knowledge. He created these pieces as components of a system, then hid them so they would only be found by someone worthy."

"Someone like you?" I couldn't keep the skepticism from my voice.

"Someone who understood." He gestured to the pieces around him. "I've spent years assembling them, using whatever resources necessary."

"Including Operation Indigo," I said, watching his face. "You created it, didn't you? Used your position in British intelligence to track down these artifacts and replace them with forgeries."

His smile was terrible in its pride. "The British government unwittingly funded the recovery of knowledge they sought to suppress. Exquisite irony, wouldn't you agree?"

Water sloshed around my legs as I circled wider, trying to see the main control panel. I needed to keep him talking. "Is that why you invited me on this cruise? To witness your triumph?"

"I invited you because you have the intellect to understand what we're doing." His voice softened, almost professorial again. "I've watched your work for years, Clarissa. Your pigment authentication techniques are unmatched. I hoped to convince you to join us."

"So, you did send that invitation. And contacted Bradford."

"Of course. I needed time to help you see beyond the narrow confines of academic orthodoxy." He waved dismissively. "I wasn't ready to tell you everything at once."

I glanced at the gauge on his control panel. The needle was climbing steadily toward a red line.

"And Quinn? Did you know who he was from the beginning?"

Montague laughed, the sound distorted by the chamber's unnatural acoustics. "Mr. Quinn reports to people who report to me, my dear. British Intelligence has many branches, and Operation Indigo reaches higher than he could imagine."

"And the murders? Were they all necessary for your 'convergence'?"

A shadow passed over his face. "Unfortunate sacrifices. Faraj recognized the mathematical sequence in the artifacts— brilliant boy. And Mullen was going to expose our work before completion."

I took another step, searching for any sign of Quinn or Hassan. "What about Mrs. Pemberton's husband? Was he a 'sacrifice' too?"

Mrs. Pemberton made a muffled sound of anguish behind her gag.

"Albert Pemberton was small-minded. He disagreed with

my methods." Montague's voice hardened. "He was going to report the modifications we'd made."

The chamber trembled again. I flinched but kept my focus on Montague.

"Risk is inherent in discovery, Clarissa. You know this." He continued to adjust his apparatus. "But the others will be here shortly to witness our success."

I caught movement in the shadows behind him—Hassan, working his way toward the control panel. I needed to keep Montague distracted.

"Others?"

"The Brotherhood, of course. Lord Ashford, Colonel Hartwell, Dr. Waverly, and the others... all here for the convergence." He checked his pocket watch. "In approximately seven minutes. Once the harmonic frequency reaches this threshold —" he tapped a gauge with a trembling finger, "—it cannot be stopped."

I needed to find a way to get to those controls.

"Why don't you explain the system, Professor? Imagine this is your classroom." I gestured at the artifacts. "One last lecture before... whatever happens next."

His face lit up with a grotesque parody of the enthusiasm his students must have once loved.

"The ancient Egyptians designed these chambers as resonance instruments. The artifacts—each contains mathematical ratios that, when assembled correctly, create a harmonic system of power."

"Yes, I've heard all this before. But power for what, exactly?"

His eyes gleamed. "Transformation. Revelation. The harmonic convergence will allow us to access knowledge beyond normal consciousness."

Of course.

"Shall we untie Mrs. Pemberton for the big moment, then?"

I felt another join the chamber behind me.

I turned to find Dr. Waverly nodded fervently, her eyes glazed.

She walked past me, reciting mathematical sequences that echoed eerily through the chamber.

Marcus followed, his face a mask of horrified realization. "Mother, please. The temple is collapsing. We need to leave!"

"We're on the threshold of transcendence," she replied without looking at him, her hands moving through the air as if conducting invisible music.

Lord Ashford appeared behind her, his aristocratic composure finally abandoning him. "Montague, this has gone far beyond what we discussed! These vibrations are destroying —!"

Montague cut off Ashford's concerns. "The stones will stabilize once we achieve convergence. The ancients understood these principles."

"Utter madness," Colonel Hartwell muttered from the darkened corridor.

And the resonance gauge clicked to 80%.

# CHAPTER THIRTY-FOUR

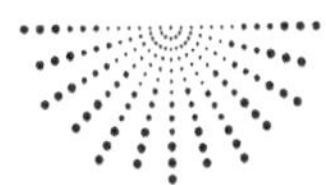

Quinn appeared at the chamber's far wall, supporting a bleeding Egyptian official I didn't recognize. He looked as if he'd been dragged through the Nile backwards—which, considering our recent adventures, was entirely possible.

"The charges are neutralized," he called, loud enough for Montague to hear.

The professor's face tightened. "You've been quite the inconvenience, Mr. Quinn. Or should I say *Agent* Quinn?"

Another support column cracked with a sound like ancient thunder. Water gushed through new fissures, rising noticeably within moments.

"Montague," Lord Ashford shouted, panic finally overwhelming his aristocratic reserve, "this has gone far enough! We agreed to test the acoustic principles, not destroy ourselves!"

"Sacrifices for knowledge are nothing new, Lord Ashford," Montague replied, his voice eerily calm amid the chaos. "The Brotherhood has always understood this."

Colonel Hartwell moved definitively toward the exit passage. "I believe we've gathered sufficient data for preliminary analysis. Strategic withdrawal seems appropriate."

"Cowards," Dr. Waverly hissed, still reciting mathematical

sequences between outbursts. "We're moments from break-through!"

I edged closer to the control panel, my archaeological training useful in an unexpected way—I knew how to move carefully around unstable ancient structures.

Slipping across the room, Marcus made a desperate lunge for his mother, trying to pull her away from the platform. A section of ceiling collapsed between them, trapping Marcus behind a pile of limestone blocks. Water surged through the new opening, accelerating the flooding.

"Mother!" he screamed, struggling to climb over the debris.

"Quinn!" I called out. "We need to disable the primary amplifier!" I gestured toward the control panel.

He nodded sharply and changed direction, wading through chest-deep water from the opposite side of the chamber.

Hassan lunged forward to dismantle the circuit, but a falling cornice struck his shoulder with brutal force. He crumpled against the wall, conscious but unable to reach the crucial wiring.

"Go!" he managed through gritted teeth.

I helped Hassan to his feet, and together we reached Mrs. Pemberton. I quickly removed her gag while Hassan worked on her restraints.

"The amplifier has a failsafe," she whispered urgently. "Built it into the primary circuit. The brass panel with the red warning plate—there's a disconnect switch beneath."

"Which you won't be accessing," came a cold voice behind us.

I turned to find Fraulein Becker—Violet Hat—training a small pistol on us. Her wig was gone, her natural dark hair plastered to her skull with sweat and temple dust.

"The convergence must proceed," she said, her accent completely abandoned. "Professor Montague has waited too long for this moment."

"And how exactly do you plan to escape the temple collapse?" I asked, buying time as Hassan continued working on Mrs. Pemberton's restraints behind my back. "Or are you as devoted to transcendent knowledge as the professor?"

Something flashed across her face—doubt, perhaps. Or calculation.

"Arrangements have been made," she replied carefully.

"For you, perhaps," I said. "What about the others? The demolition charges Quinn discovered were set to eliminate everyone after the convergence."

Her eyes widened slightly. "He found the charges?"

Hassan seized the opportunity, shoving a broken piece of equipment at her. She fired wildly, the bullet ricocheting off stone with a whine. I lunged for the control panel.

"Stop her!" Montague shouted, his academic detachment finally cracking into raw desperation.

Lord Ashford and Colonel Hartwell were already splashing toward the exit, having abandoned both Brotherhood loyalty and scientific curiosity in favor of survival. Lady Penelope was nowhere to be seen—had she already escaped, or was she pursuing her own agenda elsewhere in the flooding temple?

Montague leapt from his platform, moving with surprising agility for a man his age, intercepting me before I could reach the control panel.

"You don't understand what's at stake," he hissed, his face inches from mine. "These frequencies unlock knowledge beyond human constraint!"

"What I understand," I replied, "is that you've killed multiple people and are about to destroy irreplaceable cultural heritage to pursue a delusion."

"Not a delusion!" His eyes were fever-bright. "The convergence will prove my theories—the world will awaken to a higher spiritual consciousness!"

Hassan had freed Mrs. Pemberton and was helping her toward higher ground.

She called out over the increasing roar of water and fracturing stone: "The red disconnect switch! Pull it straight down, not sideways!"

I lunged for the control panel again, but Montague

grabbed a brass tuning rod from nearby equipment and swung it at my head.

I ducked, the movement throwing me off-balance in the surging water.

"Clarissa!" Quinn shouted, fighting his way toward us through the rising torrent.

Montague raised the rod for another strike, but suddenly staggered backward, a look of surprise on his face.

Lady Penelope stood behind him, holding what appeared to be a ceremonial knife from Montague's assembled collection.

"My husband discovered your true plans," she said, her aristocratic voice cutting through the chamber's chaos. "You killed him for it."

Montague recovered quickly, shoving her aside with surprising strength. "And now you'll die with the others."

"Quinn!" I called out. "The failsafe switch!"

He spotted what I was trying to reach and changed direction, wading toward the control panel from the opposite side.

Mrs. Pemberton struggled back through the rising water. "It won't work alone! The secondary circuit needs to be disconnected simultaneously!" She pointed to another panel partly concealed behind fallen debris.

"We need to leave NOW!" Hassan shouted, already guiding Mrs. Pemberton toward a half-submerged doorway.

"Not until we shut this down!" I called back.

Quinn reached the primary control panel, plunging his arm into the water to reach the submerged disconnect switch. I fought my way to the secondary panel, each step a battle against the rising water and intensifying vibrations.

"Clarissa!" Quinn called. "On three!"

Our eyes met across the churning water. In that moment, all the complications of our relationship—the fake engagement, the real feelings, the professional rivalry, the mutual respect—crystallized into something I couldn't categorize or file away. Something real.

"One!" he shouted.

The ceiling trembled violently, sending a shower of ancient plaster into the water.

"Two!"

Dr. Waverly broke free from where Marcus had finally reached her, scrambling toward Montague, still reciting mathematical sequences with religious fervor.

"THREE!"

# CHAPTER THIRTY-FIVE

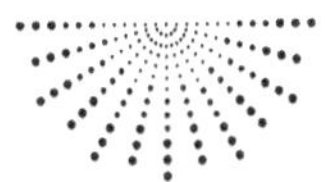

e pulled the disconnects simultaneously. For an eternal second, nothing happened.

The harmonic hum peaked in a deafening crescendo that vibrated through my very bones, then cut off abruptly as the disconnect switches took effect.

My muscles burned with constant tension as I fought against the current. The temple chamber seemed to contract and expand with each fading harmonic pulse, the acoustics distorting my perception until I couldn't trust my own senses.

Water roared around me and over me in the sudden, shocking silence where harmonic frequencies had pounded moments before.

My instincts took over—I'd read enough to know that panic hastens death.

I kicked upward, following the silver trail of my own air bubbles toward what I hoped was the surface. When my head broke through, I found myself in a transformed chamber where water had risen halfway to the ancient ceiling, leaving only pockets of air trapped against the stone.

The once-grand space had become a surreal underwater museum—twisted modern equipment now rendered useless, creating bizarre metal sculptures against limestone walls built by Ptolemy's architects. I emerged like a particularly ungraceful Botticelli Venus, if Venus had been an archaeologist with ruined Oxford brogues that had survived three digging seasons only to be destroyed by Montague's hubris.

The assembled artifacts were gone.

"Quinn!" My voice echoed strangely in the altered acoustics, bouncing off water and stone in ways the ancient architects never intended.

No response.

"Hassan! Mrs. Pemberton!"

I spotted a dark shape floating nearby—Montague, face-down in the water.

I swam toward him automatically, ethics extending even to would-be mass murderers. My throat constricted as water lapped higher against ancient stone. His shoulder bled from the wound inflicted by Penelope.

The bitter taste of fear—metallic and sharp—flooded my mouth as I rolled him over. A deep gash cut across his temple where falling stonework had struck him.

He looked beyond help, as if his life's obsession had claimed its final prize.

The water level seemed to be receding—the initial surge had equalized with whatever underground chambers had breached. I pushed Montague's body onto a partially submerged ledge, then oriented myself.

"Anyone!" I called again, fighting to keep my voice steady.

"Here!" Quinn's voice came from the direction of the primary control panel. "By the eastern wall!"

Relief flooded through me with such intensity I nearly lost my grip on the stone ledge I'd found. I swam toward his voice.

I found him struggling to free Marcus Waverly, whose leg was pinned beneath fallen debris. Quinn's face was streaked with blood, but his eyes lit with the same relief I'd felt upon hearing his voice.

"Are you hurt?" His eyes scanned me for injuries, somehow making the question sound both professional and deeply personal.

"Functional," I replied, automatically assessing the debris trapping Marcus. "We need leverage."

Together we braced against the submerged stone, creating just enough space for Marcus to pull free. His leg was clearly broken, but he was otherwise intact.

"My mother," he gasped. "She was near the platform when—"

"I'll look for her." I traced my fingers along the water's surface, though the chances seemed increasingly grim. "Can you get him to higher ground?" My eyes met Quinn's, silently communicating more than words could manage.

He nodded. "The western passage. Hassan and Mrs. Pemberton made it there. Lady Penelope too."

"And Violet Hat?"

"Unaccounted for."

We shared a look of perfect understanding—she remained a threat until proven otherwise.

As Quinn helped Marcus toward the western passage, I dove beneath the surface. The water had a strange clarity despite the debris.

And it allowed me to see Dr. Waverly's body entangled in the fallen equipment. Her eyes were open and staring, but her face bore no fear, only a serene expression of scientific certainty. She had died believing in her convergence, never witnessing its failure.

I surfaced with a gasp, treading water as I considered my next move.

A splash nearby sent me spinning in the water, prepared for Violet Hat's final attack. Instead, I found Lord Ashford clinging to a half-submerged column, his aristocratic composure entirely abandoned.

"Help me," he pleaded, his voice barely recognizable. "I can't swim."

The irony might have been amusing under different circumstances. I swam to him and guided his hand to a more stable projection of stone.

"Hold this and follow the wall to the western passage," I instructed. "Quinn and the others are there."

"The artifacts," he gasped, still focused on Brotherhood priorities despite his terror. "We must retrieve them!"

"The artifacts can wait." I pushed a floating piece of debris aside, creating a clearer path along the wall. "Lives first."

He looked genuinely perplexed by my priorities, but desperation overrode his objections. He began edging along the wall as instructed.

I made to follow him, but then something caught my eye, wedged against the base of a nearby wall.

Moments later, I clutched the Scribe's Palette to my chest. The piece I'd translated months ago, the piece that had started all this madness.

The western passage opened into what had once been a priest's antechamber, now partially flooded but with a raised section that remained above water. Hassan had organized our survivors there—Mrs. Pemberton tending to Marcus's broken leg, Lady Penelope wringing water from her fashionable clothing with remarkable composure, and Lord Ashford huddled miserably against the wall.

Quinn paced the edge of the dry space, his relief palpable when he spotted me.

"Clarissa," he breathed, wading through the water to meet me. His hands found mine with natural certainty, heedless of our audience. "I thought—"

"I'm fine," I assured him, then added more softly, "We're both fine."

His eyes searched mine with an intensity that made categorization impossible. Whatever existed between us now had evolved beyond my filing system.

Hassan approached, professional as always despite his soaked clothing. "The temple structure appears to be stabilizing. The resonance has completely ceased. Montague's effort was never going to work as intended."

"And all those deaths were for nothing," I added grimly.

Hassan nodded toward the passage where morning light

had begun to filter through. "Egyptian authorities are here. They had been delayed by the fog but arrived in time to intercept several Brotherhood members attempting to flee." He spoke with the quiet authority of someone whose ancestors had guarded these temples since the time of Ptolemy II, long before the Great War redrew the maps of control.

"The rest of the artifacts," I explained, gesturing toward the Scribe's Palette I still clutched. "I don't know if they can be recovered."

"Well, if they are, they will remain in Egypt," Hassan said firmly, with a pointed look toward both Quinn and Colonel Hartwell. "Where they belong."

To my surprise, the Colonel nodded. "I believe recent events have demonstrated the wisdom of leaving certain knowledge where it was originally placed."

Quinn's hand tightened around mine. "My superiors may have different opinions, but they'll need to take that up through proper diplomatic channels."

Hassan's expression softened slightly. "Thank you, Mr. Quinn."

As Egyptian authorities assisted our evacuation from the partially flooded temple, I had a moment to truly observe what had happened. The ancient structure had survived—damaged but intact where modern equipment had been installed, completely unharmed where original engineering remained.

The ancients had built better than Montague had calculated.

# CHAPTER THIRTY-SIX

The late morning sun painted the Nile in shades of liquid gold as the *Nefertiti* approached its destination, gliding past weathered steam launches crowding the Aswan harbor.

I stood at our ship's railing, watching the familiar bustle of passengers preparing for departure while trying to reconcile the serene normalcy of our arrival with the chaos of the dawn at Philae. Trunks appeared on deck, stewards scurried about with final bills and gratuities, and the general atmosphere suggested we'd enjoyed nothing more dramatic than a pleasant archaeological cruise.

If only they knew about the underwater chambers, the harmonic weapons, and Professor Montague's spectacular demise.

"Rather anticlimactic, isn't it?" Quinn appeared beside me, impeccably dressed despite having spent half the night disabling demolition charges in flooded temple passages. "One would expect a brass band, or at minimum trumpets to commemorate surviving what Captain Mason has taken to calling 'that cursed voyage.'"

I glanced toward the bridge where Captain Mason stood grimly supervising the docking procedures. "I suspect our captain is simply grateful to reach port without losing any more passengers to mysterious circumstances. Though I did hear him tell the harbormaster that he's never accepting another 'archaeological cruise' booking."

"Wise man." Quinn's fingers brushed mine on the railing. "Though I can't say I regret the educational experience."

Before I could respond to what felt like dangerous conversational territory, Annie appeared with Freddie in tow, both radiating the sort of determined cheerfulness that suggested Important Decisions had been reached.

"Miss Clarissa," Annie announced, "Freddie's been offered a position with the Thomas Cook company here in Egypt. Permanent-like."

Freddie beamed with the enthusiasm of a man whose romantic complications had resolved themselves with remarkable efficiency. "Lady Blackwood put in a word, she did. Says Egypt needs proper English staff who understand both hospitality and... discretion."

"Congratulations," I said, genuinely pleased. "I take it you'll be staying to explore this opportunity?" Annie deserved straightforward happiness after witnessing my own romantic catastrophes.

"Well, I can hardly leave you to manage your own correspondence and travel arrangements, can I?" Annie's practical tone suggested she'd approached romance with the same efficiency she applied to unpacking trunks. "Though I expect you'll be causing more international incidents even with my supervision."

Hassan approached with several official-looking Egyptian gentlemen in tow.

"Dr. Bell, Mr. Quinn," Hassan said formally, though his eyes held genuine warmth. "I wanted to introduce you to my colleagues from the Antiquities Service before you depart."

The introductions proceeded with the ritualistic politeness of international diplomacy, but Hassan's intent became clear when he drew me aside afterward.

"I cannot adequately express my gratitude," he said quietly.

"Though we've only recovered your Scribe's Palette so far, Faraj would have been proud to see even this one piece returned to Egyptian custody. Your commitment to cultural preservation, despite considerable personal risk, will not be forgotten."

He pressed a small object into my palm—a genuine New Kingdom scarab, its blue-green glaze catching the morning light. "From the official excavations at Saqqara. Legitimate provenance, naturally."

"Hassan, I couldn't possibly—"

"You defended Egypt's heritage when it would have been easier to remain silent," he interrupted. "Consider it a token of professional respect. And perhaps..." He handed me a calling card with elegant Arabic script. "Should you find yourself remaining in Cairo, the Antiquities Service would welcome consultation on matters requiring your particular expertise."

I tucked both scarab and card into my reticule, touched by the gesture. "I suspect Cairo hasn't seen the last of American archaeologists with questionable judgment and a talent for finding trouble."

"Let us hope the next crisis involves fewer underwater explosions and murderous academics." His expression darkened momentarily. "Speaking of which, we found Fraulein Becker's body in the eastern passage. The flooding took her. A fitting end, given what we now know of her actions."

"So, it was definitely her who killed Faraj and Mullen?" I asked.

"And according to documents found in her cabin, she was responsible for Elias Hawke as well. It seems she was Montague's personal assassin for years." Hassan's voice held a mixture of disgust and relief. "At least that much justice has been served."

"And Montague himself?" Quinn asked, joining our conversation.

Hassan glanced between us with a troubled expression. "That is... unclear. We should continue this discussion elsewhere."

Across the deck, I spotted Marcus Waverly sitting alone,

his leg properly splinted by the ship's doctor. His mother's absence hung around him like a palpable shadow, yet there was something in his posture that suggested relief alongside grief.

I approached him, Quinn following a respectful distance behind.

"Dr. Bell," Marcus acknowledged me with a small nod. "I owe you an apology. For what my mother did. For what I nearly did."

"You were trying to protect her," I said gently.

"Yes, but..." He glanced down at his hands, which had stopped trembling for perhaps the first time since I'd met him. "I realize now that what you saw that night—when I was mixing chemicals from my medical case—it was insulin. Mother was diabetic. I've been preparing her injections for years." A bitter laugh escaped him. "I suppose it looked rather suspicious under the circumstances."

"I shouldn't have jumped to conclusions," I admitted.

"It seems we all misjudged many things." His eyes met mine with newfound steadiness. "I've spent my life following Mother's obsessions. Perhaps now I can determine my own path."

I touched his shoulder briefly. "I believe you'll find it's worth the effort."

As Marcus was helped toward the gangplank by a steward, I noticed Lady Penelope in deep conversation with one of Hassan's colleagues. She caught my eye and approached with characteristic grace.

"Dr. Bell," she said, her aristocratic composure fully restored. "I owe you an explanation."

"About the documents you were passing to local contacts?" I asked. "Or about your secret meeting with Faraj before he was killed?"

"I did meet with Faraj," she said. "He believed something was wrong. So did I."

She hesitated.

"The Brotherhood insisted I bring my husband's artifact.

They would not tell me why. They implied... unpleasant consequences if I refused."

"So, you were trying to learn what they were planning."

"Yes. And Faraj thought he could help me." She smiled thinly. "I've been gathering evidence on the Brotherhood's activities for months."

"So, you weren't pursuing the artifacts for yourself?"

"Oh, I most certainly was," she admitted with surprising candor. "But not for mystical convergence nonsense. These pieces represent extraordinary mathematical advancements that deserve proper scientific study, not occult exploitation." She adjusted her gloves. "We don't always need to share the same motivations to find ourselves on the same side, Dr. Bell."

Before I could respond, Lord Ashford materialized beside us, looking remarkably composed for someone who'd nearly drowned in a collapsing temple mere hours ago.

"Ah, the brilliant Dr. Bell," he drawled, his aristocratic charm firmly back in place. "I do hope our little aquatic adventure hasn't soured you on the occasional soirée among Brotherhood enthusiasts. We're not all homicidal maniacs, I assure you."

"Just enthusiastic grave robbers?" I suggested with deceptive sweetness.

He laughed, genuinely amused. "Cultural appreciation, my dear. Though I suppose your American sensibilities might fail to distinguish the nuance." His eyes flicked to Quinn with a calculated gleam. "Should you ever tire of your current engagement, do consider my standing invitation for a private viewing of my collection."

Quinn's expression remained pleasant, though I noticed his posture shift subtly. "Lord Ashford, your persistence remains as remarkable as your timing is inappropriate."

"Merely ensuring Dr. Bell knows she has options," Ashford replied with a wink in my direction. "Until our paths cross again, which I suspect they inevitably will."

There was something in his parting smile that suggested this was neither concession nor farewell—merely tactical retreat. Behind him, Colonel Hartwell boarded a waiting launch, not bothering with goodbyes. Both men would return to England without consequences for their Brotherhood involvement, protected by wealth and position from anything as pedestrian as accountability.

A more unexpected figure appeared at the gangplank—Major Kingsley, Quinn's handler, immaculate despite the early hour and the circumstances.

"Dr. Bell, Mr. Quinn," he greeted us with brisk efficiency. "A word, if you please."

We followed him to a quieter section of deck, where the wake of our passage created shifting patterns against the hull.

"The situation has developed in unexpected ways," Kingsley began without preamble. "Montague's body is missing."

I stared at him. "That's impossible. I checked his pulse myself."

"Nevertheless, he was not where you left him." Kingsley's expression remained neutral. "Given his meticulous planning, it seems likely he had contingencies in place—perhaps a hidden passage or accomplice we haven't identified."

Quinn's face hardened. "Or someone removed his body. The Brotherhood extends beyond the passengers aboard this vessel."

"Indeed." Kingsley's gaze swept the departing passengers. "Our intelligence suggests at least thirty active members in diplomatic and academic positions across Europe and North America. This was merely one cell."

The implications were chilling. Montague—possibly alive—with resources and followers beyond what we'd encountered.

"Operation Indigo itself has become... complicated," Kingsley continued, addressing Quinn directly. "Your actions at Philae have raised questions about your priorities."

"Preventing civilian casualties seemed the appropriate choice," Quinn replied evenly.

"Yes, well, not everyone in our organization agrees." Kingsley's voice dropped further. "There are factions within British

Intelligence that found Montague's theories about harmonic weapons quite compelling, despite the lack of scientific basis. Others, like myself, see this drift toward occultism as dangerous distraction from our proper mission."

"Which is?" I asked.

Kingsley's eyes met mine with unexpected directness. "Protecting British interests while maintaining stability in strategically important regions, Dr. Bell. Not chasing mystical Egyptian super-weapons."

"And where does that leave me?" Quinn asked quietly.

"Temporarily suspended pending review," Kingsley replied. "Though you have allies. Your instincts about protecting civilians over artifacts show proper judgment, in my assessment."

The implications hung in the air between them—Quinn caught between competing factions in an intelligence community fracturing around supernatural possibilities versus rational priorities.

"I should return to Cairo, then." Quinn glanced toward me with barely concealed regret.

"Actually, I need you to return to London immediately," Kingsley corrected. "Headquarters requires a full debriefing on the Montague situation, and there are questions about your... priorities during this operation that need addressing. You'll depart on tomorrow's steamer."

Quinn nodded, professional mask firmly in place despite the emotions I could read in the tension around his eyes.

Kingsley departed with the same efficiency that characterized his arrival, leaving Quinn and me alone with new complications neither of us had anticipated.

"Well," I said lightly, "it seems both our professional futures have become rather spectacularly uncertain."

"Indeed. Though I suspect yours involves considerably less potential for court-martial." Quinn attempted a smile that didn't quite reach his eyes.

"Let's hope so."

## EPILOGUE

I arranged for my luggage to be transferred to the train station, then Quinn and I walked toward the Old Cataract Hotel. We had about an hour before my overnight train from Aswan to Cairo would depart, and tea at the hotel seemed a very good idea.

The hotel's famous terrace overlooked the granite boulders of the First Cataract, where the Nile's ancient fury had carved its channels through solid rock. Around us, British colonial administrators and their wives maintained rigid propriety in formal attire despite the Egyptian heat, while waiters in crisp white uniforms navigated between tables with practiced deference.

We settled at a corner table. The civilized ritual of cucumber sandwiches and properly brewed Earl Grey created an almost surreal counterpoint to our recent adventures, while beyond the balustrade, the First Cataract's pink granite formations gleamed in the afternoon light, polished by millennia of rushing water.

"So," Quinn said, stirring sugar into his cup with unnecessary concentration. "I suppose we should discuss the practical arrangements."

"Such as the fact that our engagement was entirely fictional?" I asked, aiming for lightness and achieving something closer to wistful.

"Actually, as mentioned, I was rather hoping we might renegotiate those particular terms." His voice carried that dangerous combination of humor and sincerity that made my blood run a little hotter. "Perhaps something with proper documentation this time."

"Benedict—"

"I realize the timing is rather inconvenient," he continued, "given that my intelligence career may or may not be ending. But I thought perhaps, when circumstances permit..." He trailed off, watching my expression with the focused attention I'd learned to associate with his more dangerous moods.

"When circumstances permit what, exactly?" I managed, though my voice emerged rather more breathlessly than seemed dignified.

"When circumstances permit, I'd very much like to court you properly. With flowers and theater tickets and all the conventional courtship rituals we've been too busy investigating murders to observe."

I twisted the lapis lazuli ring on my finger, suddenly acutely aware of its weight and meaning—or rather, its lack of legitimate meaning. The stone caught the afternoon light, as vibrant and enigmatic as the man who had given it to me.

With careful deliberation, I slid the ring from my finger, feeling an unexpected pang as the band cleared my knuckle. For something that had begun as merely a prop, it had become strangely comfortable—almost natural—against my skin.

"This probably should be returned to your handler," I said softly, placing the ring on the table between us. The absence on my finger felt more significant than it should have.

Quinn studied the ring but made no move to take it. "Actually, that particular item wasn't requisitioned through official channels."

I looked up sharply. "Meaning?"

"Meaning I purchased it myself. From a reputable antiquities dealer, with proper documentation," he added hastily, seeing my expression. "The hieroglyphs caught my attention."

"Truth emerges from darkness," I translated softly.

"Rather fitting, wouldn't you say?"

Before I could respond to this fascinating development, a hotel clerk appeared with the distinctive blue-and-yellow telegram format that had become the bane of my existence.

"Dr. Bell? Urgent message from America, madam."

My heart sank as I accepted the telegram.

FATHER'S CONDITION STILL SERIOUS STOP DOCTORS RECOMMEND IMMEDIATE FAMILY PRESENCE STOP HAVE ARRANGED PASSAGE ON NEXT AVAILABLE STEAMER STOP PLEASE

CONFIRM TRAVEL PLANS STOP REGARDS RICHARD SULLIVAN

I stared at the sign-off, common sense finally asserting itself over emotional chaos. "Richard Sullivan," I said slowly. "Not Richards."

Quinn leaned closer, studying the telegram over my shoulder. "Your former fiancé?"

"Richard still works for Father, managing some of his... more complicated business arrangements." I set the telegram on the table. "This news is legitimate. I assumed the previous message was a ruse because it came from 'Richards' — but now I think it was just a mistaken 's' added to Richard's first name."

"Which means—"

"Which means Father really is ill, and I truly must return to New York immediately." The weight of duty settled on my shoulders like familiar armor, though it felt considerably heavier than before. "How remarkably inconvenient." The words were meant to be playful, but tears had already started pooling.

Quinn's hand covered mine on the table, his touch warm and steadying. "Family obligations tend toward inconvenience. It's rather their defining characteristic. I'm so sorry about your father."

"You understand I have to go."

"Of course you do." His thumb traced across my knuckles with a gentleness that made my throat tighten unexpectedly. "Though I confess I'd hoped for more time to perfect my courtship technique before submitting it for your professional evaluation."

I laughed despite the circumstances, a sound that carried more sadness than humor. "Your technique seems quite adequate already, Mr. Quinn."

"High praise from someone with your exacting standards."

The hotel staff bustled about preparing for the afternoon train departure, creating a natural deadline that neither of us acknowledged directly. Quinn's hand remained on mine, a tangible connection in the growing awareness of impending separation.

"I don't suppose you'd consider a stopover in London on the way home?" Quinn asked with studied casualness. "I'm guessing I'll need to present myself for a comprehensive debriefing and possible disciplinary action for insubordination."

"Disciplinary action?" I felt a flutter of concern.

"If they indeed decide that choosing civilian safety over artifact recovery qualifies as dereliction of duty." His tone remained light, but I caught the underlying tension. "Nothing too dramatic, I'm sure. Probably just reassignment to somewhere thoroughly unpleasant and diplomatically insignificant."

"Such as?"

"Oh, rural Scotland. Perhaps northern Canada. Somewhere with extensive fog and limited opportunities for romantic complications."

"I do hope it's not Canada," I said. "My expertise in Egyptian pottery would be thoroughly wasted on excavating ice fishing equipment and frozen moose tracks." Despite everything, I smiled. "You could always pursue *legitimate* antiquities dealing."

"Ha!" He sobered. "For now, I think it's best I remain in Aswan until ready to go to London."

"Not coming to Cairo, then?" Disappointment settled in my chest.

"Now that you're only passing through there, no. Besides..." His voice lowered in the way that had proved so troublesome to my equilibrium aboard the ship. "I've had quite enough of the temptation of adjoining accommodations. My self-control, it turns out, has very definite limitations where you're concerned."

The frank admission sent heat flooding through me. "Benedict—"

"Separate countries seem the only sensible precaution," he continued, his thumb still tracing maddening patterns across my knuckles. "At least until we've both had time to determine whether our feelings survive the absence of murder investigations and fake engagements."

Almost as an afterthought, he picked up the abandoned engagement ring, turning it in the light. "I'll keep this safe," he said quietly. "In case it's needed again."

Whether he meant for another mission or something more personal remained deliberately ambiguous.

We walked to the train station in companionable silence, both seemingly reluctant to address the practical complications of an indefinite farewell. The late afternoon light painted Aswan's bustling marketplace in shades of amber and rose, creating the sort of atmospheric beauty that belonged in travel brochures rather than moments of uncertainty.

At the station, Quinn pressed a small card into my palm alongside my ticket. "British Embassy contacts in major cities. Should you find yourself in need of assistance with... archaeological complications."

"You mean should I stumble across more murderous conspiracies involving stolen artifacts?"

"One can hope your talent for such discoveries remains dormant for a reasonable interval." His smile carried genuine affection beneath the teasing. "Though I suspect hope may be optimistic."

The train's whistle provided an unfortunately dramatic soundtrack as Quinn stepped closer, his hands framing my face with a gentleness that made my heart perform acrobatics.

"Dr. Bell," he said formally, though his eyes held nothing resembling professional distance. The space between us seemed to compress, the background noise of the station fading as I became acutely aware of his proximity, the faint scent of his shaving soap, the slight upturn at the corner of his mouth.

"Mr. Quinn," I managed, though my voice emerged breathlessly.

The kiss that followed was neither performative nor tentative—a thorough, unmistakable declaration that left no doubt about the authenticity of our evolved feelings. When we finally separated, I found myself grateful for the train car's handrail as support.

"Write to me," I said, the words emerging as half-command, half-plea.

"Every week," he promised solemnly. "Whether I have anything interesting to report or not."

The urge to dissect the moment rose automatically—catalog it, define it, reduce it to manageable components. A temporary alliance forged under pressure. A partnership of mutual convenience. A strategic attachment.

But for once, I did not attempt to analyze my feelings. Not everything worth preserving could be cataloged.

As the train pulled away from the station, I watched Quinn's figure recede into the distance, one hand raised in farewell.

In my reticule, Hassan's scarab pressed against Quinn's contact card—tangible reminders of the partnerships and possibilities I was leaving behind.

The telegram from Richard also crinkled in my glove as I settled back for the journey north. Whatever awaited me in New York, I was no longer the same woman who'd fled her ex-fiancé's confining expectations and her father's disappointment. The categories I'd once used to organize my world—professional versus personal, duty versus desire, safety versus adventure—had proved remarkably inadequate for containing the realities of Egyptian adventures.

Perhaps that was the most valuable discovery of all.

But as the rhythmic clatter of train wheels carried me toward Cairo, a chill crept across my skin. Somewhere in the gathering shadows of Egypt, Nigel Montague—brilliant, ruthless, and possibly still drawing breath—remained unaccounted for. And something told me our paths were destined to cross again.

The Brotherhood's work wasn't finished. Neither was mine.

**Want to be notified when Book 4,
Catacombs and Curses,
releases?**

*Go to https://tracyhigley.com/get-notified to sign up for updates!*

Dear Reader,

Thank you for taking an adventure to ancient Egypt with me! I hope you greatly enjoyed *Amulets and Alibis!*

You can find lots more about ancient Egypt on my website, along with travel journals of my trips there.

And in case you're curious, here's more than you want to know about me...

I've been writing stories since the time I first picked up a pencil. I still have my first "real" novel—the story I began at the age of eight during a family trip to New York City.

Through my childhood I wrote short stories, plays for my friends to perform (sometimes I had to bribe them), and even started a school newspaper (OK, I was the editor, journalist and photographer since no one took that bribe to join me). Then there were the drama years of junior high, when I filled a blank journal with pages of poetry. {{*sigh.*}}

In my adult years I finally got serious about publishing fiction, and have since authored more than twenty novels.

When I'm not writing, life is full of other adventures—running a business, spending time with my kids and grandkids, and my favorite pastime: traveling the world. (I speak on cruise ships all over the world! How great is that?)

I started traveling to research my novels and fell in love with experiencing other cultures. It's my greatest hope that you'll feel like you've gotten to travel to the settings of my books, through the sights, sounds, smells, colors, and textures I try to bring back from my travels and weave into my stories.

I'd love to hear your thoughts about *Amulets and Alibis*, or ideas you have for future books I might write. Get in touch with me at tracy@tracyhigley.com.

Now, onward to another adventure!

(Be sure to join Clarissa's next adventure in Book 4, *Catacombs and Curses*, or if it's not yet ready, my next recommendation would be *A Time to Seek*)

# HOW TO HELP THE AUTHOR

I hope you enjoyed *Amulets and Alibis!*

If you're willing to help, I would really appreciate a review! You can review the book on Amazon, Goodreads, or my website.

**More than anything else, reviews help authors spread the word about their books.**

It doesn't have to be long or eloquent – just a few lines letting people know how the book made you feel.

Thank so much!

# BOOKS BY TRACY HIGLEY

**The Clarissa Bell Mysteries**

Hieroglyphs and Homicide

Palm Trees and Poison

Amulets and Alibis

**The Seven Wonders Novels:**

Isle of Shadows

Pyramid of Secrets

Guardian of the Flame

Garden of Madness

So Shines the Night

**The Time Travel Journals of Sahara Aldridge:**

A Time to Seek

A Time to Weep

A Time to Love

**The Books of Babylon:**

Chasing Babylon

Fallen from Babel

**The Lost Cities Novels:**

Petra: City in Stone

Pompeii: City on Fire

**The Coming of the King Saga:**

The Queen's Handmaid

The Incense Road

**Standalone Books and Short Stories:**

Nightfall in the Garden of Deep Time

Awakening

The Ark Builder's Wife

Dressed to the Nines

Broken Pieces

Rescued: An Allegory

www.ingramcontent.com/pod-product-compliance
Lightning Source LLC
Chambersburg PA
CBHW020140170726
47995CB00003BA/640